LIFE IN THE
MORGUE

LANCE ANDERSON

outskirts
press

Outskirts Press, Inc.
http://www.outskirtspress.com

ISBN: 978-1-9772-1624-3

Outskirts Press and the "OP" logo are trademarks belonging to Outskirts Press, Inc.

PRINTED IN THE UNITED STATES OF AMERICA

ACKNOWLEDGMENTS

Writing a book is harder than I thought and more rewarding than I could have ever imagined. None of this would have been possible without some of my closest friends.

Mary Winters-Sonia: For all the advice on anything and everything. The constant support and encouragement and the constant push to keep it moving. That is true friendship.

I would also like to thank Michael J. Patterson for his constant support, advice, and help with making this book a reality and constantly reminding me of things that would add to the story and offers of editorial and structuring assistance.

"Fiction is the truth inside the lie."

-Stephen King-

THE DECISION

Another long New England winter was finally coming to an end. The past few months had been especially bad this year with lots of heavy snow that started in late fall and frigid temperatures since October. Greg was an ironworker by trade, but since the "Big Dig" had just about come to an end, work was slow, and he found himself losing a lot of hours due to lack of new projects and winter weather.

As winter went on, once again construction work slowed way down, income started to dwindle, and it was time to find something else again. Greg took a job as a laborer with a demolition company, tearing down buildings. They seemed to have plenty of work, but unfortunately most of it was out of state, and the pay was not very good. He left home early on Monday mornings and did not return again until Friday nights. Greg did this for about a year when his son who was around age four or five asked him, "Why do you have to leave every week for work?" There really was no good answer for him, but his question struck a chord, so Greg decided to try and find something that was more local. He checked online and all the usual resources for a new job while staying employed with the demolition company. One day, he came across a website listing open state jobs. The posting for a morgue technician 1 stood out like a sore thumb. The mandatory requirements to secure such a glorious position were a high school diploma and a driver's license. The job description was quite lengthy, but basically it was to drive to scenes of unattended or accidental deaths to retrieve the body for the office and then assist the doctor in determining cause and manner of death, as well as a bunch of administrative duties and processing things for the lab.

Greg immediately decided that this was a job he needed to apply for. He spent a lot of time after dinner on Friday late into the night and most of Saturday morning working on and transforming his resume from that of a lifetime of construction to now highlight the fire department, rescue squad, and Red Cross - in hopes that would get their attention and hint that he had some sort of medical aptitude or knowledge. He finally got his resume ready to mail first thing Monday morning. As fate would have it, on Sunday afternoon, Greg received a call from his foreman with the demolition company notifying him that they would not be going to Portland that week but had a local job starting on Monday. Greg thought this was great news and on the drive into work that morning, dropped the envelope the mailbox in front of the local post office.

He honestly did not think he would hear back from them anytime soon as everyone knew how slow a state agency can be. The anxiety and worries started to creep in about not having enough of a medical background or any experience working with the dead. He had convinced himself that the best he was going to get was a rejection letter in about a month or two.

The demolition job turned out to be very local. It was at a small gas station/convenience store that was going to expand into a bigger store. It would only take a couple days, three tops, to finish it. It was mid-March, so the weather was not very cooperative. The week's forecast was cold and gloomy with temps in the mid-thirties and a rain and snow mix - not exactly ideal conditions for a laborer working outside. Greg managed to get through the next few days in one piece and arrive home around 4 p.m. on Wednesday, very wet and cold. He figured a nice hot shower would feel pretty good, so that was the first thing on the agenda.

After the shower he headed to the kitchen to put on some coffee. Io and behold, the answering machine was blinking. He played the message to hear an obviously older man say, "Yeah, Mr. Benson. This is Paul Rourke, the technical manager at the medical examiner's office. We need you to come in for an interview as soon as you can. Call the office and dial extension 124. That will go direct to me." Greg was amazed that he'd gotten a call and even more amazed that it only took about 48 hours for them to receive his resume. He assumed they would get hundreds of applicants for this job. He grabbed the phone and called information to get the office number as Mr. Rourke had not left it. Greg dialed his extension.

The phone just rang and rang it seemed like at least a dozen times and Greg wondered whether this guy had voice mail. Suddenly, the phone was picked up. A female voice answered in a very frustrated tone and said, "Tech station, do you have a case to report?" "No," Greg said, "no, I am not reporting a case." She snapped back, "Then why you calling the tech station? What do you want?" Caught completely off guard, Greg thought he had done something wrong. He managed to stammer out his name and that he had received a call from Paul Rourke to set up an interview for a technician position. She snapped back, "Did you call his office?" Greg responded, "Yes I dialed the extension he gave me." Then she said, still in a very frustrated voice, "It's after 4:30. He isn't here after 4:30. What the hell - I am not supposed to be here after 4:30. You need to call him at 7 a.m. tomorrow." She slammed the phone down and hung up on Greg, and they were quickly disconnected.

The next morning, Greg called the demolition company and told them he was running about 30 minutes late, so he could sit in a parking lot and call the office on his cell phone right at 7 a.m. As soon as the clock struck 7, he dialed the number and the extension. It was answered with a "This is Paul." Greg told him who he was and that he'd called yesterday to set up an interview. Paul responded with, "Benson, yeah can you come in this morning?" Greg tried to explain that he was currently working and could not make it in that day, but that he could make it Thursday morning. Paul responded, "Fine, Thursday at 10 a.m.," and hung up the phone. Despite the bad phone manners of the two people Greg managed to contact at the office, he was a very happy guy even though it was another cold, rainy day. He stopped at the main office and told the demo company that he would not be in work the next day as he had a doctor's appointment since he was not going out of town, and they seemed OK with that.

THE INTERVIEW

T hursday morning. It was still overcast and spitting rain and snow mix. Greg had his suit on and a fresh copy of the resume. He tried to calculate how long it would take to drive into Boston with the bad weather and how bad traffic was going to be. He did not want to be late for his interview so decided to leave around 7:30 to give himself plenty of time to get there. As predicted, traffic was a nightmare, but he managed to arrive around 9:20. He drove around to the back side of the building, hoping there was parking available. He managed to squeeze in between two other vehicles already parked in a pretty unorganized way on a small patch of gravel and dirt on the back side of the building along a chain link fence.

The building itself was not that impressive. It looked like it was two-and-a-half stories and made from brick. From where he was parked, Greg could see that the back of the building had two garage doors and a metal door off to the side. The back side of the building also had an enclosed area extending off the building, also made of brick. The walls were about ten feet high and extended off the building about thirty feet, forming a small courtyard. Parked inside the courtyard backed up against one wall were three white pick-up trucks and a small white minivan, all unmarked except one, which was an extended cab pick-up with a blue light bar on top.

He was barely there two minutes, and a woman in a state uniform, smoking a cigarette, came walking up to him and asked what he was doing there. She looked young, in her mid-twenties or so and had kind of a punkish look with blonde streaked hair and a fair amount of makeup. Greg explained that he was there for a 10 a.m. interview with Paul for the technician job. She laughed a little bit at that and said, "Oh boy, fresh meat for the grinder," and then asked his name. She stuck out her hand for a handshake and said, "My name is Karen. If you choose not to run away screaming, good luck." She stepped on her cigarette and walked back into the building after telling him to go around to the front side entrance and that he could not go in the garage. He waited until 9:40 and walked around to the front of the building and rang the buzzer to get in.

The front lobby had two sets of doors, which you couldn't enter until you were buzzed in. Once inside the main lobby, there was an office door off to one side clearly marked "State Police," then another set of doors that looked like they led to the back of the building where technicians worked and on the far side was an enclosed area sealed by big glass panels and a woman sitting behind a desk. She asked, "Can I help you?" Greg told her why he was there, and she told him to take a seat and she would call Paul.

After a few more minutes, Karen came through the doors and said, "Follow me." Greg got up and followed her through the doors up a stairwell that led to a large office area on the second floor. She stood at the top of the stairs holding the door and told him the conference room was on the left and again said, "Good luck."

Greg entered the conference room, and there was a very long oval-shaped table with a dozen chairs around it. Seated right about the middle of the table on the side facing the door were three people. There was an attractive woman who appeared to be about Greg's age, give or take a year, sitting there with a legal pad staring at him and looking ready to write down anything said. On her left, was an older man, who appeared to be around retirement age and a little heavy set. On his left was a sharp-dressed man in his mid-thirties, looking very disinterested in the whole process. Without even looking up from whatever paperwork he was reading he said," Take a seat." The older man stood up and extended his hand for a handshake and introduced himself as Paul, the technical manager. Greg shook his hand and introduced himself and handed him the copy of the resume he had in the manila envelope and sat down.

Just as he did, the woman who had not said anything until this point started writing on her legal pad.

The younger man in the suit finally looked up at Paul, took the resume out of the envelope and started to skim the copy. He extended his hand for a handshake and introduced himself as James Baxter, the chief administrator. He looked at Greg's resume and asked, "So do you have any experience with dead bodies?"

Not wanting to lie about anything Greg explained that the only one he had encountered was a man the rescue squad he worked with had coded and passed away in his home. James asked about the Red Cross and what Greg had done for them on a disaster scene. Greg explained that primarily he was trained for logistics and shelter management for large-scale disaster operations. James asked, "Where do you see yourself in five years?" Greg responded with the standard interview answer about moving up in the organization and trying to improve efficiency. James looked right at him and said, "Well, we don't expect anyone to be here more than two years. This is just a stepping stone job for people. Some people stay longer, whether we want them to or not." Paul asked a couple of questions, but the one that stood out was "How well do you get along with other people?" There were a couple more irrelevant questions. All the while the woman never stopped writing on her legal pad or even looked up from it. Paul stood up and extended his hand for the handshake again and said, "Thanks, we will be in touch." The whole interview was over in less than fifteen minutes. At this point Greg thought he had wasted his time and completely blew the interview. He stopped on the way home for lunch, feeling disappointed with the whole scenario.

When he arrived home just after noon time, he saw the answering machine flashing and hit play. The message said, "Hey, Greg. This is Paul Rourke. We need you to come back in for a second interview tomorrow. Be here at 8 a.m. and plan on being here for about four hours. Dress comfortably, no suit."

SECOND INTERVIEW

Knowing how heavy traffic was into Boston for an early-morning commute, Greg left his house at 5 a.m. and arrived about 6:45. He parked in back again and went to the front of the building, but it was locked. No one was at the front desk that he could see, so he sat in the parked truck out back.

Shortly before 7 a.m., Karen pulled in and parked in the spot next to Greg. She rolled down her window and laughed out loud and said, "You haven't run away yet?" Greg kind of laughed back and said, "No, not yet. They wanted me back for a second interview." Karen laughed again and said, "It's not another interview. They are going to put you in the autopsy room to see if you can handle it." She continued laughing. She got out of her car and told Greg to follow her and that she would get him situated. She was as pleasant as the day before and seemed pretty laid back.

As they walked toward the open garage door, Karen lit another cigarette and asked if Greg smoked. "Yes, I do," he replied. She said, "Well, you better get one last one in. You won't be getting a chance to smoke for a while." She went on. "When we do get a chance to sneak in a butt, we come out here, but you have to stand in this corner so you are not on camera." They stood there smoking and making small talk Greg asked her how long she had been working there. She looked at him with a grin and said, "I am almost one of the old timers here." She laughed, "Just under two years now. They hire people in groups of three to six people and see who sticks. When I was hired, they had a group of four. Out of those, it is only me and Ricardo left." Greg asked the obvious question, "Why is there such a high turnover rate?" She responded, "Well, they don't make it very easy here. The job itself is great. It's all the other bull shit you have to deal with is the problem."

Just then a dark-colored minivan pulled in, hooked toward the parking area, and started to back into the enclosed courtyard where they stood. Karen said, "Incoming," and dropped her cigarette and stepped on it. She continued, "Must have been a busy night. Great day to do an autopsy." She walked toward the back of the minivan just as a man in his early twenties or so dressed in a suit popped open the back door.

"What's up, Jimmy?" she said loudly in a very friendly tone. "What fantastic things are you bringing in today?" She spoke like they had been friends for a long time. Jimmy had a big smile on his face. "Nothing to get too excited about. These are the MVAs from early this morning in Fall River. Cars were a mess, took them a while to get the bodies out." He looked over at Greg still smiling as he pulled a stretcher out of the back of the van. Greg was sure he could tell he was very nervous about what he was about to see. Jimmy pulled his stretcher all the way out and stopped. Karen stepped up to the van and started to pull the other stretcher out for him. Now both were out in plain view in the back of the van but not in the garage yet as they continued to chit chat about things and life in general. Greg had not moved from where he stood, but could hear Jimmy ask Karen, "You guys getting some fresh blood in again?" She said, "Yeah, I guess so. You know they never let us know what's going on." They both laughed a little.

Greg was still standing there smoking his cigarette looking at the stretchers, not sure if it was relief or disappointment but there was nothing really to see. Both bodies were in body bags, securely strapped down and covered with a kind of dark maroon velvet cloth. If you did not know where you were, you would not have been able to tell there were bodies under those covers. Jimmy positioned the stretchers side-by-side right up against each other and pushed both in at the same time. Greg could hear him knock on the interior door inside the garage and then the door opening.

Karen said, "Well we might as well get this over with" and

motioned to Greg to follow her in. They got to the interior door, which had a card access lock. Karen turned to Greg and said, "I know this is all very exciting and new for new people, but just try to keep a low profile when you are inside. Try not to initiate contact with anyone unless they start talking to you. Most of the people in here will throw you under the bus if they have to. You'll figure out who you can trust and who you can't quick enough." She slid her card through the lock, and the door clicked. She opened it as wide as she could.

Inside the door Jimmy stood at a tall skinny counter writing in a long old-timey- looking ledger-type book. At the end of the tall counter on a right angle, the counter top dropped to a more normal height, and there was a phone and a computer toward the end of it with a bunch of papers scattered on top of what would have been a clear space. The walls in the entire area were painted a two-tone gray, with a darker gray on the bottom half. A technician sat behind the counter wearing a headset attached to the phone. He stood up and flipped the book around, so he could read it and started writing his own notes in it. "Thanks, Jim" he said. ""I will get you your slips in a minute." He turned to Karen. "Can I get some help processing these?" Karen said, "Yeah, I guess. Let me get changed first. I am on the road today." She walked down a long hallway that was separated from the technician desk by a heavy curtain that looked like the same material and color as the cloth covering the bodies on the stretchers. As Karen went through the curtain, she pulled it open about three quarters of the way and left it open. Greg could see the two stretchers sitting about ten feet or so down the hall, the bodies still strapped down.

The technician behind the desk finally acknowledged that Greg was standing there like a deer in the headlights. He stuck out his hand and said, "Adam, I am the nightshift guy. You working with him?" and motioned with his head toward Jimmy who was now standing against the wall in front of the shorter counter. Jimmy said with a big smile, "You know they never give me any help. He is your new puppy." Adam now smiled. "Ohhh, you the trauma dog or the nurse?" while still looking at Greg. Greg replied with a nervous chuckle, "Well, I am not a nurse and have no idea what a trauma dog is." Adam said, "Paul told me this morning there are four of you coming in - a prison nurse, firefighter/EMT, a customs agent, and an ER nurse - which one are you?" "Well I guess I am the firefighter/EMT, but I am only on a volunteer department," said Greg. "Close enough, trauma dog," Adam said. "I will call Paul and let him know you are here. Go have a seat in back," he continued as he pointed to a door leading to a back room behind the counter.

Greg walked around the counter into the back room. There was a desk with a phone and computer set up with two filing cabinets along one wall. A short distance past that there was a folding table set up with an eclectic group of office chairs, not one matching the other. Greg took a seat on the far side of the table, so he could see if anyone who came in. As he looked around the room, he saw several shelving units with various medical items and cases of Tyvek suits and latex gloves. Syringes and needles that he did not know could be so large, various test tubes with different colored tops, stacks of two different size white buckets, lids and glass jars of various sizes, and other general office supplies mixed in. He sat there just taking in all he saw and couldn't help but notice a strange musty mix of smells in the air. He thought that the smell was not as bad as he thought it was going to be.

At 7:30 a.m., Karen poked her head through the door and told Greg to go down to Paul's office where Paul was waiting for him and wished him good luck. She said, "Just go all the way down the hallway - all the way to the end. His office is on the right." Greg thanked her and got up, very nervous about the whole thing. He walked through the curtain, which had now been pulled back to a closed position.

The smell was considerably stronger on this side of the curtain. It could only be described as something rotting. There was a door on the left marked "Deco." Along that wall was a small stainless-steel counter that had nothing on it. At the end of the counter was a computer on a tall stand with what looked like a label printer. The wall formed a cubby hole about ten feet long and gave about a four-foot-deep inset. One of the bodies that was brought in was placed in this space on a stainless-steel table with a drain hole and fit just about perfectly, with a little room on each end to spare. There was a digital read out on a panel over the table and body, so it is safe to assume this was a scale. There was also a small plastic cart that had a roller and an ink pad with finger print cards. Greg paused for a second or two to look at the bag on the table. He could see blood clearly streaked on the outside of the bag. The bag on the scale was unzipped just enough to have a foot poking out, and there was a tag that read "driver 05-987." Directly opposite of this table, the hallway formed another recessed area. Two doors side-by-side, the one on his right marked "X-ray" and the left "Autopsy. On the wall on the inset part there were doors facing each other that were not marked. The other body was also placed on a stain-less-steel table and was sitting in this area.

Just then from the other side of the curtain, he heard people start to yell at each other, loud for an office environment. From what he briefly overheard, he did not want to stand there gawk-ing at dead bodies. They were arguing over who was responsible for processing the bodies since they were a night shift scene. One woman yelled, "You're on the road today, you process them. I am getting ready for autopsies." Just as Greg turned to start walking down the hall, Adam was right there behind him in plain street clothes. "What do you think, trauma dog, would you have been able to save them?" he said with a big grin on his face. "I really didn't take a look at them," Greg responded, feeling like he'd been caught doing something wrong. Adam looked at Greg still smiling. "Trust me," he said, "you would not have been able to. I am out of here, good luck." Adam started to walk away. Greg could still hear what now sounded like several people arguing from the other side of the curtain and then a big metal door slam. Greg started walking quickly down to the end of the hall figuring he'd spent too much time listening.

On the left side of the hall were a line of stainless-steel tables, all empty. About halfway down there was a break in the line of tables, so as not to block the door to the cooler where the bodies were stored, and a small electric fork lift. Opposite one of these tables was another door on the right not marked. Greg reached the end of the hallway and turned right. The hall on that side was only about six feet long. There were two doors side-by-side, one marked "Viewing." The other was wide open, and Greg could see Paul sitting behind his desk looking at a monitor and holding his phone to his ear. There was a door immediately on the right marked "Laundry." The laundry room looked like a small bomb had gone off or a teenager's room. Uniforms were in piles on the floor and on a counter. There was a standard-looking washer and dryer. The room itself was not much bigger than a walk-in closet.

Paul's office was a long rectangle only about eight feet wide but about twenty feet long. Metal cabinets lined the long wall. One had stacks of paper on every shelf. One had what looked like lab coats, and the other a mix of scrubs and uniforms. The other side wall of the office had a large cork board with papers and some photos and papers pinned to it. They did not appear to be in any kind of order. There were two very different chairs in front of Paul's desk - one with two stacks of papers on it. Paul looked at Greg now standing right outside his door and gestured for him to come in as he talked on the phone. "I don't give a shit," he said in a frustrated tone. "They are on the roster, so someone get them ready and who is cutting today? OK, I have a few for you to observe today. Let me know when they are ready." He hung up the phone and looked at Greg with a kind of smile on his face. "Did you get lost?" he asked. Without giving Greg a chance to answer, he went on. "I saw you on the monitor" and pointed to his computer screen, which had nine different camera angles of various areas of the building. "What do you think?" Now feeling like he had been caught doing something wrong again Greg managed a, "I didn't see anything. They were closed up." "Too bad," Paul said. "It's best to get the first couple out of the way." He stood up moving slowly, looking like he may be even older than he appeared and had a bad hip or back and shuffled his way around his desk "Follow me," he said moving very slowly. As he shuffled past the cabinet, he grabbed a set of scrubs and hand-ed them to Greg. He pointed across the hallway to the other side, which also only went back about six feet. "Men's locker room is on the right. Put those on. You are going to sit in on some autopsies to see how it goes."

Greg entered the locker room to change. The room was fairly small too, one stall, one urinal, and a shower on the back wall with lockers and a wooden bench. There was a man wearing nothing but a towel standing at the sink shaving. He appeared to be in his fifties and a little on the heavy side. He gave Greg a quick glance and then tuned back to face the mirror to continue shaving, never saying a word. Greg changed as quickly as he could. The scrubs were about two sizes too big, but he was not really sure what to do about that. He figured he would just deal with it. The man shaving finally spoke. "You are cutting today?" he asked. "I am just here to observe a few autopsies," Greg replied. "Are you a resident or doctor?" "Neither, I am here for a second interview for a morgue technician job." "Huh," he grunted. "It's that time again, I guess. People just don't understand." He finished rinsing his face off and turned away again.

Greg exited the locker room figuring he would return to Paul's office. Paul was not there, so he stood awkwardly in the hall out-side his door. An attractive woman came out of the women's locker room and opened the door that led down that hallway. Just as she opened the door, also on a card access, she looked at Greg and asked, " Can I help you with something?" He explained why he was there and standing in the hall. She asked," Were you just in that locker room? Did you see Freddy in there?" "I saw someone in there shaving, "Greg replied. "Oh, good. Can you tell him I need some x-rays done for Dr. Cranston? Oh, never mind I don't want to get him going first thing in the morning." Then she said, "Well, Paul isn't going to be back in his office for a while. He probably went for coffee. Why don't you follow me?" She started to go through the door. "What's your name? Where you from?" she asked in rapid fire. Greg responded, "My name is Greg, and I live in New Hampshire." She stopped and looked at him with a puzzled look on her face and said, "New Hampshire?! Why do you want to come to Boston? They shooting people left and right in Boston. Well, whatever, my name is Sharon. I think I am one of the first-shift supervisors."

They continued down the hall as she stopped at the body on the scale and flipped the tag tied to the body's shoelace still seemingly have not been touched by anyone. She muttered, "Hmm, people better be learning to slow down around here," and continued down the hall. She pulled the curtain aside and yelled out, "Who is going for coffee?" and then, "I need those bodies done, people." Sharon looked in the back room. There was a lot of talking loudly and commotion going on back there. "Greg, why don't you sit up front with me until we figure out who we are with today?" "She shuffled some papers and picked one out and started reading. "Let's see, who is cutting what today?"

Just then the door leading to the stairwell on the right side of the tech station opened. In walked a man about Greg's age , early to mid-forties, reddish-blonde hair but losing most of it on top. He carried a tray with four coffees and a bag on it. "Charlie!" Sharon said loudly. "You bring me a coffee?" Charlie said, "Yeah, and a bagel with cream cheese," with a strong Boston accent. "Oh good!" she said happily. She pulled the bagel out of the bag and spread the cream cheese around. "I need you to do me a favor. This is Greg. He is here to observe an autopsy. Who are you working with today?"

Charlie looked at her with a kind of grimace on his face and said," I am supposed to be working with Dr. Lowe today. You sure you want him to see that? He may not come back." He smiled. "It'll be fine, might as well see what we are working with here anyways." They both chuckled a little.

Charlie looked at Greg and said, "Hang tight. I'll let you know when we are starting. They are in the morning meeting now anyways." Charlie headed into the back room with the rest of the coffees. Greg sat there quietly for several minutes while Sharon messed around on her phone. The phone on the desk finally made a dull short tone. She answered, "Tech station...uh huh...OK," and hung up. "Well, here we go," she said sighing.

"Charlie!" she yelled. "Dr. Lowe is coming down. He wants the girl first. Then he will look at one of the mva's." Charlie reappeared from the back room holding his coffee and still chewing something. He motioned to Greg with an exaggerated arm wave. "Follow me. Let's get this over with." He walked past the curtain without opening it, and Charlie saw the bodies sitting there still. He looked at the tag on the body sitting on the scale. "Sharon, who is sitting in the hallway?" he yelled. Sharon yelled back, "Dr. Lowe is going to do the passenger, so one of those is yours." Then she yelled even louder, "I need those bodies done, people!" Greg heard someone yell back at her. "Those are Karen's problem. She's on the road!" Sharon responded, "She already left with Ricardo to go to Cape Cod hospital." Charlie moved over to the other body and said, "Let's take a look," and unzipped the bag. The body bag had a lot of blood at the end of the bag. Charlie flipped the flap over slowly so as not to spatter any on the wall or floor. Still holding his coffee in one hand, he stood over the head of the body on the table.

The head and neck had obvious trauma. Greg could see what appeared to be gray matter just kind of hanging over where his right ear would have been. The right side of the head and face were bashed in to a point of almost not being able to recognize this was a person. There was also a large pool of blood at that end of the bag. "He was apparently not wearing his seatbelt," Charlie said without ever looking up. "If there are no charges, he will probably be just a view with tox, so that's not bad." He placed the flap over the body again but did not zipper the bag. "I'll show you really quick how to set up for Dr. Lowe... Come on this way." Charlie turned to his left and went in the autopsy room door.

As it turned out, there were two autopsy rooms side-by-side separated by a wall with glass panels and a door, so you could see into the other room. Along the back was a stainless-steel counter with drawers and cabinets running the length of the wall. The only thing on the counter top was at the farthest end. It appeared to be about a dozen glass jars with white lids and white labels. It was hard to tell what was inside them, but whatever it was, was sitting in some liquid. On the wall with the glass panels, there was a smaller stainless-steel cabinet, which mirrored the opposite wall with the same cabinet. The front wall of the room had a large stainless-steel double sink with removable panels with holes in them on either side of the sinks. Each side has its own faucet. In the middle of this set up was a larger yellow hose attached to the back side of the double sink. In the center of the room was a large white porcelain sink with the same hose set up but no counter space on either side, and to the left of that was another large stainless sink identical to the one Charlie stood in front of.

Charlie put on a pair of latex gloves and set his coffee on the side countertop. Once again without even looking up at Greg he said, "Not much point in explaining anything to you at this point. You may not be back after today, but feel free to check out the set up when I am done." He started to rummage through the cabinet and pulled out a white, badly stained cutting board and placed it on the right side of the double sink, then he opened the draw and stuck both hands in and scooped out a bunch of items and sorted them on the countertop. Greg wasn't sure if Charlie was explaining things to him, but he picked out certain items and talked as he did. "Loafing knife, slicing knife, two scalpels, scissors, no clamps." Charlie arranged all these items on the cutting board. He opened the other drawer on the cabinet. "Pencil, marker, sewing needle," and placed them on top of the cabinet he'd just opened. He opened the bottom cabinet and pulled out one of the glass jars with the white top and opened it. There was a box on top of the counter with a spigot on it. He filled the jar about halfway and screwed the cover back on and said, "Stock jar with Formalin," and placed it on the cutting board. He brushed past Greg to the back counter and opened two drawers at the same time. "Save tubes." He pulled out one with a purple top and one with a red top and closed the drawers. He squatted down and opened a cabinet. "Blood, urine, vitreous," and pulled out three small plastic containers each with a different color top, red, yellow and, white and placed them on the cutting board. He opened the drawer on the left side of the double sink and pulled out a large stainless-steel bowl and a large and small sponge. He grabbed a bottle of bleach and a scoop of powdered soap and dumped some in the bowl with the sponges and filled it with water. He pulled out a large stainless-steel bucket and put a red bio-hazard bag inside like a trash bin inside the sink. "That's it for set up, follow me." He headed toward the center of the room and went through the door leading into the other autopsy room. He took an immediate left into another door. "This is the anteroom. You might as well hang out here. I am going to pull his bodies and when he comes down, I will show you how to suit up."

The anteroom was only about ten feet by fifteen feet, but there were two desks forming an "L" each with a computer and phone, a small file cabinet, and a wooden rack hanging on the wall with separate compartments to sort different forms and diagrams. On the far end was a shelving unit stocked with Tyvek suits in different sizes, gloves, mask, face shields, head covers, and booties for shoe protection. Greg couldn't help but notice that if more than one person was trying to suit up, it would probably be difficult in the small area remaining.

Greg could see through the window in the anteroom that Charlie had pulled a body in on one of those stainless-steel tables and had hooked it into the large double sink on the far right. He could also hear banging around on the other side of the anteroom. Charlie appeared in the room with another table, which he pushed up against the back counter. More banging and thuds, and yet a third body was brought in the room. Just as Charlie was lining up the third body with the others, he was paged on the intercom to come to the tech station. It seems like several minutes that Greg sat in the room at one of the desks. A few people came into the room and grabbed papers off the rack, including one seemingly very happy guy with a big camera slung around his neck. He greeted Greg with an enthusiastic, "Good morning." He had an accent and was possibly from the Bahamas or some tropical islands. He grabbed an apron, pair of gloves, and a surgical mask. He managed to put these on rather quickly and went into the room and started to photograph one of the bodies from several angles.

Charlie finally reappeared from the hallway door and said, "We have some extra company." Three other people followed him in, making the room seem quite crowded. Two women and a man. Charlie spoke to all of them at the same time. "OK, so we have Diana, Brad, Kate, and Greg. You guys are all here for the second interview, which is not really an interview. They just want you to observe an autopsy or two to see if it's for you." He continued. "So, we have an EMT, an R.N., a prison nurse, and a customs agent. If anyone feels like stepping out of the room at any time, feel free. Try not to get in Dr. Lowe's way or ask too many questions while he is working. I'll answer what I can, but try and hold off until the doctor is done. OK, here we go. Let's get suited up. Full-body Tyvek, small, medium, large, or XL are here. Apron over that, the sleeves over each arm, booties on your feet, skull cap, surgical mask, and then a face shield, and we are ready to go. And don't forget latex gloves," he added.

Charlie wasted no time getting fully suited up, as the four of them scrambled get ready. "OK, as soon as you guys are ready, come on in. I have to help the trooper take his photos." Charlie exited the room.

FIRST AUTOPSY

The four interviewees in the anteroom kind of silently decided to wait for all to be ready before going in. They all double checked each other to make sure they weren't missing anything for protective clothing and went into the room in single file. Charlie had moved one of the gurneys to the center of the room and locked the wheels. They lined up against the back counter, standing about five feet back from the body. Charlie had the man's arm straight up in the air and looked like he was straining slightly to hold the man on his side, exposing some tattoos on his back. The trooper snapped several photos from close ups to full-body shots. The group had to separate to allow him to step back all the way to the counter.

The body on the gurney was a good-sized male, about six foot three and two hundred and fifty-two pounds. Charlie spoke. "This guy was found unresponsive at home, not much medical history, thirty-eight years old, no suspected drug use, that's why he is here."

"You are teaching class today, Charlie?" the trooper asked with his cheerful tropical accent as he looked down at the display screen on his camera. "Possibly new technicians," Charlie replied as he attempted to gently lower the body to a lying position. "Oh, good. We need new blood in here. You never go to bed at night thinking you will end up here in the morning, the poor bastard. Charlie will figure it out. Good luck, guys." He gave a wave and a head nod as he left.

Charlie walked around the body and opened a drawer on the counter and pulled out a handful of very large syringes and a wrapped drug test stick. He faced the group on the opposite side of the body. He stabbed the needle into the body between the belly button and genitals and pulled the plunger up, filling the syringe with urine. He squirted a little on the drug test stick and said, "This will test for opiates, thc, or cocaine, but he will be an autopsy regardless." He filled the yellow jar with the remaining urine in the syringe. He grabbed the jar with the white lid and a new syringe and stabbed the side corner of each eyeball and extracted a clear fluid. "This is vitreous we send that off for testing with the blood and urine," he explained. The four of them stood in a slight state of shock, grimacing at the sight of an eyeball being deflated. Next Charlie grabbed the red top jar and a new syringe. He stuck it in the top of the shoulder and drew a good amount of blood. "This is clavicle blood." It easily filled that jar. "Dr. Lowe also likes to take femoral blood, but he will do that himself during the autopsy." Charlie lined the jars on the gurney next to the man's head. There was a small stream of blood trickling down from where he'd removed the needle from the man's clavicle.

Charlie moved over to the body he had locked into the sink and unzipped the bag. He motioned for the four to come over. "This is a rough one." He flipped the cover of the bag, exposing a teenage girl on the table. She was a small thin girl only about five-foot tall and very slim, with long blonde hair. He gently rolled her on her side and tucked the body bag under. He moved around to the other side and rolled her on her other side. He removed the body bag and placed it under the table. He continued, "She was fifteen, was out riding her horse and got thrown or fell off and whacked her head on a rock or something just right, more than likely a basilar skull fracture. They are not sure how long she was down before she was found, though." He went through the same process drawing the body fluids. "The doctor is going to do her first." He placed the sample jars next to her head as he had done with the first body.

He moved to the third table and opened the bag. "This last one is just an elderly person that was found on a wellbeing check by a neighbor. She had tons of medical history, but her primary care won't sign a death certificate because he had not seen her for a while, so she will just be a view with toxicology from the lab. She does not need an autopsy. He went through the same routine, drawing fluids and lining those jars next to her head as he had with the others.

Just then the autopsy room door burst open. In came a short, heavy-set man in blue scrubs wearing a white apron with no other protective clothing, not even gloves. He walked quickly and carried a small digital camera. "Charlie are these mine?" he asked as he approached the girl's table. He stood at the head and grabbed the girl's head, rocking it back and forth. "Yes, Dr. Lowe." The doctor snapped a picture of both sides of the toe tag. Charlie placed a small stool next to the body for the doctor to stand on to hold his camera over the body to get a full body shot. Charlie stood at the ready seemingly knowing exactly when and what position to move the body as the doctor hurriedly snapped pictures.

"Charlie," he said, "Who are these people... residents?" without ever looking at the group. "No, doctor," Charlie responded. "Possible new techs." The doctor turned to face the group with his hands on his hips. "I would appreciate it if you do not crowd my table. If I think you need to see something, I will call you over." He turned away from the group and started to photograph his other two cases. Charlie walked around as quickly as the doctor. They seemed to be perfectly choreographed. As the doctor took photos, Charlie did not miss a step. "You can block the girl," he said to Charlie as he walked toward the door. "I will be back in a few minutes." He sat at a desk in the anteroom after pulling several papers from the rack on the wall and started going through some case folders that had been sitting there.

Charlie easily lifted the girl and placed a "block" between the shoulder blades, which held the body in position for the autopsy. "He must be in a good mood today. He was kind of polite and didn't swear at you guys," Charlie said with a kind of chuckle.

Standing there fully suited up, Greg felt the temperature rising and the heat building up inside the Tyvek suit. He thought it would be a long day working in that suit for eight hours. The mask he wore did not do much to deter the odors of the room either. The elderly woman had a distinctive odor that was very musty and possibly some fecal matter smell. The large man had a vomit and urine odor. The girl did not seem to have any odor, but at this point Charlie had washed down the body , so it was hard to tell.

Dr. Lowe burst back into the room again and tossed three file folders on the back counter and pulled a sheet of peel-and-stick labels from each one and placed the proper labels on the bodies on each table. Charlie immediately starts to peel the labels and stick them to the sample jars on each table.

Dr. Lowe stood near the girl, both hands on his hips again staring at the body. He grabbed his scalpel off the cutting board that Charlie had set up and motioned toward the group to step closer. "Just make sure Charlie has room to walk around, he said. He started to make his first cuts, starting at the left shoulder toward the center of the body and then a cut from the right shoulder joining the cut in the middle just above the breasts, then a long slice right down the middle all the way down to the top of the pelvic bone forming a "Y" incision. He cut very fast, but this was not going to be a delicate surgery. He grabbed the point from the two should blade cuts and started to pull the skin up. He cut and disconnected it from the sternum all the way to the bottom of the neck. He worked the sides in the same fashion, pulling the sides of the skin away and down slicing quickly with his scalpel to separate the skin from the ribs. The internal portion of the body was not fully visible, but the ribs and collar bone and intestines were.

The four of them stood in disbelief of what they were seeing. All of them were kind of looking at each other to see if others had any reaction. Greg started to think he might not be able to handle this and felt himself getting a little dizzy and even queasy. His forehead was starting to sweat.

Charlie handed the doctor what looked like a large pair of hedge trimmers, and he started cutting the rib cage. The ribs cracked, and the cutter's blades came together with each closing of the handles. Greg really was not sure if this was for him but managed to stand his ground. The doctor handed the cutters to Charlie and removed the chest plate he had just cut, once again needing his scalpel to free it from its attachment points under the ribs. All the internal organs were now exposed. Greg took a half a step backwards toward the counter, just as Kate decided this was not for her and started to walk away and back into the anteroom.

Dr. Lowe with his scalpel in hand started to remove the heart. He sliced the pericardium sac and with his right hand and scooped the heart upwards as he cut the aorta with his left hand. He placed the heart in a hanging scale over the sink and wrote the weight on the cutting board. He put the heart on his cutting board and took his loafing knife and sliced it right down the middle. He cut a section of each half and dropped them in the stock jar and tossed the remaining pieces of heart into the bucket with the red bio bag in it. "You can start the head. I am saving the brain," he said.

Charlie picked up his own scalpel and positioned himself at the head of the body and took another head block and placed it under the lower skull and neck, holding the head in a better position. He parted the girl's hair as best he could, folding most of it over her face. He started to make his incision from underneath the right ear around the underside of the skull and back up to the opposite point of the left ear. Then using his thumbs, he worked them underneath the skin he'd just cut. The skin peeled away from the skull. Once it was loose enough, he got a firm grip with both hands and started to forcibly separate the skin from the skull. It literally folded over the face, making a tearing kind of sound as he made enough progress to expose the entire skull. Dr. Lowe stopped what he was doing and stood at the head near Charlie and ran his hands around the bottom of the skull. "OK, you can open it," he said and went back to removing and weighing the organs.

Now feeling very sweaty and even a little weak, Greg watched as Charlie plugged in a Stryker saw, used to cut bone and in this case the skull to remove the brain. His knees nearly buckled when Charlie started cutting. Bone dust flew off, and the smell was similar to the one made when your dentist drills your teeth. He made a short straight cut back from the ear and then a short straight cut down. He guided the saw around the back-bottom side of the skull all the way around to the left side. At this point the four had stepped all the way back to the counter. None of the four were handling this well or expected it to be like this. Charlie completed cutting all the way around and picked up a stainless-steel "T" that had a wedged end. He stuck the wedge in the cut he'd just made and twisted the handle. The skull made a loud crack and pop sound. The released portion of the skull was clearly detached but clung in place by the dura inside the skull.

Dr. Lowe once again stopped what he was doing and stepped into Charlie's spot. He ripped the skull cap free of the dura to expose the brain. The brain started to droop and fell out of the skull. Dr. Lowe grabbed the top of it with one hand and cupped the bottom with the other and worked it free. He carried the brain and placed it on the scale, writing down its weight. He went back to examine the inside of the skull.

He motioned the three left to come over. He had a finger stuck deep inside the skull going down into the spinal cord. He wiggled his finger a little bit back and forth and said, "Basal fracture," and moved back to his cutting board. "You can sew up the head," he said to Charlie. Charlie jumped into action again, replacing the skull cap and unfolding the skin and pulling it over the skull cap. He grabbed his sewing needle and made about six sutures in a few different points. He used his hands to comb the girl's long hair back in place. One could not tell the head had been opened anymore. Dr. Lowe removed his gloves and told Charlie he was all set. He could close her up.

Charlie took the red bag out of the bucket and tied it shut and placed it inside the body cavity. He replaced the chest plate and folded the skin back into place and once again used a half dozen strategic stitches to close the body cavity. He ran a stream of water over the body and wiped her down with a large sponge. He placed her back in the body bag.

Charlie told the group it would be about thirty minutes until the next autopsy, so if they needed a bathroom or smoke, now was the time.

They removed the protective clothing in the autopsy room and placed it in a bio-hazard bin. Diana asked Charlie, "Do we have to stay for another autopsy? I have an appointment. I did not know I needed to be here this long." Charlie said, "Just check in with Paul before you leave. I don't know what he wanted you guys to do." Brad chimed in that he needed to go as well. Greg kind of wanted to stay to see if he could handle at least one more. Paul had told him to plan on about four hours. He told Charlie he was going to step outside for a few minutes and that he would be back. Charlie informed him there was a store about a hundred yards away and he could grab a coffee if he wanted before the next case. The next case was going to be the big guy. The elderly woman was just going to be a view. So that is what Greg did. He grabbed a coffee and sat outside the building in back.

Greg was back in the anteroom in exactly thirty minutes and started to suit up again. Both sides of the autopsy room were empty except for the big guy who was now locked into the sink where the girl had been done. Charlie came back in the anteroom and told Greg that Dr. Lowe would be down in about ten minutes. He said Charlie could start. Charlie suited up again, and they went into the room. The body was already on the block and ready to go. Charlie stood on the side as Dr. Lowe worked on and grabbed a scalpel and started to make the "Y" incision. Greg stood on the other side of the table in amazement. He was thinking to himself that they might be expecting him to do this! It did not take Charlie more than ten or fifteen minutes to have the body eviscerated with all the organs removed and weighed and sitting on the cutting board intact waiting for the doctor.

Heart, left and right lungs, liver, and spleen. Charlie put the head on a block. He explained, while he worked on opening the skull, that Dr. Lowe liked to string out the intestines instead of taking them out in a block and would probably save stomach contents on this one. This was a case that would not be resolved until toxicology results came back. The man did test positive for THC, but that would not have killed him. He had little medical history, at least none that would have caused an early death, so unless Dr. Lowe saw something with the heart or brain that was obvious, this would probably be a pending case and unable to list a cause on the death certificate, other than pending.

Dr. Lowe finally made an appearance, and his ten minutes turned out to be about thirty. He asked Charlie if he saw anything obvious. He took his spot at the cutting board and started to slice off pieces for the stock jar. Charlie responded that he did not see anything obvious. Greg watched as Charlie sewed up and cleaned the body just like he had the last one. Once again, after Charlie sewed and cleaned, it was hard to tell the body had been autopsied. Greg helped Charlie re-bag the body and started to remove the protective clothing. Charlie asked him what he thought about the whole thing. Greg told him, "I think I could give it a shot." "Good," Charlie said. "We need a lot more help around here. Go tell Paul you're all set here. Autopsies are done."

Greg walked down the hall to Paul's office. His chair was once again empty. Greg waited in the hall for a few minutes and decided he should go back to the tech station. The locker room was just right across the hall, so he figured he would change out of the scrubs. Greg entered the locker room, and Freddy was sitting on the wooden bench, staring at the wall, wearing scrubs.

"You know," he said, "I don't mind them hiring more help, but I am sick and tired of new techs coming in here and bossing me around. I have been here twenty-seven years and people just think they can come in here and tell me what to do. I did this in the military, too, and the same thing happens all the time. Sharon has only been here twenty years. How can she be a supervisor already? People just don't understand." The only response Greg could muster was, "I am not coming in to boss people around. This is all new to me." He changed as quickly as he could and headed toward the tech station.

Greg walked down the long hallway. He could see Karen and

Ricardo had just come in with two more bodies, and they are transferring a third body to a funeral home's stretcher. "Hey, how did it go? Did you make through an autopsy? Hey, Rick, we are getting new techs again," Karen interrupted. "Cool," he responded. "We need them." Greg stopped to look at the bodies they'd brought in. They no longer looked real. They looked like they were made of wax. He said proudly that he managed to sit through two autopsies and a view with Charlie and Dr. Lowe. Both bodies were in the same gray body bags the others he had seen had been in but also wrapped in sheets and plastic inside the bag. "Just hospital cases, nothing exciting," Karen said. "I hope the good doctor behaved himself today." Rick seemed to find that statement amusing. "You never know with him," he said with a big smile. Sharon poked her head through the curtain. "I got a scene when you're done there." "No lunch again today," Karen remarked. She double checked the toe tags to make sure they had the right information, and she and Rick pushed both gurneys toward the cooler.

Sharon walked past the curtain. "Why did you change your clothes? You are leaving us already?" she said, looking at Greg. "Shifts don't end until 3:30." "Well, I guess for today, Paul told me four hours to observe a few autopsies. I saw two and a view. Pretty sure Charlie said they were done cutting today." "Oh, I guess if Charlie said you were done, you might as well go then. Did you tell Paul you're leaving?" she asked sighing. "He was not in his office. I waited a few minutes for him." Still in a sighing tone, Karen said, "I will tell him you are all set when I see him. Thank you." She moved to the door labeled "x-ray" and looked in the small thin window like she was looking for something then poked her head in the door. She closed the door and turned around and looked straight up at the ceiling and yelled," Anybody seen Freddy! I need some x-ray's done!" She walked slowly toward the locker room area. "I'll see you tomorrow," she said as she did a zombie-like walk down the hall. Sharon yelled from all the way down the hall as Greg was leaving. "I am going to lunch, people!" and a door slammed behind her.

Greg was feeling proud of himself and hopped in his truck and headed home. Traffic was not that bad leaving Boston this early on a Friday, so Greg decided to stop on the way home at one of his favorite roast beef places for lunch. "I guess if I can handle a roast beef sandwich with all that sauce on it, I should be good to go for this place if they call me," he said to himself. It took just about two hours to get home, including the stop.

Greg put on a pot of coffee and got ready to hop in the shower. He wasn't sure why he felt the need to shower but took a nice long hot one. The answering machine flashed, indicating that he had a message. What were the odds, he thought, that the morgue would already be calling? He did not get a chance to see Paul before he left so who knew. He hit the play button and heard unfortunately the voice of his boss's wife, who ran the office of the demolition company. "You need to be here at 4 a.m. Monday. You are going back to Portland next week. If you take Monday off, you won't have any work the rest of the week. Thanks." She hung up the phone.

Well that slapped Greg's thoughts back into reality, and it sucked that he must go back to Portland. He poured himself a cup of coffee and went into the living room to watch TV. About an hour passed and the phone rang. He answered, "Hello." The voice on the other end said, "Greg Benson, please." "Speaking," Greg responded. "This is Paul from the ME's Office. How did you make out today?" "Fine, I think. I stayed for two autopsies and a view." "Good, good," said Paul. "When would you like to start?" Greg was taken completely off guard by this. "Really?" he managed to say. "Ummm, I need to give my notice to my current job, so I guess two weeks from today." "Well, just give me a date," Paul snapped back. "Well, today is the nineteenth, so let's see." Paul interrupted him as he tried to fig-ure out the date. "I don't have time for this. Just be here Monday for 7 a.m. Everyone starts with six weeks in the autopsy room for training. We are bringing in three new techs. I want to start you all at the same time." "OK great, I will be there," Greg stammered back. "Good enough, see you Monday," Paul said and hung up the phone. Not much for goodbyes, thought Greg. Now he must make the dreaded call to the demolition company. Greg got lucky. No one answered, and it went to voicemail, so he left a brief "I will not be coming back" message and hoped that they would not call him back for an explanation. Which they never did. Suddenly it dawned on him, he never asked about how much the new job paid, benefits, or a work schedule. It had to pay pretty good, right? He guessed it was too late to inquire, but he was still excited for Monday.

THE FIRST DAY

Monday morning arrived. Greg was up way too early, very nervous and excited at the same time. He left his house at 5:15 to give himself plenty of time to get there, and arrived just a little after 6:00. There was plenty of parking where he had parked previously. He sat in his truck and waited, hoping that Karen would pull in soon. She seemed kind of friendly the other day. He sat in his truck until about 6:50, but she did not pull in. "I guess I am on my own, but I do not have the card access yet so someone needs to show up soon," he thought to himself.

Greg walked into the enclosed area, thinking he would just stand by the door until someone showed up for work. To his surprise, the card access door was closed, but the garage door was wide open. Talking to himself, he said, "I guess they are not as secure as they think." He entered the garage and took a quick look around. The bay he entered was empty. There was a small area with large cardboard boxes marked "bio-hazard" off to his left, stacked neatly along a chain link cage that took up the entire second bay of the garage with stacks of long skinny boxes and a shelving unit along the wall full of those small and larger white buckets. There was a gate on the end toward the tech station side with a large padlock on it. The opposite wall with the card access door had a row of upright refrigerators and chest freezers along it. He still has the card access problem with the interior door.

Greg could see Adam sitting behind the desk through the window, but he wasn't facing him. He knocked on the window three times, and without looking to see who it was, Adam reached up and pressed a large square button on top of his desk and the door popped open. Greg walked in. Adam still did not turn or look to see who came in, but he held up his left hand, palm facing Greg to either stop him from moving or talking, so Greg stopped there and did not speak. "The medical examiner will decline jurisdiction. Have a good day," he said loud and clear and then spun around in his chair. "Trauma Dog! You are back for more," he said with a big smile.

"Yup, I guess I am officially a technician as of today," Greg said smiling back. "Go have a seat out back." Adam pointed through the door leading to the stock room. "Sharon will be here eventually, maybe even Joel, too. I have to catch up on my paperwork." He spun back around and started typing on his computer. Greg headed into the back room and saw Diana sitting at the table. "You back for more, too?" he said smiling still. "Yeah," she said. "Can you believe how fast they called?" They sat and made small talk for a few minutes. It was well after 7.

They heard a big metal door slam and then loud voices. Someone told a story about something someone did yesterday and they all got a good laugh out of it. They burst into the back room. A young-looking, very attractive woman with Sharon, Charlie, and another person looked at Diana and Greg, and said, "Oh Lord, here we go again." She laughed while looking at them but walked right past.

Sharon looked at them with a smile. "These are new techs, Greg and Diana. I think I got that right." The other woman said loudly, "Well, they ain't working with me until they know what they are doing. I ain't got time for these reindeer games. You can put them with Charlie and Freddy. I got to go find me some food." She walked out of the room.

"Charlie, you mind working with Greg again, I'll get Freddy for Diana.?" I got to send them upstairs first to see Dana in human resources. I can't have them do anything until they get their paperwork done, but after that you can have him." "I am not really a trainer," grumbled Charlie. Then he said to Diana and Greg, "No point in getting scrubs yet if you have to go upstairs. Just sit tight." Diana and Greg sat and waited until 9:00 for Dana. There was almost no interaction with anyone for most of the morning. Sharon was "busy" with whatever she was doing at the front desk. She did check on them a few times to see if they were OK. Charlie and Freddy never made an appearance in the back room, and the other young woman was nowhere to be found.

HUMAN RESOURCES

Dana finally came in. They heard Sharon telling her they were there and waiting out back. Dana was pleasant enough - very friendly but a little disorganized. She was carrying an armload of papers, a couple of binders, and a travel mug of coffee in her other hand. She was a little past middle aged, shoulder-length hair

She popped into the back room, struggling to hold all her papers "Hi, I am Dana Mahoney, the HR manager. What don't you guys come with me, and we can get you situated and ready to start." She turned around and went through the door on the other side of the door Greg and Diana exited. This door led to a back stairwell to the second floor where all the office staff and administrators worked. The stairs led to a door on the second floor into a long hallway similar to downstairs. Dana gestured with her hips and elbow while saying, "Why don't you guys have a seat in the conference room, as long as they are done the morning meeting. I will get your paperwork and stuff and meet you in there in a minute."

Greg and Diana walked to the end of the hall, but there was a crowd all seated around the large table. There was a row of chairs outside the room, so they both sat and waited. Dana came down the hall carrying a binder and a bunch of loose papers. "Damn it, what time is it?" 9:15," she answered herself. "OK, come with me. We will see if Jay is in and get your ID badges done." She turned and walked back down the hall.

They walked back down the hall and stopped about three quarters of the way, at a row of three cubicles. Dana poked her head in one of them. "Can we get some ID's done?" A man groaned. "No one told me we are getting new people. I have to go pull the equipment out of the closet and get it set up." "I'm sorry, Jay. No one told me new people were starting today either." Dana turned to Greg and Diana and said, "OK, let's just go have a seat the meeting should be done by 9:30 or so."

They eventually get into the conference room and filled out the paperwork, watched a couple of videos on sexual harassment and work place violence. It was just about noon time at this point. Dana came back in and asked if they had any questions. Diana asked what the pay rate was. Dana looks a little confused and said, "Whatever the tech one rate is. I'll have to look it up. We should take thirty minutes for lunch, and we will get your ID's taken care of."

Greg and Diana returned from lunch and went back upstairs to get their badges done. They knocked on Dana's door and entered. "Oh, good you are back. Jay is ready to get the badges done, and I looked up the pay rate. It's not very good, I am afraid, only $9.62 an hour. After ninety days you will be in the union officially, and they have regular increases as you get time in." "Geez, I hope so," said Diana.

Dana added, "You both will have six weeks in the autopsy room for training and then you will be rotating on different shifts to get the full training, and as far as schedules, Greg, you will be Tuesday to Saturday, and Diana you will be Sunday to Thursday. Everyone has to work one weekend day. There are no Monday to Fridays."

They got their ID's done, and it was now about 2:00 in the afternoon. Dana told them to go downstairs and tell Sharon they were all set to start. They went downstairs. Sharon was still sitting at the desk playing on her phone. Greg and Diana let her know Dana said they are all set. "Good," she said, "but you guys might as well go home at this point. I don't have anything for you to do this late. I'll see you in the morning, though."

DAY 1

T he next morning, Diana and Greg were both there before any other technicians in the parking lot. They entered through the garage together and were greeted immediately by Adam with a cheery, "Good morning, good night last night, should be a good day. Find an empty drawer in the yellow filing cabinet you can use as storage for your keys, cell phones, and anything else you might need during the day, and then go get some scrubs on. Dr. Lowe and Dr. Grady cutting today, only have four on the roster. Two overdoses, a suicide, and an unattended at home."

They found a couple empty drawers and headed for the locker room. "I guess we are official now," said Diana. They rummaged through the piles of laundry in the laundry room to find some scrubs and headed to their respective locker rooms to change.

Greg entered the men's locker room to change. Freddy was sitting on the bench in a towel. "Well, I guess I am going to have to show you how to do x-rays." "I am here to learn and do whatever," Greg responded. "My name is Greg, by the way." Greg started opening lockers searching for an empty one and couldn't seem to find one. "Are there this many people using the locker room?" he asked. "No, most of that stuff is mine," Freddy said.

Greg finally found a very small one on a bottom corner and got changed as quickly as he could. Freddy did not seem to be in any hurry as he was still sitting on the bench in his towel, which made Greg feel very awkward. "Well, I guess this is it. I am off to the tech station to see what's what." As Greg started to leave the locker room, Freddy said loudly, "Just watch yourself down there. Don't fall into their bullshit." Greg left the locker room to head back down the hall.

Diana ran down the hall to catch up to him. "Oh, my God," she said, "poor Sharon just walked into the locker room, and this other girl just starts ranting and bitching about everyone and everything to her. Tough way to start your day."

They arrived at the tech station. Charlie was in street clothes behind the desk. Adam was giving him the rundown of what was on the roster. Diana and Greg stood on the opposite side of the counter listening. Adam finished filling in Charlie and said, "I am out of here." Charlie looked up at Greg and Diana and said, "Go have a seat. After I get changed, we will go grab a coffee and then get the room set up. Looks like it is going to be a pretty easy day. Doctors won't be down until 9:30 or so." He walked around the counter and headed for the locker room, about fifty feet behind Adam. Diana and Greg stood there. No one else was around, but they could hear Sharon and the other woman talking loudly coming down the hall.

For the most part, the morning was uneventful. Charlie had returned from the locker room wearing scrubs. Karen and Ricardo were on the road again. Freddy, as far as Greg knew, was still sitting in the locker room, and Sharon and the unidentified woman were behind the desk at the tech station just talking about things in general. "Nicky, this is Greg and Diana. They're starting their training today," said Sharon. "OK, what do you want me to do about it?" was the response from Nicky. Nicky continued, "Stay in your lane, new guys, or I will roll over you."

Charlie stuck his head in the back room, and with his big exaggerated arm wave said, "Let's go. I'll show you where we get coffee and lunch some days." It was the same place Greg had had previously gotten a coffee. Just a small convenience store that made sandwiches and had a coffee station. As they were walking, Charlie was full of questions about Greg and Diana's personal lives and experiences. He did not talk much about what was expected of them or even about the agency in general. He did stop before swiping his ID in the door before they went back inside and said, "This is a good job, lots of benefits and overtime, but be careful on what you say to people in here. This is the only place I have ever worked that eats its own young." He swiped his ID and opened the door to go inside. The two of them reentered the back room. Charlie stopped at the front desk to deliver coffees that he bought for Sharon and Nicky and then came back to sit with Greg and Diana to drink his coffee. They sat and drank their coffee. About half way done, Charlie got up and said, "We might as well go get set up. We can come back after to finish the coffee and grab a smoke." The set up was the same as the first day, nothing new there. The hardest part was just being able to find the right instruments for whatever doctor they were working with. According to Charlie, there was no point in explaining each doctor to them until they were working with them. He went on, "Each doctor is just a little different and even a little quirky, but you will figure out who is who after a while." They finished setting up and went back to finish the coffee.

At 9 a.m., Charlie motioned them to follow him again. "There are only four cases today, so we might as well pull them all out and put them in the room. The doctors are in the morning meeting now to figure out who is doing what today. I will do the first autopsy, and then, Greg, you will do the second. I guess you are working with Freddy, Diana. He knows what he is doing. He has been here twenty-something years. Just try not to ask too many questions while we are doing the autopsy. It is best to just stay quiet until the doctor is gone. The less you speak here the better is the general rule. Freddy may go on one of his rants about how everyone in life has screwed him over. Just take it with a grain of salt."

They suited up when the doctors come down, nothing different from the second interview. Greg watched Charlie intently on what he did so he didn't mess up with Dr. Lowe. The first case was a suspected drug overdose. He was about five foot eight inches tall and very skinny and had a crew cut. He was done rather quickly. There was not much in the way of looking at anything in particular on him. His results would come from lab tests on samples taken. Dr. Lowe was very quick with opening the chest, cutting the ribs, and removing organs. It appeared he was moving even too fast for Charlie, but he managed to keep up with the doctor's pace in almost perfect sync.

The doctor grabbed his clipboard and copied down the organ weights on his form. "I am all set. I will be back in ten minutes," said Dr. Lowe as he walked toward the anteroom. "Going to be one of those days. He must have court this afternoon," said Charlie. He took a large rubber stopper shaped like a cork and plugged the drain hole in the table, unhooked it from the sink, and moved it off to the side. Grabbing the hose attached to the back of the sink, he started to rinse off the blood and small pieces on the doctor's work station, even used an S.O.S. pad to erase the organ weights off the white cutting board. He handed Greg the hose. "Clean up our side. We need to reset for the next one. We will clean up and sew the first one after this." His side looked just like it did before they started. He changed the blades on two scalpels and handed Greg a new blade for his scalpel.

Charlie moved the second table into position and locked it into place at the work station just as the doctor opened the anteroom door to come back in. "Are you ready?" asked Dr. Lowe. "Yes, we are all set, doctor, and I am going to have Greg handle this one." Dr. Lowe stood on the side of the table and put both hands on the edge while looking down and said, "That's fine." Charlie stepped back from the table , and Greg took his spot standing on the other side.

"You might as well start the head. It will probably take you a while," said Dr. Lowe as he proceeded to make his "Y" incision. Greg took his position at the head and placed it on a head block and grabbed the scalpel. Dr. Lowe snapped his scalpel down on the table and held his right arm out over the body to where Greg stood and had his left hand on the edge of the table again, looking down at his feet. "Rib cutters." Dr. Lowe stood in the same position with his head down. Charlie twitched his head to the left toward the cutters sitting on Charlie's side of the sink. Greg stepped over as quickly as he could and grabbed the cutters and handed them to the doctor backwards. He dropped them on the body and picked them up correctly.

Dr. Lowe quickly cut the right side he was standing on from the bottom up, as Greg stepped to move back to the head. Just as he repositioned himself, Dr. Lowe puts his left hand back down on the table and held the cutters in his right hand over the body. Apparently, Greg was supposed to stand there and cut the left side. He was pretty sure Charlie was smiling under his mask and might have even chuckled a little. Greg did his best to cut the ribs in the same fashion as the doctor. The cuts were nowhere near as straight or clean as Dr. Lowe's.

Greg placed the cutters down on the sink counter and moved back to the top of the table for the third time to start the head. He felt very flustered and nervous. He picked up his scalpel again and placed the sharp edge behind the right ear. He gave a quick glance at Charlie who gave a slight nod with his head. Greg made his first cut. It was not as easy as Charlie had made it look on the cases he did. Greg started to cut around the back of the skull. Charlie spoke softly. "Not too low. Start curving back up to the back of the left ear. You will have a hard time with the scalp if you go to low. Now use your thumbs, work them under the scalp, and start to separate the skin from the skull. When it is loose enough, you will be able to fold the skin over and just peel it over the face." Greg managed to expose the skull. It was a strange feeling to peel someone's scalp over their face, exposing the grayish white bone of someone's skull Charlie stepped in with the scalpel and scored the skull to make a line. "Just follow the line, a nice easy shelf cut," as he handed Greg the saw.

Greg made the cuts into the skull then took the church key and stuck it in the cut and twisted. The skull made a popping sound and was free. Dr. Lowe was already done with the body and taking his samples. He stood there waiting. "Stop there," he said. "I will get the brain." He moved to Greg's spot. He made quick work of it and was back at his cutting board with the brain in less than a minute. "You can sew up the head," he said as he sliced into the brain matter. He took a few pieces of brain and dropped them into the jar. "I am all set, Charlie. Thank you." He tossed his gloves into the trash bin and walked out of the room.

"That wasn't so bad," Charlie said. "We just need to get him back together and clean up." He handed Greg a big sewing needle and instructed him on how to put a few stitches in to hold the skull cap in place and then tied the viscera bag closed with the discarded organs, placing that in the body cavity. He started to hose the table down and rinse off the body. Handing Greg another sewing needle, Charlie said, "Sew up the body the same way. Use about six or so stitches. Lowe must be happy. He didn't throw anything. You will get faster each case you do."

They finished up with the body and had the entire station cleaned and shiny again. They placed the body back in its body bag and transferred it to another clean gurney and pushed it back into the cooler. Charlie said," I just need to label the tox and then we can go to lunch if you want." The rest of the day was uneventful.

GREG'S FIRST HOMICIDE

The rest of the six weeks in autopsy training went by pretty fast. Diana and Greg were not allowed to do any high-profile cases since they were still new, but they were both working on their own and had a little contest going on how many heads they had opened. Autopsies were fairly easy to do once you figured out the doctor you would be working with. As a matter of fact, it became routine and almost boring except for a few random cases.

One morning about three weeks into autopsy training, Dr. Lowe came into the office around 7:30 in the morning. He made a point to stop at the tech station and tell Sharon that he wanted to work with Greg that day. Sharon tried to explain to him that he was probably going to be assigned the homicide case, and he might want someone with more experience. Dr. Lowe insisted that Greg would be fine, and it was time he moved on to other types of cases. Sharon was not going to argue with the doctor, so she said that would be fine with her and she would have Charlie sit in to guide Greg through the process of handling a homicide case.

This particular case was a suspected drug dealer from New Hampshire. Law enforcement was speculating he had a drug deal go bad and was murdered and dumped into the river. The body had not been found for eight or nine days and had been decomposing in the river until it finally surfaced and was found. Both local and state police representatives were going to observe the autopsy.

When a suspected homicide case was brought in, the processing was handled differently. The body itself was to be left as untouched as possible. All the clothing was left on the body, so techs only made notes on what they could see. The case would also get a set of full-body x-rays to look for any signs of trauma, broken bones, or bullets. In this case, the x-rays showed what appeared to be several bullet fragments in the chest from possibly two bullets.

Charlie was there listening to all of this and agreed to show Greg how to set up for the homicide case. All the autopsy instruments that Dr. Lowe liked stayed the same. They needed some extra jars for toxicology and a different color test tube to take some extra blood for testing in addition to the saved tube they already had. They also needed large white bucket to save what was left of the brain and several different sizes of brown paper bags. Charlie explained that each item of clothing was hung in a drying chamber and what was found in his pockets needed to be bagged and marked separately, and then all the small bags could be placed into larger bags to send for testing. He also retrieved the x-rays and placed the chest pictures on the light to see the bullet and fragment locations. He explained all the pieces had to be removed and placed in a special envelope to be sent to the ballistics lab.

The morning meeting was finally finished around 9:30 or so. Dr. Lowe had called the tech station to say he did in fact have the homicide and that he would be down at ten to start. The state police were also ready to take their photos, and the local police had two detectives sitting in the anteroom waiting. Charlie and Greg went in to suit up. There were two men in suits. Greg assumed they were the local police detectives and the state police photographer he had seen take photos on the day of his second interview. He later found out his name was trooper Arnie Madeleene. As he had the day Greg first saw him, he greeted them with a big smile and a "good morning, good morning, good morning!" with the tropical accent. He asked Charlie if the body was out yet. Charlie told him to give him five minutes and they would pull it out. The trooper responded with a big smile. "Excellent, just let me know when you are ready for me, cool man!"

Charlie and Greg finished suiting up. He followed him down the hall to the "deco room." This room was only about one-tenth the size of the main autopsy room. It was positioned on the same side of the hallway as the main cooler because this room had its own cooler built into it with an interior wall that was the end wall of the main cooler. It only had nine shelves and room for three tables if packed in properly. Only one autopsy station and one white porcelain sink, the counters and work station were considerably smaller too.

The body was one of the most recent brought in and was on a table right in front so that it was easy enough to pull out and lock into the sink. Even being fully suited up with the mask on, one could smell a strong combination of decomposing body and what can only be described as low tide of a dirty river. Greg asked Charlie if they ever used Vapo-rub under the mask. Charlie said with a laugh, "You can if you want to, but it only makes it worse when you open your nasal passages." The body was dark green and black in spots. It was very bloated, and the eyes were bulging and opened wide. Greg was silently dry heaving a bit and not sure he would make it through this one, but he managed to help Charlie roll the body out of the bag and laid it down flat on his back on the table.

Just as he finished folding up the bag and placing it under the table, Dr. Lowe and Trooper Madeleene entered the room. Dr. Lowe was still in his scrubs with no gloves on, and the trooper was wearing everything but the full-body suit and face shield. The trooper started taking pictures, much as he had done on the cases Greg saw him working on before. Dr. Lowe stood looking at the body with his hands on his hips. The trooper asked Greg to roll the body on its side, so he could take back shots. Greg did not notice that Charlie had left the room. Arnie took all his photos as did Dr. Lowe with his own camera. Greg returned the body to the lying down position as Charlie re-entered the room with the two detectives all suited up. One of them said loudly, "Oh, God, that is gross." Dr. Lowe opened one of the drawers on the work station and produced a small jar of Vapo-rub and handed it to the detective. "Try this," he said. Both detectives used a generous amount under the mask.

Dr. Lowe told Charlie that they could undress the body. Charlie positioned both of the man's arms up over his head and started to remove the shirt. As he did, several layers of skin peeled up with the shirt. Greg turned six shades of green. The smell and now the sight of this was really getting to him. Charlie noticed Greg's reaction. "Just what is called skin slippage, Greg." Dr. Lowe stepped over and was standing at Greg's left side, obviously noticing he was losing it. He even tried to give Greg a little pep talk telling him to try and think of something else or trick his brain into smelling something else. Just don't use the Vapo-rub and he would be fine. He continued with, "This guy was from New Hampshire. You are from New Hampshire, aren't you, Greg? Did you know who he was?" When Greg was uncomfortable with a situation a dry sarcastic wit kicked in. He heard the doctor's question and not sure if he was being serious, answered with, "Yes, Dr. Lowe, we met at the "I am from New Hampshire" cook out last weekend." Charlie, the trooper, and both detectives laughed. Dr. Lowe on the other hand just kind of rolled his eyes and said, "OK, I am going to suit up. I will be back in a minute," and left the room.

Charlie and Greg finished undressing and laying out the clothes from the body to be put in the drying chamber as one of the detectives and the trooper continued to take photos from several angles. The photo shoot was done, at least temporarily, until the body was opened. Charlie and Greg stood against the counter waiting for the doctor to return. Charlie was washing off some items under the faucet and said to Greg, "You know Lowe must like you. He would not have asked for you if he didn't. There are only certain techs he will work with." That made Greg feel a lot better about his decision to stay there.

Dr. Lowe came back into the room fully suited up this time and stared at the x-rays under the light. "It looks like the main slugs almost went all the way through. Let's roll him over and take them out first." Charlie and Greg rolled the body, so he was lying on his face. The bullets clearly caused large bumps on the back of the body. Dr. Lowe made a quick slice over the bumps and removed both large pieces with his fingers and handed them to Charlie, who rinsed them off and placed them in a small glass jar. Greg stood on Charlie's left, closer to the body's lower legs. Dr. Lowe asked him if he saw anything on the back of the man's legs. The calf muscle on his left leg closest to where Greg stood was split open from the decomposition. Greg told Dr. Lowe about the split, so he asked Greg to look inside it to see if there was trauma. Greg used his hands to spread the split open a little bit more and saw four small tannish crabs crawling around. Dr. Lowe said, "So what - do you see, anything?" Greg responded, "Yes, doctor, he has crabs." Dr. Lowe leaned over from the other side of the table to look into the calf muscle. He stood up and placed his hands on his hips again, looking right at Greg. He might have had a smile on his face under the mask because he said, "I think you are going to fit in just fine here. Now get a small white bucket and save those for Ricardo. He likes those things." Greg did as he was told and removed the crabs from the leg.

They rolled the body back over, and the autopsy was just as typical as those he had seen performed a few dozen times at this point. There was nothing remarkable about it other than trying to fish around for as many bullet fragments as could be removed. The internal organs, for the most part, were still intact and identifiable. The head was a little different as well. The skull seemed very thin, but Greg did not want to ask if that was because it was decomposing. Charlie handed him the large white brain bucket and told Greg he was going to need that as the brain had probably started to soften at this point. Sure enough, as soon as Greg popped open the skull, the brain started oozing out in a thick, soft jelly-like state. Greg placed the bucket directly under the skull and captured as much as he could.

After Dr. Lowe examined the inside of the skull, he turned to the detectives who were still observing and told them his early impression was that the victim was shot at close range in the left side of his chest, one bullet piercing the left lung and the other directly into the left center of the heart, which would have been the one that killed him. "I'll have my report done as soon as I can. If you have any questions, just give the office a call." He turned toward Charlie and Greg and said, "I am all set. Thanks, guys," and left the room. Charlie and Greg finished sewing up the body as best they could and cleaned the room

CONTINUED TRAINING

Diana and Greg were about four weeks into the rest of their training in autopsy, which had become routine. There were only a few cases that needed special attention, and there were certain technicians who wanted to do those. There was definitely some ego involved with those. There were also some cliques of technicians, which made it hard to get along with everybody. Sharon seemed very indifferent to everyone. Charlie stood firmly on the fence between them. He managed to not get involved other than work and small talks with anyone by just keeping himself busy with daily tasks and cleaning unless he was on the road. He seemed to get along fine with everyone when he was on the road.

There was a second day-shift supervisor named Joel. Greg had very little interaction with him. He did not work most of the week that Greg worked. Greg was told Joel was a great technician but was getting ready to retire from working for the office after twenty-two years or so. He was burning up a lot of earned time and vacation days. He seemed OK but was definitely sided with one clique with two other technicians, Nickie and Catrina. These two were the ego and attitude among the technical staff largely responsible for the low morale and teamwork. They seemed inseparable, always worked together, and were able to pick and choose their assignments with doctors or cases on the road that needed to be picked up and did almost no cleaning or mundane tasks. That caused a lot of problems with the remaining staff. As far as Freddy, it seemed not many people wanted to work with him in general, including doctors. He was really good at taking x-rays, but when no x-rays were needed, he just seemed to wander the hallway or hang out in the locker room. No one wanted to go on the road with him either. He had an incontinence problem, and on several occasions had accidents, which made for a long ride home.

With Diana and Greg being new, their days were confined to getting in scrubs and setting up the autopsy room and working with the doctors on the standard cases. They spent the rest of the day cleaning.

Second shift started at 3:30 and was supervised by a man named Dale. He was in his mid-fifties, gray hair and an average build. The best way to describe him was he was the "Eddie Haskel" of technicians. He was as polite with his manners as possible with the "please" and "thank you" and using people's titles to address them such as doctor, Mr., Ms. even a "sir" or "madam" if he did not know them as long as they weren't techs. Everything he did or said was done by the book to the letter. On his shift was a large man named Bill, a younger tech named Arthur, and an older woman named Mary.

Bill was the epitome of what people think of a state employee. He would do as little as possible and take as long as he could to do it. If asked a question even as simple as "what time is it" it would take him a few seconds to formulate his response, and he would usually start any sentence with "ummm" as he calculated in his mind what he was going to answer. He was a nice enough guy with a good temperament and was more than willing to train and show new techs the ropes, if they had the time.

Arthur was in his twenties, with a laid-back street-smart attitude. He attended community college during the day, majoring in business. There wasn't much to say about him. He kept to himself, did what he was told to do, and went home at the end of his shift.

Mary was quite a unique character in her early sixties, with almost thirty years working for the Commonwealth. She was very out of shape and rather large, bad knees and back, quite incapable of performing any kind of physical labor. She had a drill sergeant-like disposition and attitude. She was also a by-the-book to-the-letter type, as any variance in protocol would result in being disciplined, in her mind. As long as it was not her start time, she was friendly enough in a paranoid sort of way. She seemed to think everyone in the office was talking about her behind her back and always conspiring to get her. Staff could be standing somewhere talking, and she'd sneak up or peek around the corners of the hallway to hear what was being said.

She usually arrived about thirty minutes early and would sit in the back room and try to listen to the supervisors in front. She would question anyone in the back room as to what happened during the day and who talked about who. If anything was going on, she should know about. Another quirky thing she did was wait until the day shift women left to get changed back into their street clothes. She trailed behind them in the hallway at a slower pace and waited until they were in the women's locker room. She would even give a minute or two and stand outside the door to see if she could hear what was being said inside before she entered to get ready for her shift.

One afternoon about 3:15 or so, Diana and Greg were sitting in the back room adding a powdered chemical in a small dose to the blood jars to help preserve the sample. Mary was sitting on the other side of the table firing questions at them about the day shift. Sharon poked her head in around the door frame and told Mary that Bill was not coming in. He had called in sick, and Arthur had a scheduled personal day for a family obligation. It was just going to be her and Dale. She went on to say that they just called a case down that needed to be picked up and that she might have to go with someone from dayshift. This was one of Mary's worst nightmares to be sent out on the road. She was terrified of having to drive one of the office trucks and even more terrified to have to go physically pick up a body.

Mary in a complete panic asked Sharon, "What kind of case is it?" Sharon said from what they told her on the phone, it is a badly decomposed body, found in the woods on a chicken farm property. It appeared it was a homeless person who was living in a tent out in the woods and had died some time ago. Sharon said, "Let me page

Charlie and see if he wants some overtime." She went back to her phone and the overhead speakers loud and clear paged Charlie to the tech station.

Charlie showed up after a couple of minutes and was talking to Sharon at the desk. The group could hear her explaining to him the nature of the case and that Bill would not be in and he might have to go with Mary. Charlie immediately and without caring if Mary heard him expressed his unwillingness to do a removal with her. He even suggested that he and Dale go when he got in and that Mary could run the desk.

Mary hearing all of this, got up as fast as she could and started to argue with Sharon that she needed to stay in the building and her duties would be restricted to cleaning or doing case intake on the phone, processing cases in, or releasing bodies to funeral homes. One person couldn't possibly handle all of the tech duties by themselves. With two technicians out, they would have to contract the removal to a funeral home.

Charlie said to Sharon, "Why don't I just take Greg with me?" Sharon said that would be fine with her if Greg wanted to go, but Mary fired right back that a new technician is not allowed on the road until the six weeks in the room were completed. All three of them were arguing about who should do the removal. Greg figured he would throw his two cents in and joined in the conversation. He was a little excited about being able to go do a removal.

He went to the front desk and stood by Charlie and told them he was more than willing to go. Mary went into yet another rant about a new technician getting overtime and going on a removal. Sharon looked right at her with a bit of attitude in her face and said, "Well then, do you want to go?" This made Charlie laugh out loud. Mary continued with her rant about overtime and a new tech doing a removal and that she would have no part or responsibility for this decision. This made Sharon laugh out loud. "You have no say anyways. You are lucky I am not making you do it. I am doing Charlie a favor this way." This was the first time Greg had seen Sharon assert herself as some kind of supervisor.

Charlie told Greg to go down the hall to the laundry room and find a road uniform that would fit and get changed while he got the truck ready. As Greg was walking away, he could still hear Mary and Sharon arguing over the decision. He managed to find a uniform that was close enough to fitting and got changed. Dale was in the locker room already getting ready for his shift. Freddy was sitting in street clothes on the bench just looking down.

Greg had not spoken to him much, but he seemed friendly enough, so Greg filled him in on what was going on. He looked at Greg with a big smile on his face. "Excellent," he said. "Does Mary know this is going on?" "Yeah, but she doesn't seem too happy about it," Greg responded. Still grinning from ear to ear, Dale said, "Excellent... this is going to be a great night. I'll talk to you when you guys bet back." Greg returned to the tech station desk. Charlie was standing there with a clipboard and a body bag under his arm "All right, off we go."

They left through the garage, and as they were walking Charlie started speaking. "Always good to get out of that building and get out on the road. We are going to Marshfield. Should take us about an hour to get there. It should be an easy removal depending on where the body actually is. They never really give us accurate information. Dale might end up sending us somewhere else if a scene comes in or a hospital case needs to be picked up. When we get back, I will show you how to process a case in. This should be good for about four hours of overtime. We are taking truck three-eighty-seven."

Three-eighty-seven was a Chevy extended cab four-by-four, with a third door and a cap on the back with two doors that opened sideways, painted all white except for the medical examiner logo stickers on the door. It was loaded with all the bells and whistles, a full light bar with blue lights, wig-wag headlights, strobes in the taillights, and siren with PA system.

"We don't need lights and siren for this. It's not that big of a deal." Charlie seemed much more relaxed in the truck than he was in the building. He was very friendly and talkative and gave Greg his life story pretty much while they drove. He wanted to be a nurse and was currently in school, lifelong Boston resident, single no kids, and was taking care of his mother who now lived with him. Right before they hit the highway, Charlie pulled into a Dunkin' Donuts drive through.

They grabbed coffee for the road and hit the highway. It took less than an hour to get there. It was a chicken farm, and land was being cleared for a new barn. That is when they discovered the body. They had no idea someone was living out there in a tent.

Charlie turned down the farm's driveway and continued all the way around the house. Charlie had already spotted the access road and saw the police cars flashing lights about a half mile down a dirt road near a wooded area. He pulled up behind the state troopers' SUV. There were two uniformed local police officers and one state trooper in plain clothes with a camera. There did not seem to be any sort of investigation, so Greg assumed they had done whatever it is they do on a scene like this. The trooper was just waiting for them to take back shots when they could roll him over.

Greg was thinking this was going to be a very official-type investigation, so he was a little nervous not really knowing what he needed to do or expect. The police on scene just seemed to be hanging out and talking but not about the scene, just general conversation. Charlie handed Greg the body bag, and he grabbed a stretcher from the back of the truck as they walked over to the scene. He could see the very faded, worn-out-looking tent, some clothing, a small fire ring, and some blankets tossed on the ground near a tree. The ground was soft and muddy. It had recently rained, so it was a little mucky, and Greg was wearing sneakers. He looked around the area still not really seeing a body anywhere. He was thinking it must be in the tent, and his feet were starting to get wet from the mud. He walked over by the tree and stood on a blue plaid blanket that was on the ground thinking this might be a dry spot. Charlie seemed to know the trooper, and they exchanged a bit of small talk and then talked about the scene. Charlie asked him if he was all set and if they could remove the body. The trooper said, "Yup anytime you are ready. I just want to take some pictures of his back."

Charlie told Greg to lay out the body bag, so he started to unfold it and get it laid out and had to ask where the body was. The trooper started to laugh and said, "You are standing on it. It's under the blanket!" Charlie started to laugh as well as the uniformed cop. Charlie still laughing said, "I wanted to see how long it would take you to notice."

Greg was very embarrassed and felt like he had just learned his first lesson on removals. He pulled the blanket off the body. It was almost a skeleton. The parts of the skin that remained were blackened and almost mummified, but from the skull and ribs, it was clear the body was very thin. Charlie knelt on the body bag and rolled the body on its side. The trooper snapped a few quick pictures and said, "OK, I am good." Charlie tucked the bag under the body and zipped it up and loaded it on the stretcher. He and Charlie loaded it in the back of the truck.

"Not bad for your first removal." said Charlie. "I should have told you were standing on him, but I thought it was kind of funny," he said with a big smile. "Looks like he has been there for quite a while. I told you they never give us accurate information. You hungry? We can hit a drive through on the way back. I just need to give Dale a call to see if we need to go anywhere else." Sure enough, they needed to go to a hospital on the way back to pick up another body, a thirty-two-year-old female, suspected drug overdose.

THE INSIDE SCOOP

Charlie was very talkative suddenly. it seemed being out of the office and on the road made it safe to talk. He wanted to explain the office and its politics and just who was who. He started with the Nicky and Catrina situation.

Nicky had been working there for more than three years. She was very good at her job, and even Dr. Lowe liked her. She was trained by Joel who Lowe also liked, but Joel was a supervisor and did not do autopsies anymore. When Nicky started it was apparent that she was the best candidate to work with him. There had always been speculation that she was hired because of a minor political connection with a state representative and possibly a connection to one of the main Boston newspapers.

Charlie went on to say that for whatever reason, the *Globe* seemed to have it in for the office and would print any negative happenings it could, but that had been happening long before Nicky was hired. She was never proven to be any kind of mole or source of information for them. There was also an administrative person upstairs who had a connection to a local television news reporter by a marriage in the family but also unable to prove she would leak information.

Catrina became a good friend to Nicky after she was hired. Nicky trained her, and soon they became good friends and almost inseparable in the office as far as assignments. Catrina also seemed to be able to take advantage of Nicky's ability to do whatever she wanted for the day at work.

Just a few months ago, three other technicians had quit after only a short time there, mainly because of the hostile work environment caused by Nicky with her loud demands and almost bullying tactics to get her way. Several people wrote formal complaints about her actions and things she said and turned them into Dana in human resources. A Union representative was called in to defend her in what was supposed to be a formal hearing. But a few days before the hearing, the file with the written complaints went missing and no copies had been made. The hearing was cancelled and was never mentioned again.

Sharon was a quiet sort of supervisor and had given up on trying to run things the way she wanted. Joel overrode any decision she made even though he was only working two days a week to cover her days off. Nicky with Catrina in tow would only do what she felt like doing, but they were on friendly terms and Sharon did not want to force any issues and get caught up in some sort of disciplinary hassle. Upper management had already made it clear to Sharon that she would not get any support from them.

Freddy, a long-time state employee, had been trained in the military for morgue and x-ray work. According to Charlie, he seemed to be in a constant state of shell shock and would wander the hall all day waiting to take x-rays on a case. He had also just gone through a divorce on a very long-term marriage and had a large unpaid taxes debt and child support that was automatically deducted from his paycheck. He was in such a financial mess that he was living in the morgue's locker room. Most of his personal possessions that meant anything to him were stored in areas like the unused bay of the garage or upstairs in the storage area of the building. If you asked him why he would stay there his answer was that people just didn't understand that he doesn't get paid on the first of every month. It was well known in the building that he was living in the locker room, which should not have been allowed, but no one seemed to really care.

Paul Rourke had almost fifty years working for the medical examiner's office and was ready to retire in the next few months. He'd started as a technician in a small satellite location north of Boston at a state hospital that was also a psych ward. That office had closed due to budget cuts many years ago, and he was transferred to Boston. He knew the techs' job better than anybody but was now more or less confined to administrative work and shuffling papers for the upstairs management, so he had little involvement with the techs.

Charlie ended his spilling of the office dynamics with "just be careful of what you say to anybody in the building. If it's good enough, it will end up in the papers the next day somehow. Also, you need to be careful with making jokes or sarcasm. That will get you pulled upstairs quicker than you can blink."

They arrived back at the office with both cases, and Charlie showed him how to process them in. As they were pushing the gurneys into the cooler, Greg couldn't help but notice Mary standing at the end of the hall, peeking around the corner watching everything they did.

CONTINUED TRAINING

Time was passing quickly at the morgue. The six-week training in the autopsy room was over. They were free to go on the road when needed and to start learning the administrative tasks associated with being a technician.

As it turns out, when there were no administrative people upstairs, it fell on the techs to take cases over the phone. Techs took over case intake after 4:30 p.m. until 8:00 a.m. and on the weekends. There was always a doctor on call to make the decision on whether a case was accepted or declined. Most doctors did not want to be called at all hours of the night, so they would check in when they woke up in the morning, and the techs would give them a brief rundown on any calls. It was easy to decide which cases should be brought into the office, so it was rare when a doctor went against a tech's decision.

Greg and Diana were both going to be left on the first shift as they were the ones who needed the help. Diana suddenly developed a problem with having to wear all the protective clothing, saying it was too constricting and causing her to become claustrophobic. She wanted to go on another shift that did not do autopsies.

Paul moved her to the third shift to help Dale. Dale with his military background and training was a little hard to work with for her. He expected a lot, primarily doing one-person removals from hospitals while he took calls. Picking up bodies is not the easiest thing in the world to do alone. It takes some good upper-body strength. After about a week, Diana developed a problem with driving at night and said she was no longer able to do that. So as long as he was going to have help on his shift, Dale decided he would go on the road and let Diana handle the calls. It was not long after that Diana resigned her position as a technician.

Greg, however, had become good at the job. He had a good understanding of what was expected and what needed to be done on most of the standard cases that came through the office. He routinely grabbed overtime on the second shift and went on the road to hospitals on his own to retrieve bodies or pick up an entire shift when he could as someone was always looking for the time off. He was well liked by all the technical staff and even most of the doctors he worked with.

One afternoon just before the end of day shift, Adam came in to work for Dale who had taken a personal day. A homicide case had been called in earlier, and the office was just waiting for the call saying they were ready to remove the body. It was a domestic violence situation were the estranged husband broke into his ex-wife's home and stabbed her multiple times. The autopsy later determined forty-two stab wounds in various parts of the body, including defensive wounds. The suspect was already in police custody.

Arthur and Billy were ready to go as soon as the scene called, but Adam chimed in and asked Greg if he had been to a homicide scene yet. Greg had not. Most of the actual scenes, as they were called, were taken by certain people in the office. Mary immediately had an issue with Greg going, stating he was still too new, and it should be handled by experienced techs.

"Well, then," said Adam obviously agitated that she would question him, "go get a road uniform on and you, I, and Greg will go to the scene. Billy and Arthur can handle the office while we are gone."

Mary did not know what to do or say now. Her own military-like attitude was going to keep her from disobeying a direct order. She reluctantly walked slowly to the locker room to get changed.

She finally reappeared after twenty minutes. Adam had shown Greg the process for getting a truck ready for a scene like this and had all his paperwork in order and ready to go. They took truck three-eighty-seven with the third door and back seat, which Greg squeezed in easily and off they went. Mary didn't say a word to either of them. Adam drove and made casual conversation with Greg. The scene was local not far from the office, so they arrived in about fifteen minutes.

The police had the side street blocked off at both ends, but the truck was waved right through. Two of the major local news station trucks were parked right before the police road block. Greg tried not to look like he was looking at the reporters standing in front of their cameras giving their live reports to their respective stations.

Adam laid out his plan to both. They would pull up to the front door. All three of them would put on Tyvek suits with the shoe booties. He would take the clipboard with the paperwork. Mary would grab a body bag, and Greg would get a stretcher out of the back of the truck.

They parked in front of the house and did just what they were told. Adam and Greg carried the stretcher up the front steps into the house with Mary trailing behind carrying the body bag. The body was on the floor in the living room. There was blood splattered everywhere. It appeared that the woman had been trying to get away from her attacker and running from room to room. Her body was lying on its back, and there was a large pool of blood around it on the hardwood floors. It was quite a gruesome scene Adam told Mary to stay put and for Greg to follow him into the kitchen to talk to the lead detective to make sure they were ready for removal of the body.

Mary did as she was told and stood almost at attention with the bag as Greg and Adam walked into the kitchen. Adam seemed to know everyone in the kitchen, and once again it seemed like they were all old-time friends. Conversation was about their own lives and not homicide related at all. One of the local police was telling a story about his vacation at the beach the previous week and something about one of his kids doing something funny. This caused a small outburst of laughter from the kitchen, which triggered Mary's paranoia. She could not stand knowing what was being said and without thinking started to walk toward the kitchen.

Suddenly there was a loud outburst of laughter coming from the living room area from other cops on the scene. Dale stuck his head out the door to investigate the living room and started laughing as well. He motioned with his hand to come look.

Greg, the detective, and the two uniformed cops all came over to look. There was a very out- of-shape Mary, on her back in the pool of blood next to the body, arms and legs were flailing around like a giant white turtle on its back trying to right itself. Adam could not control his laughter, nor could anyone else. "Are you hurt? Do you need to seek medical attention," he yelled out to her. "I told you to wait out there. Look at the mess you're making!"

Two crime scene techs helped Mary to right herself and stood her back up. She was mortified and struggled to get the blood-soaked Tyvek suit off. "I will be waiting in the truck!" she yelled angrily at Adam. After the laughing settled down, they bagged the body and loaded it on the stretcher. Adam was doing his best to try and train Greg on proper scene etiquette, but it was hard without continuing to chuckle. "OK," he said, "wipe the smile off your face. We need to get her in the truck. You would be surprised how good of a camera shot those news people will get even from down the street."

Mary was livid on the ride back to the office. She threatened to file reports on everybody who was at the scene, claiming she was set up to be made fun of and hazed. Adam's very calm response was that his report would have to reflect how she was told to stay put and not follow him into the kitchen, which is directly disobeying a senior technician. He might also have to mention that she was unfit and unable to perform her duties as a technician as evidenced by the incident with several witnesses. Mary was no closer to calming down but sat back in her seat fuming over the whole incident. Adam continued to say that if things stay civilized, he would not mention this to the other office staff.

The training on second and third shift was only two weeks each. It was more focused on taking calls, arranging removals, processing bodies in, and releasing finished cases to funeral homes. Greg picked up on all of this rather quickly, even the incoming calls to report cases seemed self-explanatory as to what should be brought into the office for examination or autopsy.

He liked working with Dale on second shift, and occasionally there would be a removal that caught his attention where he would take Greg and handle it himself to get out from behind the desk.

One hazy, hot, and humid day in late August, a body was found in a dumpster in Chinatown. It was ninety-two degrees about 5 p.m. with very high humidity. The Boston police had called in a case. They had little to no information about the circumstances. They suspected it was a homeless man but were not sure if any foul play was involved. They also reported that there was a news crew on the scene that they were holding back at a safe distance. If the techs get there sooner than later, they would appreciate it. Arthur and Billy were already out in a truck picking up a couple of hospital cases and were not due back in the area for a few more hours.

Dale not wanting to miss an opportunity to mess with Mary, called her out to the front desk from the back room where she liked to hide. "OK, Mary," he smiled at her. "We have a removal in town. Why don't you and I go handle it?"

Dale new all too well that she had been hiding around the corner of the door jamb listening to his call as he took the case. "I can't possibly get a body out of a dumpster! Did they already pull him out?!" "How did you know that he was in a dumpster?" Dale asked. "You talk too loud," she said angrily. "Call a funeral home. They can get him. We can't spare two more techs. That would only leave one person in the office." She immediately retreated into the back room.

"Well," said Dale, "I am going to take Greg and get him since you are refusing. You will have to deal with the office until we get back. It shouldn't take us long. Unless you are going to refuse that directive as well, then I am running out of options on how to handle this." "Fine." she yelled from the back room, "but I am closing up the building and only handling phone calls until I have help!"

Dale and Greg took one of the remaining rucks. Dale was having a good laugh out of the situation. "Just so you know," he said to Greg, "I had no intention of sending you with Mary on your own. I know she can't do removals, but I figured it would be fun to get her going. This will take less than an hour to get back, but I will bet you a coffee the office is a mess," he laughed some more.

The traffic in town was not too bad. They arrived in about ten minutes to the address given. It was a restaurant, and there was a police cruiser parked in front. Dale pulled in behind the cruiser. As he did, a uniformed officer got out and walked toward the truck. "You'll need to go around the back and up the alley, but I got to say I am glad I don't have your job today. This is not pretty."

Dale pulled out and went around the block. They could see the news van at the entrance to the alley way with a big camera set up on a tripod. Dale pulled up and could see the alley was blocked off by crime scene tape. The man running the camera seemed oblivious to the approaching truck. Dale slowly drove right at him with his turn signal flashing, but the camera man never looked up.

Dale was about twenty feet or so from having to make his turn into the alley - camera man still not budging. "Everything must be the hard way," mused Dale. He stopped the truck in the middle of the street - camera man still not looking at them. Dale gave him a loud "whoop whoop" from the siren on the medical examiner's truck. The camera man jumped backwards almost falling over. The camera stayed in place. They both laughed a little at this as the camera man grabbed the camera off the tripod and pointed it directly at the medical examiner's truck as another man grabbed the tripod.

Dale told Greg to hop out of the truck and break the crime scene tape and tie it back together after he pulled the truck through. Greg did as he was told and opened the access to the alley as Dale pulled the truck through enough for him to re-tie the tape. The camera never stopped pointing toward him, so he tried very hard not to look like he was having a good time. He tied a hasty knot to rejoin the tape and hopped back in the truck as they proceeded down the alley.

It did not take more than a minute driving down the alley to suddenly become aware of the over-powering stench of discarded and rotting seafood. As they approached the parked Boston police cruisers, they could see the alley formed a courtyard-type area, and there was a line of four dumpsters in a row, all with the sharp sloped front for the trash truck to just hook up to and dump.

Dale parked next to the unmarked car of the detective, and they hopped out of the truck. Dale grabbed the clipboard, and Greg went to get a stretcher from the back of the truck. The uniformed officer wearing a surgical mask walked toward Greg with the stretcher. "How's it going?" he said like he and Greg were old friends. "You guys have some of those fancy white suits? Because you are going to need them."

Greg grabbed a couple of Tyveks suites from the compartment, just as Dale came walking over saying they were going to need suits. Dale pulled out two more suits for the cops on the scene as well. "We may be needing some help," he told the detective with a big smile on his face.

The four men, all covered in protective suits and masks, walked toward the row of dumpsters, Greg pulling the stretcher behind him. "He is in the end one," said the detective. Greg looked inside the dumpster. The smell inside the container was ten times worse than in the courtyard. He could barely see an arm bent at the elbow sticking up in the back part of the bin.

"Well, one of us is going to have to crawl inside and try to get him in a bag," said Dale, looking right at Greg. "I am guessing that that is going to be me judging by the smile on your face." "You would be guessing correctly," said Dale still smiling. "Have the bag unzipped and open and try and tuck the flap underneath and pull it all the way around. He should slide right in and then you can zip it closed, and we can pull him up and out. Try not to bag the pile of squid that is next to him, but make sure nothing falls off his person that might be important."

Dale stood with his hands together and slightly bent over so he could help Greg climb in the dumpster. Greg slid down the slope inside the dumpster, and to his surprise both feet and legs up to his knees, slid right through the trash and down to the bottom of the dumpster. The dumpster was not as full as it looked, but it did have a large amount of standing water that the trash inside floated on. "If he is floating, that will make this a lot easier," said Dale. "Oh, my God. This is disgusting," exclaimed Greg. "The sooner you bag him the sooner you are out," said Dale.

Greg tried to move slowly so as not to disturb the debris and water around him. He managed to accomplish just what Dale suggested and found getting the body in the bag was not that bad, but the smell inside the dumpster was really overpowering. "See if you can send him up head first, and we will grab the handles on the bag and pull," remarked Dale. Greg managed to spin the almost-floating body so it could be removed head first. Dale and the uniformed officer leaned in over the top of the dumpster to grab the heavy nylon handles on the bag, Greg positioned himself at the legs of the body and tried to push at the same time.

"OK on three, one, two, three." Dale and the cop pull hard as Greg tried to push the legs. No one seemed to notice that as they moved the heaviest part of the body up, the sloped side the dumpster became top heavy and started to tip over. The front of the dumpster slammed on the ground with a loud bang as the water and trash poured out over the two men standing in front of it as Greg flopped on his face on the body bag. The detective burst out laughing as Dale and the cop were now soaked with the dumpster water. Greg was seemingly spared what could have been a disaster, but he was on the back end of the water fall. "Well, he is out," exclaimed Dale with a laugh. Greg also laughing climbed out of the bin and helped Dale place the body on the stretcher, and they loaded it in the truck. Fortunately, all the news cameras captured was the body being loaded in the truck, which looked very professional from a distance.

Both men had a good laugh about the removal on the short trip back to the office. Luckily the Tyvek stopped them from getting wet underneath the suits. Dale remarked on the way back to the office that they would treat the case as suspicious unless they heard otherwise from the police. They had only been gone about forty minutes and were just about to take the last turn to get back to the office. "Still betting a coffee that there is going to be problems at the office?" he asked Greg. "Sure, why not," Greg laughed, as they turned into the access road for the parking lot.

Dale pulled in and made the sharp left into the gravel area so he could back into the courtyard to unload but had to stop before he could back in as the courtyard had two minivans already in front of the garage door. "Never fails," Dale said with a slightly disappointment tone in his voice. I don't know how that woman has kept this job so long." He parked the truck where it sat with the body, and he and Greg started to walk toward the office as the driver of each minivan got out of their driver's seats. "Guess you owe me a coffee," Dale said to Greg.

"What's up, guys?" said one of the drivers. "Thought you were closed today for some reason. I was getting worried. I must have my client ready for a viewing in the morning." "No, just had to leave Mary alone in the building. You know how that usually works responded," Dale. "Yeah, that explains it," said the driver. "I'll get the door open as soon as I get in," he told the funeral director.

Dale entered the card access door followed by Greg. As they entered the tech station area, Mary was nowhere to be seen. The phone on the desk was ringing, and papers were scattered on the counter top. Dale walked over and hit the garage door opener for the funeral directors waiting outside. "Mary!" Dale yelled. Mary came out from the back room and looked sternly at Dale. "I am on the phone." And she disappeared again. Dale stood at the doorway waiting. Greg could hear Mary speaking very softly so he couldn't understand what she was saying. Dale obviously frustrated said to her, "When you are done pretending to be on the phone, can you please tell me what the hell is going on here. We were gone less than one hour."

Mary very angrily said to Dale, "I told you, you can't leave one tech in the building. This is what happens." "What happens? asked

Dale. "There is only one tech in the building every night on third shift even second shift used to only have one technician after 6 p.m. How many cases did you take? Did you release anyone to a funeral home?" "I couldn't release anybody. I was tied up on the phones," she snapped back. "Well, how many calls did you take? The desk looks like you handled a mass casualty incident." Mary was still very angry. "I only had one call from a hospital, but I could not reach a doctor to run it by. I don't know who is on call and couldn't find the list, and I have been trying to get medical history from the primary care doctor. I don't have time to deal with funeral homes."

"Well, if you only took one call from a hospital, who were you just on the phone with." "That was something else," she snapped again. In the meantime, Greg was pulling the bodies out of the cooler for the funeral homes and getting them, all signed out. They only took a few minutes each and they were on their way. Mary and Dale were still arguing back and forth, and it was obvious that Dale was just trying to push Mary's buttons to get her going. Mary, however, was not the least bit amused and really felt she was right about one tech being left alone in the building, regardless of just how often that happens to any given number of other techs.

"Clean up your mess on my desk and put whatever case you took over the phone in the computer," Dale said to Mary. "Greg, why don't you back the truck in, and we will get our guy taken care of for the night. Maybe we can get Freddy out of the locker room to take some x-rays if he is going to be labeled suspicious." Greg did as he was told and backed the truck up and brought the body in. By the time he had taken down the height, weight, and incoming photo, Freddy was already wandering his way down the hall to take the x-rays.

The case did not turn out to be suspicious. The body was identified rather quickly and was well known in that area as a homeless veteran who stayed in that particular part of town. The local VA had confirmed a lot of medical history, and there were no signs of any foul play.

CHANGES COMING

T ime was passing quickly for Greg. He was now considered one of the senior technicians and was enjoying the job tremendously. He was quite good at all functions. He worked on all three shifts and frequently took double shifts and overtime whenever it was open.

The comment Mr. Baxter had made during his interview always stuck with him, about this being a stepping-stone job and that they did not expect techs to be around more than a few years. In a sense he was right. Greg had been there about eighteen months. Several people had come and gone in his short time there. Some of them just couldn't hack it. Others truly used it as a stepping stone to other jobs. After all, it looks great on a resume even if it was only for a short time.

Now there were big changes in the works. A new governor had been elected, Dr. Grady was stepping down as the chief, James Baxter was moving on to bigger and better things in the Department of Public Safety, and Paul Rourke was retiring sooner than later.

Initially the changes were not so bad. The woman who took notes during Greg's interview was now director of operations, and her name was Katelynn Fletcher (nobody saw that coming). There were lots of rumors on how exactly that happened. The chief's job was in the process of being filled, and Paul's job was left vacant until a new chief was named. Things continued as they had been since Greg started

It only took a month after the new governor took office for a new chief medical examiner to be appointed, a Dr. Harold Cavanaugh. He was a well-known and highly accredited doctor from Chicago.

He arrived and took charge immediately and made some of his own appointments of people he had brought with him. One individual who came with him was a man named Richard Finely. Richard was to be his right-hand man with the title of personnel director and equal in status to Katelynn. He would be involved in most of the decisions on how the office handled things. He spent a good portion of the budget remodeling the building and upstairs offices including his own and some remodeling downstairs in the actual morgue. All of these changes seemed good. One of the biggest changes downstairs was the removal of the wall that separated the main autopsy room, so now it was a giant autopsy room.

One of the unfortunate things that was not considered by the new administration was that the current budget was much lower than they were used to. So, they had to come up with a way to get more money from the state to function as they were used too. One way they figured they would do this was to increase the case load of accepted cases by making it harder to decline a case that was being called in from a hospital. The daily case roster quickly jumped from six cases on average to twenty-five to thirty-five on a daily basis.

The technical staff was completely overwhelmed with this kind of jump. Costs for overtime and contracting funeral homes to transport bodies in was skyrocketing. It did not take long for a huge backlog of cases from all areas. Cases soon took days to be ready to release to funeral homes, and the doctors were unable to finalize any cause of death. They had to list "undetermined" as a cause of death until toxicology results came in.

After a short time, they hired several new doctors and opened several new tech positions. One of their ideas to attract better quality technicians was to hire people with higher levels of education. Greg decided to take advantage of this and applied for and was given a technician II position. This was a nice pay raise for him and gave him a little more clout with new techs. He also offered to be a sort of training officer for new hires. Greg was seemingly well liked by the new administration for some reason, even though they didn't know him for very long. He kind of took a little advantage of this by asking if he could bring a long-time friend named Nancy, who was training to be a nurse into observe an autopsy. She had been asking for a while ,as most people did when they found out where Greg was working. He first asked Dr john if he would mind an extra person observing and he was fine with it. He even made the arrangements with the upstairs administration and came down with the proper paperwork that she needed to sign to be able to do this.

Nurse Nancy singed off on everything and made arrangements to come in the following week for a day to observe.. Unfortunately for her, Dr john only took the routine cases, so she just saw, but did get to participate in, a suspected drug overdose case and an unattended person with no medical history.

It did not take long, and soon there were six new people starting as techs and reporting for training. It was an eclectic group. Three were currently in college in criminal justice majors and two were very much blue-collar types. One woman named Allie worked for a funeral home and was going to school to become a funeral director.

There were also six new full-time doctors and two part time. Most of the new hired doctors were young and looking to make a name for themselves in the medical community. There were two more experienced doctors who were both neuropaths and specialized in brain studies.

The case load at the office increased dramatically. The office took in three bodies for every one released to a funeral home, which didn't take long to create a huge inventory of cases in the office. The main cooler had a capacity of one hundred and twenty bodies and the deco room cooler could only hold about sixteen. Both coolers were now well over capacity, with bodies stacked three to a shelf and two on every gurney. At one point they were even stacked on the floor to free up tables for autopsies

There were now six doctors handling cases every day. The workload was tremendous, and most days would now start with lining up cases in any available space in the main autopsy room. All six stations would have a body, with a body positioned between stations. Others would be lined up along the back side of the room on any free table that could be found. The morning meeting still took place at 9:00, but the techs would start drawing toxicology from the cases as soon as they were pulled out of the cooler.

Most days the doctors being overloaded with getting paperwork together had the technicians do the autopsies and have the bodies ready for inspection by the doctor when they were finally able to make it downstairs. The techs would put a rubber stopper in the drain hole on the table and perform the autopsy right were the body was lying.

The work load was almost non-stop. Most days autopsies ran into second shift, so the cost of contracting funeral homes and removal services skyrocketed. They would hire new techs in batches of four to six at a time, but most would just stop showing up within the first month. There was, however, usually one or two who rode it out a little longer.

One of the major changes Richard Finley introduced was a concept of having medical-legal investigators. Several people were hired and trained to more or less try to investigate circumstances that may have led to the death. It was apparent that he did not realize that state police and local police had their own detectives and were not particularly fond of people stepping on their toes.

Generally, the majority of homicides happened after hours, so Richard and his investigators were not getting much call to action. Their days were spent in the office on the phone gathering medical history on previous cases. Richard was getting frustrated with this consistently happening, so he instructed the technical staff to call him the next time a homicide was called in, as he wanted to respond to the scene personally.

It did not take too long. Late one August evening there was a fight at a subway station, and a man was punched or kicked off the platform onto the third rail electrocuting him to death. The case was called in by the police department, and the call was put out to Richard. He could not have sounded more excited on the phone when Dale called to tell him of the case. He ordered Dale to have a truck ready with two technicians and a camera and said he would be there in thirty minutes. Dale told Greg and Bill to get ready, but they had to wait for Richard to arrive.

It took him about an hour to get back to the office from wherever he lived as traffic getting in and out of the city was bad. He arrived in a suit, carrying a large black duffle bag, which he deemed his homicide kit bag. All three men got into the truck to proceed to the station of the incident.

They arrived about twenty minutes later, and the trains had already been shut down for about two hours. The transit police and Boston police had their people on scene, which was blocked off to the public with crime scene tape. He insisted that all three must be fully suited up before they walked onto the scene, which was a little embarrassing but technically he was the boss.

After putting on the full Tyvek suits and foot wear, they grabbed a stretcher and body bag and started walking to the platform. It did not take long for the summer heat and humidity to make them start sweating in the full suit. The body was lying on its back right across the third rail, which was now shut down.

They arrived at the platform. A Boston detective told they were all set and could take the body. Richard looked confused and questioned the detective. "What do you mean you are all set? We need to take pictures. Has the body been moved? What are the circumstances?" The detective looked right at him and asked gruffly, "And just who are you?" I am Richard Finley the chief investigator for the medical examiner's office. The detective still looking at him and not impressed one bit came back with, "We don't need any more investigators. We have it covered." Richard now a little gruff himself said to the detective, "Well, there is a new sheriff in town, so you better get used to it." The detective laughed a little bit and responded with, "We'll see. You guys do what you got to do, but he is ready as far as we are concerned."

Greg and Bill hopped down onto the tracks with the body bag while Richard stood at the edge of the platform digging through his duffle bag and pulling out two brown paper bags and a roll of electrical tape. "Take some pictures of the platform and the body. Then we will take some measurements to see how far he fell," he ordered. "Tape the bags onto his hands so we don't lose any evidence. But after you take pictures, when his hands are bagged, we will roll him over and take back pictures as well."

Bill and Greg did as they were told, and as they were bagging the hands a transit cop came over. "Hey, you guys might want to hurry it up a little. The line goes active in ten minutes, unless you want to have two extra cases tonight." Greg grabbed the camera as Bill rolled the body up on his left side and snapped a few quick pictures and started to tuck the bag under the body. They got him zipped up, and with the help of a few officers on scene passed him up onto the platform to be loaded on the stretcher. Richard stood on the platform talking into a small recorder, taking his own notes on the scene.

The body was loaded into the truck, and they were finally able to take the Tyvek suits off just as the Boston detective came over to the truck to talk to Richard. "Look," he said, "I am not sure what directive you are working under, but we do our own investigations. We have video of the fight and the man falling off the platform. We have witnesses to the incident, and we have the other man in custody. The more reports that are filed on one case the more confusing it gets and the more likely the defense will get off on some technicality, so let us do our job. Your office is supposed to be impartial and find the cause of death, whether it's electrocution, falling on his head, or from the punch or kick that knocked him off the platform." Richard did not like hearing this at all and fired back at him angrily, "I saw several things just walking up to the scene that were not done properly. There are national guidelines on how these things are to be handled! You know how I know that? Because I wrote the guidelines!" The detective laughed a little again and turned and started to walk away. "We will see, we will see," he laughed.

The drive back to the office was awkward. Greg and Bill just sat silently as Richard rambled on into his recorder about the incident with the detective.

They arrived back at the office with the body, unloaded him, and brought him to the processing area. Richard micro-managed the entire process of processing and logging the body into the morgue register. As they were about to start rolling the body off the scale and into the cooler, Freddy popped open the x-ray room door. "You can just push him in here and I will do the x-rays tonight, so he will be ready for the morning." "Not without being fully suited up!" yelled Richard, who now seemed even angrier than he had on the ride home. "People are going to have to learn there are new procedures to be implemented immediately around here!" Freddy just stood there with a glazed look on his face. "Umm, OK. I will get suited up, I guess," he mumbled as he shuffled toward the anteroom.

The autopsy was done the next morning by Dr. Grady who now worked as just a regular medical examiner with Nicky as his tech and the Boston homicide detective to observe. According to the detective, the other man involved in the fight was going to be charged with homicide as the video from a surveillance camera on the platform showed a solid round-house-type punch to the side of the victim's head causing him to fall off the platform and land on his back smashing his head onto one of the railroad tracks.

Just as Dr. Grady was about to start his "Y" incision, Richard Finley burst into the autopsy room with only half of his Tyvek suit pulled on, so it looked like he was trying to run with his pants half pulled up and holding a surgical mask over his mouth. He demanded that the doctor stop the autopsy until he could examine and take his own photos of the body. He approached the side of the table where Nicky stood. "Who undressed and washed the body already," demanded Richard glaring at Nicky. "I already took my photos and so did the detective," stated Dr. Grady.

The detective turned around and was face to face with Richard. "Look, I told you yesterday the investigation is handled, and Dr. Grady has done his share of homicides. We do not need anyone else's input on this." Dr. Grady put his scalpel down and approached the two men standing face to face speaking very softly. "The detective is right, Richard. This is pretty clear cut that it will be blunt force trauma to the back of his skull from hitting the rail. There are no signs of any other trauma to the body externally and no obvious signs of any electrical burns, but if you want to take some photos, feel free. I will give you a few minutes, but I have to be in court today as well, so I really do not have much time to waste and I will not include your photos in my file." He turned to Nicky. "Can you help him take his photos, please." "People got to learn to stay in their own lane," mumbled Nicky. "Exactly," replied the detective. "I'll be back in ten minutes," said Dr. Grady as he walked toward the anteroom. Richard still struggling with his Tyvek suit started to follow him out. "Where are you going? Do you want your photos or not?" questioned the detective. Richard replied sheepishly, "I have to run upstairs to my office. I forgot my camera." Nicky laughed out loud. "Ohhh man, people got jokes around here, don't they?"

It was less than a week before rumors started to circulate around the office that a letter from the governor's office had come stating that Richard and his medical-legal investigative team were not to leave the building to respond to scenes.

Now their main function was to sit upstairs in their office space making phone calls to try and gather medical history and track down family members.

MORALE PROBLEMS

The case load at the office was still non-stop. They did manage money in the budget to hire more doctors at a much lower salary than the more experienced. They were much younger and looking for their stepping stone and experience. They also hired new technicians every month. As expected, most of them did not stay, but out of every six new hires one or two would soldier on for the experience. They also changed the hiring practice and now started techs at a higher pay rate than some of the older technicians who had been there for a while made. The justification was that they were looking for people with some college or still in school to get a better-quality person. All this really did was piss off the more senior technicians.

A new technical manager was hired as well. Deborah Wingate was a large woman around forty years old or so. She had some surgical experience but was clueless as far as what the technical staff did. She was supposed to be the promised one to save the technical staff from killing each other and restoring morale. She made it clear after her first week there that she was not there to babysit the techs. She was an administrative manager and not a supervisory manager. She would be tracking efficiency and production. She also said she was only there on a five-year plan and then moving on to other things.

This, of course, was upsetting to the other longer-term technicians who had worked their way to supervisory positions as the tech manager job was handled by someone who had never been a tech. Nicky, Greg, Ricardo, and Karen were all bumped up one pay grade to level-two techs, which was a nice increase in pay, in exchange, of course, for training, new techs. Each one would be assigned a new tech to train out of the ones who made it more than a week. Greg, Ricardo, and Karen were fine with it. Nicky did not want to be bothered but wanted the increase. Training was easy. The job was not rocket science, and there were plenty of repetitive procedures to do and no shortage of bodies to do them on.

Nicky was rude and sometimes just mean to the new techs she was supposed to train. There were several complaints filed against her that went up to human resources. Bright-eyed eager-to-learn college kids did not expect to be thrown into the wolf's den like they were. The woman Nicky was training asked if she could be trained by someone else after her first week.

It got to a point were Dana Mahoney had to speak to the technical staff individually and in secret to see who wanted to file a written complaint against Nicky so that they could take some action without the union getting involved. But as usual, word got out and rumors started spreading within the week and a union rep was sent to the office. They scheduled a hearing with Nicky, the union rep, and Dana for the following week. The hearing never happened, though Somehow the file with the written complaints mysteriously disappeared, so there were no written complaints to dispute.

This did, however, divide the technical staff into its own small cliques. Nicky and her minions tried to figure out who said what to who. It was impossible to tell, though, as so many people had come and gone in the past few months. One of the newly hired technicians was Diana, a woman in her mid-twenties, very attractive who had some experience working in another state's medical examiner's office, quickly became a threat to Nicky. She was very fast, knew the job, and able to manipulate people as well as Nicky. It didn't take her very long to convince the new technical manager to turn the small laundry room into an office for her. Her reasoning for this was to be able to process the toxicology samples in a quiet private setting to avoid errors. In the past, this process was done in the body processing area without any issues. Now, however, there were so many bodies coming in and so many cases being autopsied that the task seemed almost overwhelming and time consuming.

Even with the cliques and some bad blood and in-fighting, the office was now fully staffed. They were able to have two trucks on the road during the day and four or sometimes five techs in the autopsy room, depending on the day. The flow of bodies coming in was still constant. Livery services would bring them in in pairs as well as the two morgue trucks, but bodies were still being released at an incredibly slow pace. A lot of this had to do with the medical -legal staff under Richard's newly implemented protocols. Certain criteria had to be met on information before bodies could be released.

Training new techs was quite enjoyable despite the office politics. Most of the new hires were young, college age, and quite happy to be working there. The days would fly by working with someone who was pleasant to be around. The mandatory six weeks of autopsy was no longer enforced due to the number of cases, and it was great to be on an every-other-day rotation to be on the road.

One particular day, Greg was on the road. He was asked to take two of the new techs with him. Both were just about to finish college and were planning on much better careers than this. One of the girls named Diane was only a few classes away from her bachelor's degree in criminal justice. She was duped into thinking this job would be like it is portrayed on television, but it didn't take more than the first day to see that it is not even close.

The other girl's name was Lisa. She was in school to become a funeral director and wanted to learn embalming. Greg was on the road with her the previous week and learned a lot about her personality. She was very much into the macabre and horror scene and had several subject-related tattoos to prove it. She told Greg on the road that the best present she ever got from her boyfriend was a mummified bat that he found on an attic cleanout.

Lisa and Greg were driving through a very rural part of the state and passed by a field with about ten horses grazing in the pasture. Greg happened to like horses, and as they drove by made a comment about horses. Lisa's response was, "Yeah, they're OK." A little further down the road they passed by another field with a large red barn and one black and white cow standing on its own in the middle of the field. Lisa was now as excited as a three-year-old, exclaiming "A cow, a cow!" So obviously cows were her thing instead of the typical horses.

Greg, Diane, and Lisa were going to go on the road one morning when a call came in from the state police that a car had been found in a culvert's drainage ditch. The water level had been unusually high the last few days, and now that it had dropped a little the top of the car could be seen from the road. This was peak traffic time to get out of the city, so it was going to take a bit to get there unless they could use lights and siren to respond. Greg got permission from the supervisors to go with lights but to stay on the hard shoulder in the breakdown lane and no siren. It would still take a bit to get there, but it beat sitting in traffic, so good enough.

They all hopped in truck three eighty-two as the club cab was already on the road with two other techs and headed out. The highway was less than two miles away, so that part of the trip was quick, but it was bumper to bumper and all you could see was brake lights

"You're going to have to be in charge of the flashing lights, Diane," Greg said, as she sat in the middle of the regular cab truck. Greg was not going to reach between her legs to reach the control panel. She seemed very excited to be able to do this and pleaded a couple of time to just give a couple of whoop whoops on the siren. As tempting as it was to clear a little traffic, Greg gave in and said, "Yeah, what the hell, just until we can get a clear path to the breakdown lane, though." "What a power trip this is going to be!" squealed Diane.

Greg took the left to get onto the ramp heading north on the highway, trying to stay to the right side to get on the shoulder. It was backed up with people who didn't know how to merge on a highway, but in their defense, people won't let you just cut in either.

"Now?" says Diane with a huge smile on her face. "As good a time as any, I guess," replied Greg. "Well here we go," she said and started flipping the row of switches one at a time. In her excitement of being able to run the lights, she flipped the switch for the siren as well, which let out a very loud wail, more than likely causing heart attacks in the line of cars in front as well as the three of them in the truck. She was now in panic mode and flipping all the switches on and off in rapid succession trying to find the siren switch as it continued to wail on and on. The traffic in front of the truck had no idea what was going on, and drivers tried to part like the Red Sea for Moses. Some cars were pulling off to the far right, which is exactly where Greg was trying to get to. Others pulled to the left, while still others for whatever reason pulled up alongside the car in front of them. Lisa sitting in the passenger seat on the right side of the truck was laughing out loud hard, "This is awesome!" she laughed.

Greg was starting to get a little nervous about getting in trouble. This was taking way too long to resolve. Traffic on the ramp was now so screwed up on the right side that he had to cut left and bob and weave his way onto the highway. After making it the half mile on the ramp, cutting left and then right and then squeezing down the middle, he finally was able to see a clear shot to the highway's breakdown lane. He got in it as fast as he could. "No more sirens for you," he laughed. "I am so sorry," Diane said apologetically. "I just got so excited." "Everyone is going to do that at least once," laughed Lisa.

They rode down the breakdown lane but at a slow pace for fear of someone seeing the lights and cutting over in front of them. But moving forward was still better than standing still. They cruised this way for about five miles with no issues when suddenly coming up fast behind them in the breakdown lane was a state police cruiser, with all his lights flashing and giving the short whoop whoops on his siren. Now Greg was very concerned he had been busted for doing something he wasn't supposed to do but could not figure out what. Driving down the breakdown lane with lights going was a common practice when a scene was causing traffic problems or a major disruption. He pulled as far right as he could and stopped. The cruiser drove up on his left side, half in the right travel lane and half in the breakdown lane, the front ends of both vehicles lined up like they were going to drag race.

The trooper, who looked like he had just graduated high school, hopped out of his cruiser and ran over to Greg who was sitting with his window down wondering if he needed to get his license out. "Hey, you guys heading to the car they found in the culvert under water?" he asked. "Yes, sir," responded Greg feeling a little confused. "Great," said the trooper. "Follow me. You think that truck can keep up with me?" "I can try," "smiled back Greg. "Great," said the trooper. "Let's go."

The trooper walked around the backside of his cruiser. There was a steady stream of cars slowly moving past as best they could with his cruiser taking half the lane. Without missing a step, he held his left hand up in a stop motion and the lane froze. He had a clear path to get in his car. He paused briefly before ducking into his car. OK, let's go use your lights and siren, too," he said still with a big smile. He popped himself into his cruiser. He hit his siren and pulled out in front of the medical examiner's truck. It did not take him long to get to about sixty miles an hour in the breakdown lane with his lights and siren going. Greg was kind of terrified driving this fast. There was no room for any margin of error or one clown panicking when he saw the blue lights and pull over to the right to make this a very bad day. Fortunately, they were not going to be on this highway much longer. They were quickly coming up to an intersecting highway they needed to take. The cruiser hit the off ramp at just about sixty miles an hour. There was no way this pick-up truck was going to do that. Greg had to slow down in a hurry to take the ramp and the sharp right-hand curve to enter the next interstate. By the time they got to the end of the ramp, the cruiser was about a football field length ahead and had already cut over to the fast lane. This highway was not as congested. There was some traffic, but it was flowing at speed limit pace.

The cruiser was slowly pulling further away from the truck in the fast lane. Greg glanced down at the speedometer. He was going seventy-five miles an hour, and the cruiser was still pulling away.

"Punch it. You're going to lose him," yelled Diane and she slammed her left hand down on Greg's knee to force it down on the accelerator. Greg floored the gas pedal, now approaching over ninety miles an hour and still not really gaining any ground on the cruiser. If he did, it was because the cruiser backed off a little but not much. After fifteen miles or so Greg finally saw some break lights on the cruiser. He thought to himself, "Thank God. We must be getting close." The cruiser now only about fifty yards or so ahead of the truck cut across three lanes to the right to take the exit. Greg had no idea how fast he was going, but he had the truck's accelerator floored for quite some time, but he was afraid to look down at the speedometer.

"Oh my God, that was awesome. I think we hit one hundred and five miles an hour," Diane exclaimed. "I need a cigarette!" "That was incredible, Lisa joined in, "I need a cigarette, too, and I don't even smoke!" she laughed. The scene itself was only about ten minutes off the highway and was mostly secondary and back roads. The cruiser had killed his siren and was just driving with lights flashing and doing the posted speed limits. He probably realized he got a little crazy on the highway and wanted to avoid any chance of getting in trouble with his barracks. The back road was blocked off by another cruiser. The cruiser Greg was following stopped right in front of the other and got out of his car and joined the other trooper standing outside his cruiser. He waved the truck in as they exchanged their own small talk. He gave Greg the hand up "stop signal" as he was about to pass them. Greg stopped and rolled down his window. "There you go," said the trooper with a big smile. Diane still very excited about all of this leaned out the window over Greg's lap. "Thanks, that was awesome!" she said to the trooper still smiling from ear to ear. "My pleasure, just a little professional courtesy to get a job done," responded the trooper. "All right I got to take off and go mess up some traffic somewhere. Take it easy, guys," he said and got back in his car and drove off.

The trooper blocking the access road spoke. "You guys got here quick. They called it in early figuring you would get held up in traffic.

The tow truck got here about fifteen minutes ago, but we had divers get the body out so he should be ready for you. Just about half a mile or so down the road. You can't miss it." He waved the truck through.

They drove down the road and pulled up to the scene. There were several unmarked cruisers, a fire department rescue truck, engine company pump truck, and a state police dive team unit truck. They did, in fact, have the body up on the bank strapped down on a back board, and the tow truck was already winching the car out of the ditch. The body was in a good spot. Greg was able to pull up right next to him, so this would be an easy removal. The body was in early stages of decomposition, indicating it had probably been there for four or five days. Greg went over with his clipboard to talk to Trooper Madeleene who had been called to the scene a few hours earlier to see if they were ready to have the body removed.

"Hey, man, how you are doing?" he said with his strong accent. "We are ready for you this time," he continued with a big smile on his face. "I already took my scene pictures. I will photograph the body tomorrow before autopsy. There is nothing suspicious here. He may have just had a major medical event or just drove off the side of the road. You guys are the best. You'll figure it out. We ran his car registration and driver's license, so we are pretty sure it is him. He was reported missing about three days ago by his family. They said his work had called their house because he was a no-call no-show that day. He did not come home that night, so they reported him missing the next morning. You can take him whenever you are ready."

Greg had him sign off on his paperwork, giving him permission to take the body. On an outdoor or public scene, the sheet is left blank other than the signature giving permission to take the body. Normally you would have to document everything the person has on its body before getting the signature. Greg walked back to the waiting girls and let them know they were all set. It was a very easy pick up with three people and the body being in a good location. They loaded the body and drove back to the office.

The drive back was much less intense. Traffic was not as bad going the opposite direction, and they made it back in about an hour. They brought the body in and started to process him in as Sharon walked over as if to inspect what they are doing. "You guys do OK?" she asked. "Yeah, no problems. This was an easy one," remarked Lisa. "Good, good to hear," Sharon replied, while looking the body over. "Greg, when you are done processing him can you go upstairs and see Katelynn. She called down here and asked to see you when you got back." "Ummm, yeah sure," said a very worried Greg. "I don't think there is a problem, but she asked to see you. I will have Freddy do some x-rays on this guy since he is starting to turn." She turned and walked back toward the tech station. Lisa said quietly, "We got your back, Greg, right, Diane?" "Absolutely, we didn't do anything wrong," agreed Diane.

They finished the processing and logged the case in the book. "Well, I guess I am going to go upstairs," Greg said to Sharon who was sitting behind the desk texting someone on her phone. "All right, good luck. Can you send the girls to lunch before you do?" she said without looking up from her phone. "Yeah, sure," he said as he turned to walk down the hall to find out where the two ended up.

Greg went upstairs and knocked on Katelynn's door. "Come in," she said. Greg opened the door and started to walk in. She turned away from her computer screen and looked right at Greg. "Oh, good. I wanted to talk to you. Did you go on the removal in Topsfield this morning?" "Yes, we just got back and processed the body in," he said. "Oh, good, no problems on the removal then?" "No, not at all, Ms. Fletcher. It was actually a very easy removal. The body was ready to go when we got there." "Oh, OK, that's good, but I was curious as to why channel 7 news would call the office and ask what is going on?" "I am not sure, Ms. Fletcher, but I am pretty sure the story will make the news if it hasn't already." "They said their news chopper clocked the truck at one hundred and ten miles an hour and wanted to know what was going on that warranted that kind of response. We had a state police escort that met us along the way, and he told us to follow him and keep up. I can't say we were going as fast as that though, but truthfully I did not look at the speedometer." "Did you use lights and siren?" "Yes, ma'am, as instructed by the trooper giving us the escort." "All right then, no problems getting to the scene and the body is here. OK that is all I wanted to know. Thank you." Greg turned and left the office and went back downstairs. The incident was never brought up again.

The autopsy was done the next morning by Dr. Grady. Arnie was there all bright eyed and bushy tailed to take his photos. The trooper gave Dr. Grady the rundown on the case, telling him he was reported missing a few days before he was found, and that he was seat belted in his car with no signs of foul play. Dr. Grady did his external exam and agreed with Arnie. "No, I do not see any obvious signs of trauma or even drowning for that matter. There is no frothing around the nose and mouth and his eyes look OK, no burst blood vessels, but we will open him up and see."

The autopsy was performed, and it turned out the man had a lengthy history of cardiac issues and it appeared that he had what is called a "widow maker" heart attack and was more than likely deceased before his car plunged into the water. There was a 100 percent blockage of his left anterior descending artery, and there were no signs of drowning in his lungs. Dr. Grady told Arnie that he would not classify this as a drowning and would list it as a cardiac event on the death certificate.

One of Greg's other favorite trainees was a young man named Jake. He had finished his masters in forensics and was also here for a stepping-stone job, but really wanted to work in a lab environment. Greg had quite a good sense of humor, and Jake seemed to be afraid of just about everything to do with dead bodies. Greg seized the opportunity to exploit this and was constantly pulling pranks and practical jokes on him. On one occasion even he went as far as hiding in a coat rack filled with lab coats and waiting until Jake walked by and grabbed his ankle as he passed. This sent Jake running down the hall out of the locker room.

Jake also had a good sense of humor and took all of this with a grain of salt, vowing to exact his revenge in some way as soon as he could figure out how. He was also very good at his job, picked up on everything quickly and was as strong as an ox.

NORMAL OR PARANORMAL?

As with any morgue situation or place that handles the dead, there are going to be accounts of strange happening or sightings in the building. The infamous heavy funeral home-type purple velvet curtain that was used to separate the long hallway where bodies were processed and the tech station seemed to sway back and forth randomly or just one corner or end of it would, making whoever was sitting at the tech station think someone was about to walk through. This often went unexplained as there were no air vents around and any sort of air flow to move that heavy curtain would have to be fairly strong. Skeptics said that air currents would come in through the garage, which was normally closed most of the day, or even more absurd was the theory that air was coming in through the front doors of the building. The front of the building had two sets of double doors to get outside and then inside had another set of doors and still another after that to get into the one-hundred-foot hallway and so wind would have to pass through all of that and still maintain enough strength to make the curtain sway or just one side of it move.

After a while the new administration removed the curtain and installed an automated sliding glass door to separate the two areas, much like those at store entrances. They also installed a sink on the side tech station side of the curtain so techs, livery service people, and funeral directors could wash their hands after handling the bodies. They also installed a paper towel dispenser that was on a motion sensor to dispense the paper towels. After the changes were made, the door would randomly open itself and the paper towel dispenser would randomly spit out a towel or two.

The deco autopsy room was located only a few feet from the door on the other side. There were also rumors of what was called the "deco room doctor" who seemed to hang around that area. One morning, Dr. Armstrong, a part-time medical examiner who came in to take cases when needed, was assigned a badly decomposed body for autopsy. She came down to get suited up in the anteroom, and Nicky was going to be working with her. Nicky and Greg were behind the tech station counter and could see through the glass slider that Dr. Armstrong was standing at the deco room door looking into the small rectangular window. She was there for the better part of thirty seconds or so and then put her hands on her hips as if she was agitated. She came through the glass door to approach Nicky and Greg. "I thought I was working in the deco room today!" she said in an agitated tone. "You are," said Nicky. "I have him all set up in there. We are just waiting on you." "That's my case set up in there?" she questioned. "Yes, it is. I was going to get suited up when you came down," replied Nicky. "Well, there is already a doctor in there looking the body over," stated the doctor more frustrated than before. "No, there isn't. Everyone else is already down here and cutting in the main room," said Nicky now just as frustrated as the doctor. "Let me go see what is going on in there." Nicky walked around the counter and through the glass door, popped open the deco room door in a fashion that was meant to startle anyone who happened to be in the room. She poked her head inside the door jamb and looked back and forth. "They aren't anybody in her but your body. Now quit stalling. I will go get suited up," she said in a laughing tone. "People always trying to play games around here," she laughed. The doctor stood there looking at Greg, "I saw someone in there taking notes and looking at the body," she said to Greg in an I- know-I-am-right tone. "I don't know anything about it, doctor." Everyone else is in the main room. I don't think anybody else wanted to do this guy. I can't imagine they would voluntarily do an external on him for you." The doctor turned and went over to the deco room door and looked inside again through the window and then slowly opened the door to the room and entered. Just as she took about two steps inside the room Nicky came in right behind her, walking at a fast pace. "Get in there, you scardy cat. Let's get this done," she continued laughing.

There was one-night Greg would never forget when he volunteered to work an overnight shift when someone called out sick. The phones had been relatively quiet and not a lot of calls coming in, so it was setting up to be a good night. There were a couple of hospital cases that were ready to be picked up, so he sent the two junior technicians on the road to go grab them so they would be there for the morning roster. They were happy to oblige. Both stops would take the better part of the early-morning hours before they got back, and they would only have a couple of hours left on the shift.

They got the truck of choice ready and headed out. Greg was left alone in the building. Phones still sat silent after the truck left, and it was eerily quiet in the building as Greg shuffled paperwork around and updated the roster for the morning. It was about 2 a.m. He had taken one phone call since the truck pulled out, and it was a declined case from a hospice house of an elderly woman with metastatic cancer and loads of other medical history. It was an easy decline but was going to be lots of typing. He decided to run upstairs and grab something out of the vending machine and a cup of coffee before he started to type the case into the system. He quickly ran up the back stairs to the kitchen area, grabbed his snack and coffee from the Keurig machine, and headed back down stairs. Just as he opened the door at the bottom of the stairwell, the automated sliding glass door just finished closing itself. Greg put the coffee and his package of cookies on the counter and looked through the door. He could clearly see the entire one-hundred-foot hallway was clear. "Well, that's creepy," he thought to himself, "Maybe it's Freddy coming in way too early or something." He grabbed the cordless phone and walked down to the locker room. He cracked open the locker room door "Freddy?... Freddy you here early again?" There was no response. He stepped into the locker room and looked around, but the room was empty. No one in the shower, and the toilet stall door was wide open. "Well, this is weird," he thought and exited the locker room. He thought maybe one of the girls had come in, so he knocked on the girls' locker room door. "Hey, did someone come in early?" he said loudly after knocking on the door a few times. Nothing but dead silence. It was so silent he had to check the cordless phone and hit the on button to make sure he had a dial tone, which he did. He knocked even harder on the door this time. "Hey, I am coming in!" he yelled and walked into the girls' locker room. It was the same set up as the men's locker room, but they had a couch in there instead of a bench. "OK," he thought to himself, "this isn't fun anymore." He started his way back down the long, dimly lit hallway toward the tech station. He peeked in the window of the autopsy room door, trying to look in both directions. The room was almost pitch black with darkness. He continued down the hall and opened the anteroom door. It was completely empty, and the only light was the dim light from the hallway. The main cooler was on the other side of the hall. He could see through the window on the door that the light was out in there, too. No need to look in. He walked at a quick pace down the rest of the hall, so quick the sensor barely had time to recognize someone was there. He had to stop and wait for the door to open enough for him to get back to the tech station. He crossed the threshold of the door way and noticed a couple of paper towels on the floor that had been spit out of the dispenser. "This is not funny, Jake!" he yelled down the empty hallway as the slider was closing. Greg picked up the paper towels and put them in the trash and walked back around the counter to his seat. He turned the cordless phone on again to check for a dial tone and placed it back on its charging stand.

"What the hell, man," he thought as he opened the computer program to start entering the case, as he opened up the package of cookies. He spun around in his chair to face the computer and started typing in the demographics for the patient. The desk phone as phones do when someone is calling, burst into a loud double-ring-type tone, signaling an outside line was calling. It seemed twice as loud as normal and really startled him while he was trying to type. "Medical examiner's office," he said into the head set. "Hey, it's Keith. We got the first one. We are going to head back toward Boston and grab the other one. We should be back to the office in about an hour now." Keith was one of the newer techs who was hired specifically for doing removal on third shift, but he was really good at taking cases over the phone as well. He was on the road with another newer technician named Phillip, who was a good guy in general but didn't seem too bright. "All right," responded Greg, "but hurry up. I might need you guys back here." "Is it getting busy?" asked Keith. "No, not busy, just weird," said Greg with a laugh. "We will do what we can," laughed Keith. Greg hung up the phone and went back to typing.

Greg finally finished typing in the case, printed out his report, and made the folder and put it in the declined folders pile. He grabbed another cookie out of the pack and took a sip of his coffee. It had gone ice cold. It had only been sitting about twenty minutes or so. It should have at least been warm, but this seemed like it had been iced. The building itself was at its normal temperature. Heat was working fine. Greg dumped the cold coffee into the sink near the sliding glass door, grabbed the cordless phone again, and headed up the back stairs again to get another one. The kitchenette and break room were immediately on the right when exiting the stairs. On the left were the long stairs past all the offices, and around the middle of the building there was a large open area where the administrative girls worked. There were no walls, but the four desks were separated in a square-type pattern as if they each had walls. Each admin worked for at least one doctor and typed up notes on the cases.

Greg opened the cabinet and stared at the coffee selection. He couldn't find any more regular coffee. All that was left was flavored stuff, which he was not a fan of at all. "Well, this sucks," he thought as he started to sort through to find something at least acceptable. While he was sifting through the selections, he heard what sounded like someone talking possibly even working in the admin area. He grabbed a hazelnut-flavored one and placed it on the counter and stopped to listen to see if he could identify who would possibly be in at three in the morning to do admin stuff. He heard a voice - maybe even two - having a conversation, but he couldn't hear what was being said or tell whose voice it was. He walked back out into the hall way and peeked around the corner. He heard an office chair sounding like it was being rolled on one of the hard-plastic mats placed under them and papers being shuffled around.

Greg was convinced at least one person was working but was confused at the same time. There were no lights on upstairs, and why would they be talking to themselves? He bravely stepped around the corner and stood facing down the darkened hallway. Suddenly, everything looked creepy in the dark, and he was hesitant to even walk past the closed office doors or even worse the three cubicles with no doors opposite the offices.

He yelled out, "Someone come in early? Hello, who's here?" There was no answer. It seemed quiet, and he could not hear any talking or shuffling around. He stood there for a few more seconds. It was dead silent now. "Hey, is someone here early?" he yelled down the hallway again. Still no answer. He walked back toward the stairwell door to turn the lights on and flip the switch. The lights in the drop ceiling started to flicker on until they were as bright as they got. "Hey, is someone here?" he yelled down the hall again. Still nothing but dead silence. "This is nuts," he thought to himself. "The building is locked. No one can just walk in. If someone did come in with their card access, the panel at the tech station would light up to let me know which door was opened." He stood there for another thirty seconds or so. Still not a peep to be heard.

He walked back to the light switch and put his fingers on it. "Last chance to let me know you came in early!" he yelled. Still nothing but silence, so he flipped the switch and the lights went out. He stood there waiting for someone to yell about the lights going off, but nothing. He went back in the kitchenette to make his coffee. The Keurig made its usual noises and finally spit out its last bit of steam and water. He waited for the last drop to hit the cup and grabbed it. "Well, at least this one is hot," he said to himself. He turned to walk out of the kitchen. Just as he was about to open the door to the stairwell, he heard a bang. He was no expert on loud bangs, but that sounded like someone just slammed a file cabinet drawer closed. He took his hand off the door handle and waited for the next sound, but there was nothing.

He started talking to himself. "OK, if I don't go see who is here, I am going to be more freaked out the rest of the night than I already am, and there is definitely someone down there working at three a.m. for whatever reason. I would look stupid if I called the cops in on this and it is an admin." He stood there silent, waiting for more noise, but there was still nothing. "All right here goes nothing," he said to himself out loud. He flipped the lights back on and waited for the flickering to stop. "Hey, is someone working!" he yelled one more time. "I am doing a building walk through. If you are down there working, say something!" It was just as long a walk as it was downstairs, the row of cubicles on the left and the closed office doors on the right. Greg walked slowly as he approached each cubicle and stayed on the right side of the hall by the wall. He could see the lights were not on in any of the offices as they each had a long rectangular window next to the doors. The opening for the cubicles was the last panel by the corner of each square, so if someone was hiding, they would have to be opposite that as there was a flat wall separating it from the next cubicle.

First cubicle was clear, no room for anyone to hide. Second was clear, and the third was empty, too. "Of course," he thought to himself, "the noise was coming from the admin area, your big chicken." About forty feet or so into this adventure, he passed three offices and cubicles. The next big obstacle was the door on the left side that led into the long hallway that mirrored the downstairs hall way. He crept over toward it and could already see the lights were off in the hallway. He opened that door and poked his head in. "Hello!" he yelled into the empty hall. No answer, as expected. Admin area was now about five yards away, and he has not heard anything since he heard the big bang. He was close enough so figured he would try one more time. "Hello, someone working early?" Still no answer, and no sounds coming from the area. Greg took a few more steps closer. He mustered all his courage and did not stop and walked right into the admin area and stopped in front of the girl's desk. He figured if someone was there and he was acting like he was scared; the hazing would be relentless from everybody. "Hello!" he yelled one more time, but no response. He walked between the two front desks toward the back wall just to make sure no one was hiding under a desk or having some kind of medical crisis, but still nothing, no noises, or people,

"Well, you have come this far," he thought to himself, "might as well go down the front stairs. There was no one from where you just came." Not seeing anyone or hearing any more noise, he was starting to feel better about things, so he moved at a much quicker pace. He cruised past the property closet and the counter area where funeral directors signed out the bodies they were picking up and headed for the doors that led down the front stairwell. Even on his quicker walk, he could see the conference room had the lights off and so did all the management offices on the opposite side. Greg stood by the door leading out of the office area. "Last chance!" he yelled one more time. Still not a sound. He flipped the switch at this end of the hall for the lights, and it went dark again except for the red glow of the exit sign lights. Still no one yelled out to turn the lights back on.

He made a quick trip down the stairs still carrying his coffee and stopped at the glass double doors leading into the lobby. The reception desk was unoccupied, the lobby was darkened, and the office door for the state police was dark - no lights on in there either. One last long walk down the hallway to the tech station, past the main cooler and the autopsy rooms. Greg took a couple of big steps to trigger the motion sensor on the sliding glass door that was installed on this end - same type of door as the other end leading to the tech station, but this one had frosted glass so you could not see through. This was just in case a civilian or non-morgue person needed to get upstairs without having to see anything. Greg walked through the door still walking at a slightly faster pace than normal but got kind of spooked as he approached the main cooler door. He grabbed one of the stainless-steel tables used for autopsies that was lined up against the wall and rolled it as he walked forward. He positioned it so it was across the cooler door and pulled it about six inches or so from resting right against it then locked the wheels on his side. By doing this, if the cooler door was opened from the inside it would bang into the table making a loud bang or tip the table over all together with the wheels on one side locked. There was no way he wouldn't hear that.

Greg made it back to the tech station. Everything was right where he left it. His cookies still sat in their plastic on the counter top next to the computer, and the folders of declined cases were stacked neatly next to the computer. Suddenly the phone came to life with the all-too-familiar double ring of an outside line with a case being called in. He picked up the phone. "Medical examiner's office," he answered. It was a state police trooper calling in a motor vehicle accident, but it was not on one of the major highways rather on a two-lane road that was regularly patrolled. The trooper did not have any information other than a single occupant had hit a tree at high speed and was pronounced dead at the scene. The fire department was going to need some time to extricate the body, so no rush on the removal.

This was a well-known trick or tactic by people who knew what to say when calling in a case. The trooper knew the medical examiner had to take the case because it was a motor vehicle accident, but he didn't want to waste his time giving all the patient demographics and information. He simply had to state he has no information at this time. The case would come in as an unknown driver and the medical-legal people would fill in all the blanks on exactly who had been picked up, and the trooper could be on his way with the rest of his shift. It was an easy case to enter into the system as well, would take less than five minutes to enter, make a folder and put on the roster. It was also a good distraction from what the last twenty minutes or so had been like.

Greg entered the case, got its case number, and made the

folder. He felt pretty good about how the night had been going as far and the number of phone calls coming in. He sat there and ate the rest of his cookies and drank what was now a slightly warm coffee as the phone came to life again. This was not the familiar outside line double ring, though. This was the long, loud, single tone from an inside line dialing the tech station. Greg looked at the caller id screen on the phone. "What the hell," he said. It was extension one zero six calling. That was one of the phones in the ante room. Greg grabbed the receiver. "Tech station," he said a little confused. No response. "Tech station. This is Greg. Who is this?" There was a crackling sound and some static and then a hang up. Greg was really spooked now. He jumped up and ran around the counter and looked through the slider as it opened when he hit the sensor and stared down the hall. The autopsy table was still in front of the cooler door. "Who could that be?" he thought to himself. He walked down to the ante room. As he got closer, he could see the light was not on in the room. "What the hell?" he thought and opened the door and flipped the lights on. Nothing was disturbed in the room. The chairs at each desk were pushed in, and no one was standing there. He could see the autopsy room through the window. The lights were off in there. Greg turned the lights off and backed out of the room and let the door close. He then walked quickly back to the tech station. He sat there trying to think of something logical to explain what had just happened, but he was a little freaked out.

It had to be Jake getting back at him was what he was starting to think. That's what made the most sense, but how had he sneaked in the building? He was working day shift. Did he hide all day and wait until three in the morning to pull a prank? If he did, kudos to him. This was good one. "I might even admit he got me," Greg laughed to himself to try and calm his nerves. A few more minutes passed. Greg checked out his Facebook on his phone, but his head was on a swivel in case anything else happened. The phone let out another long, solid tone for an inside line again. Greg looked at its extension - one zero seven, the other phone in the ante room. Instead of answering it, he got up and ran on the other side of the counter and hit the sensor for the sliding glass door, so it started to open. He reached over the counter and grabbed the phone. "Tech station," he said with a smile on his face because he was going to catch Jake in the act. Instead of anyone answering, there was nothing but static or white noise coming from the phone. Greg dropped the phone on the counter and ran down to the anteroom. The lights were still out as he popped open the door and yelled, "Gottcha!" as he flipped the lights on. But no one was in the room. Greg jumped over to the door leading to the autopsy room. "Come out, come out wherever you are," Greg said in a kind of sing-song voice as he flipped the lights on in the room. The room just sat there silent. No one was in there. Jake could not possibly be fast enough to have made an escape. Greg back tracked to the main hallway and looked up and down both directions. Both sliding glass doors were closed. The table was still in front of the main cooler door. The only place left that Jake could be hiding was the x-ray room, but how could he have moved that quickly and silently to not be detected? Greg creeped up to the x-ray room door and tried to peek in the small rectangular glass window but could not really see inside. The lights were off in there, too. He burst through that door and flipped the lights on. "Ha!" he yelled into yet another empty room. Greg was starting to lose his mind. It was not possible that Jake made it to the locker room as Greg almost jogging down the hall went through the glass door and entered the locker room. It was empty, too. Was Jake smart enough to hide in the girls' room? Greg burst into that room - also empty.

Greg was absolutely convinced without a doubt it had to be Jake. He started to head back to the tech station. About half way down the hall he yelled out, "OK, Jake, you got me. This was a good one!" Greg got back to his seat behind the counter waiting for Jake to make an appearance and laugh at him. But he sat there for several minutes, and it remained silent. Greg looked at the alarm panel. No external doors had been opened all night, so Jake had to still be in the building. Greg decided to use the paging system. He picked up the receiver, hit the page button, waited for the loud double tone to ring out on the overhead speakers throughout the building, and said over the intercom, " OK, Jake. You win. That was a good one, but I will not surrender. Come down to the tech station, and I will buy the coffees." He hung up the receiver and waited, but Jake did not come down to the tech station or even call the desk.

Greg waited about fifteen minutes and still no sign or word from Jake. He grabbed the phone again to do another overhead page "The jig is up, Jake. You win. Come on out." He hung up, but still no response. Just then, Greg saw the truck that had been on the road all night backing into the courtyard on the security camera. "Well, at least they made it back," he thought, now very relieved to not be alone in the building. He reached over and hit the button to open the garage door. As it starts to open, the light on the alarm panel went on. "Well, that's still working," he thought to himself. Keith and Phil came in single file, each pushing a stretcher. "How has it been?" said Keith with a big smile. "Has it stayed quiet?" he asked as he pulled the stretcher by with Phil right behind him. "For the most part," responded Greg. "Hey, how many cars are in the parking lot?" asked Greg. "Just our three," said Phil.

Keith and Phil processed the bodies in and put them in the cooler. "What's with the table in front of the door?" yelled Keith. "Nothing," yelled back Greg. "You can move it." "Are you expecting a zombie uprising," laughed Keith. The rest of the night was uneventful. Greg took a handful of calls at the hospitals' shift change time, and most of those were declined cases. Only one other possible overdose case was accepted.

Greg could not wait for 7 a.m. to see Jake face to face, but 7 a.m. came and went and no sign of Jake. Greg waited until 7:30 and decided to send him a text. He typed in his phone to Jake: "HaHaHa you got me, that was a good one. I was freaked out half the night, but I will not surrender you will get it back ten-fold now lol."

Greg waited to see if there was going to be any response, but it never came. Ricardo was working the tech station, so Greg asked him if Jake had taken the day off or something. Ricardo told him Jake had taken the whole week off and was on vacation. Just then Greg's phone went off. It was a return text from Jake who responded: "I have no idea what you are talking about. I have been in Florida for the past three days, but HaHaHa I am glad someone finally got you!" Greg decided it was probably best to keep the story of last night to himself.

The only other time Greg experienced anything he could not explain was another night working third shift. One of the nightly procedures on third shift is a cooler inventory -that is each body that is in the cooler has to be double checked to make sure it is in the system. A printed list of bodies that are supposed to still be in the building is double checked against each toe tag. This is very time consuming because of the number of bodies being taken in versus the number of bodies released. The list gets longer every day.

One-night Greg was the senior technician on duty, and this inventory was his responsibility. Keith was also working that night, but Phil had taken the night off for a family event. All the hospitals changed their shift at roughly the same time, so there was a peak hour when they called their cases in, usually about an hour before the hospital shifts ended. Once that shift change happened, the phones stayed quiet for a bit unless there was an emergency or accident.

After the quick run of a few phone calls from the hospitals with nothing really exciting being reported, Greg printed out the list and told Keith he was going into the main cooler to do the inventory. He grabbed his list and clipboard and headed to the cooler. Keith was going to handle any phone calls that came in. Greg had been in the cooler for about forty-five minutes, still taking his inventory but not finding any problems and making what he thought was pretty good time. Keith opened the cooler door and told Greg he had to go to the bathroom but was taking the portable phone with him. Greg said that was fine. He was almost done in the main cooler anyway. He spent another fifteen minutes completing the inventory and finished it with no issues or problems. He left the cooler. He stepped into the main hallway and out of the corner of his eye thought he saw Keith through the frosted glass as the sliding door closed. He stood in the middle of the hall switching the inventory lists to find the deco cooler one. He was thinking Keith had been down there for a while and hoping he was OK. After a minute of fumbling with his paper work, Greg finally looked up and turned to his right to head for the deco room. He now saw Keith sitting behind the counter at the tech station. Greg opened the sliding glass door and asked him how long he'd been back at the desk. "About ten minutes. I only went to take a leak," replied Keith. "Did anybody come in?" questioned Greg. "Not that I know of," said Keith. Greg put his clipboard down on the counter and quickly headed for the locker room. He went in the men's room and no one was in there. he knocked on the girl's room, and there was no answer. He went all goose pimply and said, "Nope, I am not doing this again," and headed back to the tech station to get his clipboard and finish his inventory. He planned on spending the rest of the night where ever Keith was.

TROUBLE IN PARADISE

Another interesting incident that Greg particularly enjoyed occurred on a sunny Saturday morning. Dr. Grady was scheduled for autopsy as part of his part-time agreement, and so was Dr. Cavanaugh, the new chief. The two men had some history as quite a few years prior Dr. Cavanaugh applied to the office to become a medical examiner, and Dr. Grady did not think he had enough experience to bring him on, so his application was denied. This was something that Cavanaugh did not forget and had caused some bad blood between to the two. Now that he was the chief, he was calling the shots.

Dr. Grady was not fond of working on Saturdays as it was, and that day, he had an important lunch date so wanted to get in and out of the office as fast as he could. He cherry-picked a few cases off the roster when he came in at 9 a.m. and instructed Greg to pull the cases and draw all the toxicology and take the photos if he had time. He would be down at ten to start.

Greg did as he was told. The doctor had marked the cases as views or autopsy so he could get everything ready. He took six cases, which Greg thought was pretty ambitious for only having about two hours, but Dr. Grady had marked four of them as just external views. Now it was well known in the office that Dr. Cavanaugh did not like doing only external views just in case something was missed. It was equally well known that Dr. Grady preferred doing a view with toxicology when he thought medical history would determine the cause of death.

Dr. Grady was one of Greg's favorites to work with. He learned all kinds of things working with him, even though Dr. Grady went much faster through cases than other doctors. The doctor would often point out things like external symptoms and diagnose the cause of death before an autopsy was done. His record of accuracy was about 100 percent, and it became sort of a game when working with him. On rare occasions when Greg guessed one right, the doctor would make a big deal out of it and take him to lunch.

Unfortunately, this was not going to be a free lunch day, as Grady was just looking to finish and leave. Dr. Cavanaugh was already cutting two stations over with one of the newer technicians. All his cases were slated to be autopsied, which was going to make a long day in that suit.

Dr. Grady came down a few minutes before ten, and Greg was just finishing up taking the photos. The two cases he was going to autopsy were both homeless people found unresponsive but unrelated to each other. There was no medical history on either of them as they were pretty much unknowns. Living on the streets of Boston in the winter would be enough to do most people in. Out of the other four cases, two were elderly people found at home on well-being checks, lots of medical history, nothing suspicious and nothing that toxicology would not reveal as a cause of death as far as the doctor was concerned. Sometimes the primary care physician was not willing to sign the death certificate. As in both of these cases, the doctors claimed that they had not seen the patients for several months, so were unwilling to list a cause of death. Unfortunately for these people, that warrants a trip to this office. The third case was a suicide of a man in his forties who placed a twelve-gauge shotgun under his chin. He left a lengthy note detailing his decision, and it was deemed that no foul play involved. An autopsy on him would not show anything. His cause of death was blatantly obvious.

The last case, however, was, at least according to Cavanaugh, needed an autopsy. He was a man in his mid- to late fifties with a history of heart disease, but his doctor would not sign the death certificate, claiming he was being properly treated and on several prescriptions. Dr. Grady took one look at the man and even asked

Greg to make a diagnosis as he had several external symptoms of an advanced heart disease issue.

Greg looked over the body, and the first thing he noticed was the earlobes had diagonal creases. "At first look," Greg said, "it looks like he has 'Frank's sign' and his fingernails are looking like they could be clubbing. If I had to guess, I would say it's definitely a cardiac issue." "Very good, very good," said Dr. Grady. "Do you see anything else?" Greg looked closer at the man's corpse lying on the table. "There seems to be something with his face, but I can't put my finger on it," replied Greg.

"If I had more time today, I bet you would see the other signs, but I will point them out this time. Next time you will know what else to look for. OK, here we go. Do you see the halo around the iris in his eyes?" Dr. Grady stood there with a pair of tweezers pulling open the eyelid. "This is called Arcus Senilis. It does not make it conclusive but is an indicator of heart disease. But if you look at his lips, they are slightly discolored almost a blue shading in the corners of his mouth - also an indicator - this is cyanosis. His cardio system is having trouble delivering blood and oxygen to his tissues. So, you are right about his face not looking quite right. These are just some subtle hints that most people would not notice. I am willing to bet that if we did a closer examination in his mouth, we would more than likely find some loose teeth or problems with his gums. The one that clinches it for me, though, is if you look at his elbows and his knees you can see what is called 'xanthomas.' These little fatty bumps are a great indicator that there is a serious problem. Xanthomas are most commonly seen in people with a genetic disease called familial hypercholesterol-emia. People with this condition have exceptionally high levels of low-density lipoprotein cholesterol - so-called bad cholesterol. The levels of this cholesterol are so high they become deposited in the skin. Unfortunately, these fatty deposits are also laid down in arteries that supply the heart. You are right about the Frank's sign and the Hippocratic or clubbed fingers. So, with his history and all the tell-tale signs, I don't think he needs an autopsy, and I will sign him out as ASCVD, arteriosclerotic cardiovascular disease when I get the blood work results."

Dr. Cavanaugh was apparently eavesdropping on Dr. Grady's little class a few tables over and came to look at the body himself. Without looking up at Grady he said, "Just because he has some symptoms and history of cardiac issues does not mean that is what his cause of death is, doctor. He needs a full autopsy to determine exactly where the problem is." Greg could tell by Dr. Grady's change in posture he was frustrated. "Well I don't think I will have time to do a third autopsy today. If you insist he needs an autopsy, then he will have to wait until Monday. I have some other commitments I have to take care of today. Push him off to the side for now please, Greg. We will get the other cases that warrant an autopsy done to-day." Greg did as he was told as Dr. Grady stepped over to start his first case that was already set up. "We will have to go a little faster than normal today, Greg. I already wasted too much time arguing over an obvious view."

The atmosphere in the autopsy room was pretty thick. Cavanaugh was just about back at his table, but Grady made a point of speaking loud enough for him to hear his comment. They fin-ished the first autopsy in about thirty minutes. Dr. Grady was still flustered and didn't talk much during the process, so Greg was not sure if he saw a cause of death or not. The doctor finished tak-ing his pieces of organs for the stock jar as Greg finished sewing the head back up. The doctor used his loafing knife to scrape the remnants off his cutting board into the viscera bucket and pulled the bag up and placed it in the chest cavity. "Could you sew him up after, Greg? I need to start the second case." Greg plugged the table so as not to make a huge mess on the floor and swapped out the tables for the second case. Before Greg was back over to block the body in position, Dr. Grady had already started making his "Y" incision. Greg stood waiting for a long enough pause to lift the body and place it on a block. The autopsy could be done if the body was flat but needed to be blocked, so Greg could place a second block under the head to remove the brain. Dr. Grady was well aware of the situation and gave Greg the pause he needed. Greg properly blocked the body and started to work on the head. Dr. Grady was moving at what seemed lightning speed. "I will take the brain out myself," he told Greg. "I saw something indicating he had a possible hemorrhage, but in this case, I need to see it for myself." The doctor was already done removing organs and stood waiting for Greg to finish opening the skull. As Greg started to pull the skull away, Dr. Grady stated, "Ohhh, look at that. He looks like he may have had some mini strokes. I am willing to bet he had a major one that did him in." He stepped into Greg's spot to remove the brain, also at lightning speed as he dropped it in the scale and proceeded to split it down the middle on his cutting board. "This looks like a major stroke right here," he said as he took a large sample.

"All right," he said to Greg, "thanks for your help. I am all set here." He stepped back from the work area and started to remove his Tyvek suit. "Sorry about the mess. We will do lunch when I have more time. I have got to make it to my meeting today." Cavanaugh made a beeline toward Dr. Grady. "This man needs an autopsy today!" he demanded at Dr. Grady. "He does not need to be cut up. He has ASCVD. If you really feel he needs an autopsy, then you feel free to add him to your list today," said Dr. Grady as he continued to remove his protective suit. "You are no longer in charge here, doctor, and I say he needs an autopsy and he is your case!"

Dr. Grady now completely unsuited not willing to admit defeat but not willing to disrespect the new chief yelled back, "Fine, he will get an autopsy! Greg, can you please get him set up and open he chest for me." Greg swapped out the tables as quick as he could. Both doctors stood there watching him as he placed the body on a block and stepped back. "I am not going to suit up again, Greg. Can you open the chest and remove the heart for me?" Once again, Greg did as he was told and started to wonder what kind of repercussions he was going to face from the chief. Working as quickly as he could, he made the "Y" incision and cut the ribs. "Just remove the heart for me, will you, and use the loafing knife and split it down the middle." As Greg was doing what he was told, Dr. Grady put on a fresh pair of latex gloves and stood next to him at the cutting board. "Just as I thought," he said as he scooped up the two halves of the heart in his palms and turned to show Dr. Cavanaugh. "His heart is completely plugged with plaque. Doctor, I think we have his cause of death." He turned and let the two sections of heart slide back into original cavity where the heart was located. "I am all done for the day, Greg. You can sew him up." He tossed his gloves into the trash and headed for the door.

"This isn't over, doctor. I will see you in my office on Monday morning," Cavanaugh said sternly. "I have court on Monday and Tuesday. I will let you know when I am available, doctor," responded Grady as he left the room. Greg was pretty sure he would have slammed the door if it was capable of being slammed. He never did find out the outcome of the incident. It seemed to have just vanished like all the other problems in the office.

GOOD TIMES

There were more changes in the staffing of the building and more upstairs positions had been added, including case intake people, to lighten the load on the tech station. This was an election year, so it stood to reason that favors would be called in for endorsements and campaign help. The jobs being posted didn't exist previously, but now the building could not function without them. This worked out well for Greg and some of the other technical staff. Greg was promoted to level II technician, as well as two other technicians, one for each shift plus an additional one for the very busy day shift, and a couple of new doctors,

There were only two new technicians. One happened to have gone to school to become an x-ray technician. Once this became known, Freddy really started to lose his mind. A month after the new technician was hired, they replaced the very old x-ray machine that still required hooking up jugs of chemicals and running the slides through a developer with a brand-new state-of-the-art machine that produced almost instant high-definition digital images. In addition to the new guy, Brad being trained on the new machine, Greg, Freddy, and three other techs were also trained so they could take x-rays around the clock if needed.

Brad was an interesting individual, in his late twenties, single, not the most attractive guy you would see, and had a slight stutter when he spoke. He was constantly cracking jokes and telling funny stories, probably compensating for his lack of immediate appeal to the female persuasion.

One morning Greg was smoking by the garage in the smoking area with one of the seasoned female techs who had been hired a few months prior. Her name was Patty. She was in her thirties and had a carpentry background. She and Greg got along great. She was attractive, in shape, and worked out regularly, not a bad body, but a little smaller on the top side. Her uniform shirt was not properly sized. It was at least two sizes too big, and as they were standing smoking Brad joined them. Patty knelt down on one knee to tie her boot lace, which gave Brad a clear look down the front of her shirt as the top of it now hung about four inches from her collarbone and she was not wearing a bra. "Hey, you should get that mole on your chest checked, Patty!" "What are you talking about? I don't have a mole," she said, looking down her shirt front. He started to laugh hard out loud. "Oh, never mind that is just your nipple." He was laughing so hard at his own comment he had to turn and go back into the building.

He was great to go on the road with. He entertained the entire time. He did have a sort of OCD thing when he was not on the road. He had to count out the number of paper towels he used on his autopsy set up because it had to be a certain number or he went in the x-ray room to make sure the system was functioning, then rearrange the x-ray files of the shots other people had taken to make sure they were good enough.

James, the second new technician, was brought in as a supervisor for second shift. It ruffled a lot of feathers to hire an outside person as a supervisor. The justification was that he had been and still was in the funeral business. He was a nice enough guy, in his fifties, balding, and married with grown children. When Greg's father passed away, he helped him out a lot with the funeral services and even got him a cremation urn at cost.

There was a woman, named Francine slightly younger than James hired for a legal position upstairs. She was hired right around the same time as James. She was not the most attractive, but ok, overweight, and had a bossy, condescending tone whenever she dealt with the technical staff, which was often in her created job title. Greg and she got along just fine. There was not a lot of banter or joking between them, and as long as he was able to do what she asked, she was OK to deal with. She usually came into work much later than most of the administrative people, which meant she was at the office later in the evenings than anyone else upstairs. Rumors around the building were that she and James both achieved their positions by favors being called in, but that was unsubstantiated.

One night Greg was called in early to cover the last four hours of second shift and then work the overnight hours. He arrived about thirty minutes early and apparently went undetected on the security cameras. When he walked into the back room coming in the open garage door and entered the back room, he caught her straddling James' lap with his hands on her hips. James promptly pushed her off and laughed. She turned around very red faced and said, "You did not see anything, Greg." She told James, "We will talk later" and went upstairs. The fortunate thing was that they were both fully dressed. Who knows what he would have walked into fifteen minutes later.

The technical manager, Deborah Wingate, also came in late in the mornings and could often be found in the building later at night. It was not unusual to find Francine sitting in her office chatting away.

MORE NEW STAFF

The tech staff had grown significantly since Greg started working in the morgue, and there were a few standouts in the crowd who actually stayed and enjoyed the work. Despite the morale problems and the politics of the inner workings at the office with the more senior techs, new techs came in with a good attitude and under the assumption that coworkers were a good thing. This was the case for most of the new people. Ego and attitude were nonexistent with anyone employed less than six months. The unfortunate thing was it didn't take long for people to be deemed stupid and lazy by others in the office. For the most part, everyone liked Greg. He had a good attitude and was funny and generally a nice guy to everyone. The new techs gravitated toward him, Karen, and Ricardo, while a couple seemed to side with Nicky and Catrina. They soon learned that was a mistake and would not last long before they turned on them, too.

One of these people quickly became a favorite work buddy after she started there. Her name was Tracey. She was an older woman - about ten years older than Greg - and had a loud but funny outgoing personality. She was also a gym rat and went every day after work, so she was in great shape. She had several kids of her own, so she knew how to handle herself when presented with attitude. She was also the only other technician willing to work with Dr. John another recent hire.

Dr. John was from the South and had a no-nonsense attitude. Being at work meant you worked. Dr. John had worked for a few other states as a medical examiner and had a long career already under his belt. He was in his seventies when he started after being forced to retire from another state. He was full of "dad jokes" and told them all day long, even if you heard them already. Dr. John was in at 6 a.m. every day and grabbed most of the mundane cases just to get them off the list. If no tech was there, he pulled his own bodies out of the cooler and started on them himself. It was not unusual for him to have four or sometimes five cases done before the morning meeting. There came a point shortly after he was hired that Greg and sometimes Tracey came in early just so he didn't have to work by himself. Other techs avoided being seen in the building when he was scheduled to autopsy so as not to interrupt their breakfast time.

There were a few other new doctors, most of them young, who probably thought the job was more glamourous than it actually was. They worked at a slower pace than the more experienced doctors. Most of them were great to work with, though. They all had their own personality and quirks, but for the most part were friendly and showed some respect to and appreciation of the tech staff.

On one case, one of the newly hired doctors, Dr. Barkley, who happened to be a neuropath doctor specializing in the brain, disagreed with Dr. Lowe's determination on a cause of death in court. The case involved two older teens who were bullying a slightly younger mixed-race boy. The abuse went too far one day, and they started a fist fight. When the younger boy got the upper hand in the fight, the other friend kicked him in the side of the head, knocking him unconsciousness. He eventually fell into a coma and died. In his report, Dr. Lowe determined that the victim suffered brain swelling and hemorrhaging, both signs of a severe beating caused when the brain shifted inside the skull from the kick. The entire fight was caught on video, so it was obvious what had happened, but Dr. Barkley testified in front of the jury that the kick did not necessarily cause the boy's death even though it did show a brain injury. The jury didn't buy it especially after seeing the video. Both teens were convicted of the lesser charge of manslaughter, but the repercussions at the office of Dr. Barkley going against one of their own made her stay there short, and she moved on to other things.

Or maybe that wasn't it, as some of the other new younger hot shot doctors also moved on after a short time. The techs could make a doctor's life pretty difficult if they did not like working with them or if they felt disrespected.

As luck would have it, Tracey and Greg were on the same schedule for the work week and autopsy room and removals Saturdays became the favorite day to work as they were both on the road and both regularly on time if not early for their shift. They would have a truck ready to roll right at 7 a.m. and hit the road while everybody else was still hanging out in the locker room stalling on getting the day started. There were always hospital cases to pick up, so they would take the two furthest from the office and take off. If no scenes came in, they could be back at the office by eleven and half the shift was gone. They always had a good time on the road, discussing their home lives and just making jokes and having a good time all day. Tracey even described herself as Greg's work wife one day.

One of these Saturday mornings they had taken their truck and picked up their first hospital case about an hour from the office. Just as they were about to call and let Ricardo, the supervisor for the day, know they were on their way to the next, their phone started to ring. It was the office, and they had a scene and it was at least a two-hour drive from the current location. It was a house fire that had happened overnight, and two bodies had just been discovered now that the fire was out.

It was decided that since they had to pass the office they would drop the first body off and head to the scene. The fire department would not be ready for the removal for a bit anyway. There was a slight sense of urgency, though, as a truck needed to be on scene when they were ready to remove the bodies. They made good time back to the office in about forty-five minutes and dropped the body off. Ricardo offered to process her in so they could head right back out, which they did.

The scene was north of the city, which for whatever reason seemed to be much less frequent than south, so it was like a whole new road trip. Traffic on a Saturday leaving the city was almost non-existent. Still feeling a slight sense of urgency, though, they used all the flashy lights with no siren. This was not 100 percent effective, but for the most part once people saw the flashes, they moved over.

They arrived at the scene and drove up as close as they could. They grabbed the stretchers and body bags and walked down the driveway toward the home. It looked like a total loss. It was a dormered cape-style house, probably pretty cute in its original condition. The yard was well taken care of so no reason to assume the home wasn't. Although a large portion of the roof and front wall was completely gone, you could actually see inside the second floor of the home. What was left of that side of the house and remaining roof was totally blackened. All the windows were smashed out with a little white wispy stream of smoke still coming through.

Greg found the man in charge at the scene to see if they were ready for removals and to find out how they wanted to do it. Fire scenes could be tricky. Scene safety was a priority. You can't just walk into a burned-out building and assume the floors or walls won't collapse around you. Some departments would not let you enter a burned-out building at all and felt it was their job to remove the bodies from the building. In this case, the fire chief was quite all right with letting Tracey and Greg go in and handle the removal, but he sent two firemen with them to assist. Greg and Tracey walked in behind the firefighters carrying their body bags, looking around and checking things out and formulating a path back out while carrying a body. Greg saw the tell-tale sign of a bright blue tarp on what the kitchen floor had been. He assumed those were the bodies of the couple. One of the firemen asked, "Are you taking the dogs, too? That's what is under that tarp. They had five big dogs. None of them made it." As animal lovers, this was heartbreaking news to both Greg and Tracey. The fireman continued. "The bodies are over here in the back bedroom. They are not burned up too bad. My guess is the smoke and heat got them first." Greg and Tracey stretched out and opened up the body bags, rolled both of the cases in, and zipped them up. The two firemen grabbed the larger man, and Tracey and Greg grabbed the woman and the four proceeded to back track their way out of the house to the waiting stretchers on the front lawn by the door. Both bodies were placed on the collapsed stretchers. As they were being strapped down, the fireman's radio announced that animal control had just arrived on scene for the dogs. Tracey noticed that one woman was driving the animal control van. "We should stay and help her," she said to Greg. "That's a good idea," he responded and killed the engine on his truck. Greg was feeling a little choked up about the dogs and doing his best to cover it up. He noticed that Tracey's eyes were welling up a little, so she was doing the same.

The animal control officer pulled up next to their truck. Tracey rolled down her window to talk to the woman as she got out of her van. "H , I am Tracey, and this is Greg," Tracey said. "Would you like a hand? We were told they had five large dogs." "Oh my God, that would be great. I am Janine," she replied. "I hate these kinds of calls. It's heartbreaking. I hope they didn't suffer before they passed. You guys must think that's crazy. All your calls are like this only with people. I just need to grab some bags. Five of them you said?" Janine walked to the back of the van and opened the door to pull out some body bags for the dogs.

Greg and Tracey got out of the truck and waited for Janine. A fire fighter walked over as Janine walked back toward them. "The dogs can go anytime you are ready," he said to Janine. "OK, I am ready if you are," she said as all four of them headed to the path leading to the front door. They walked past one of the town's fire engines. Two firemen standing on the front side of the truck were rolling hoses. "Franklin, come give us a hand," the fireman who was walking with them said, placing his hand on the back side of one of their shoulders. Franklin did not say a word. He just stood up straight and followed them into the burned-out home.

All five of them entered the house and headed to the room where the dogs were covered by the tarp. They lined up at its edge just standing there, almost like giving the dogs a brief few seconds of silence out of respect. Janine went down on one knee to remove the tarp. She picked up the corner and passed it down the line of the five of them to unfold it exposing the animals. The room immediately filled with the smell of wet dog and burnt hair. It was a little sickening. There was a harlequin great Dane, two huskies, a German shepherd, and a boxer. None of the animals looked like they were burned too badly though. "Poor pups never had a chance," Franklin finally spoke. "They were all up in that front room," he continued pointing up at the gaping hole that used to have a roof. "We had no way of knowing they were in there. They must have been dead when we got here." When we finally go to the point where you could enter the house for an interior attack on the fire, the door on that room was closed. They couldn't get out. They must have been barking like crazy. I can't imagine the owners didn't hear them.

Each person managed to carry a dog on their own, so it was a one-trip removal. They walked out single file each gingerly carrying their dog back to the van. Janine carried the boxer that she gently placed in the back and then hopped in to slide him forward to make room for the rest. Each person gently placed their dog down as Janine dragged them all the way in.

Janine hopped back out carefully stepping over the last dog and closed the van door just hard enough to secure it. All four who helped her stood behind the van as Janine turned and said, "Well, thanks for your help, guys. You made a terrible day a little easier." The two firefighters acknowledged the thanks with a "Take care,", and a "No problem, anytime," and headed back to their firefighter duties. Greg responded with "you're welcome and anytime." Tracey gave her a hug and a "you're welcome," and they both got back in their truck and waited for Janine to leave first.

Greg gave her about a fifty-yard head start and then pulled out to head back to the office. Neither of them said a word. After ten minutes or so, Tracey asked Greg, "So what is your worst case you have had to deal with so far?" "Geez, I don't know. I guess burn victims and broken bones are the ones that I find disturbing," answered Greg. "No, not like that. I mean what case did you see that really got to you that you're not going to forget, like hit you right in the gut?" "Well, to be honest, it might sound a little corny, but not long after I started here maybe three months or so, we had a livery service bring in a case from the South Shore somewhere. It was an eight-year-old boy that just finished his Little League game, and for whatever reason his father thought it would be a good idea to let him ride home in the back of his pick-up truck. Long story short, the truck got t-boned in an intersection and sent the boy flying out of the back of it. He was pronounced at the scene, so he was coming directly in and when he got here, I was going to process him in. When he arrived, I moved him onto a table and unzipped the bag and I had to look twice. He was the spitting image of my son. Smaller than your average eight-year-old, blond hair, blue eyes and still in his baseball uniform. He even still had his glove on and his ball cap. His uniform did not have a speck of dirt on it. It looked like it just came out of the wash, bright white pants and a royal blue jersey. He was laying on the table with his head facing to the right, and when I turned his head to face looking up so I could remove his hat and shirt, the whole right side of his head was just smashed, with grey matter showing. I will never forget it or what he and the damage looked like."

"That's awful," she said. "Well I don't think I will be forgetting this one. All I can think of is those poor innocent trusting dogs. They must have been barking their heads off trying to get help."

"Well, I hate to say it, but there are probably more bad scenes and situations coming. One of the things I was told when I started here is never say 'now I have seen everything' because guaranteed you will see something new." They were both very quiet for the rest of the ride back to the office.

THE NEXT DAY

T he next day, Tracey and Greg where both scheduled to work in the autopsy room. Tracey was going to work with Dr. Grady on the woman from the house fire and Greg with Dr. Lowe on the male victim. On the surface, both cases seemed to be no brainers due to the circumstances. Dr. Lowe had started on the man a few minutes before Dr. Grady, drawing toxicology and taking his pictures. Nothing externally obvious that he had any signs of trauma or injuries, but the autopsy would confirm he died in the fire by smoke inhalation or excessive heat.

Dr. Grady, on the other hand, stood looking at his case. "Tracey, could you block her please so I can see the neck?" he said with just his forearms extended like a t-rex and wiggling his fingers. Tracey did as she was told and blocked the body and tilted the head back. "Look at that," he said to Tracey. "It looks like a ligature mark." Making his signature t-rex arms with wiggling fingers gesture again, he said, "Can you open her eyelids please." Once again, Tracey did as she was told. "She has petechiae in her eyes, and I would bet you a cup of coffee that is a ligature mark around her neck. I think she was strangled before the fire. Dr. Lowe, could you come over here for a minute," he called over from his station.

Dr. Lowe had his body open and had started to eviscerate already but put his scalpel down and walked over. "What are you seeing"? he asked Dr. Grady. "I think this woman was killed before the fire. Look at the ligature marks and petechiae in her eyes. I will know more once I get her open, but I think we need to call the trooper in here to get some more photos." "I am on it," said Tracey as she headed to the anteroom to call the trooper in. "Nothing on your guy over there?" he asked the doctor. "No, nothing so far," remarked Dr. Lowe. "I will go check his lungs right now to see if there are any signs of inhalation. I will get stomach contents as well, just to be safe." Dr. Lowe returned to his table. Dr. Grady had ceased on his case until Trooper Madeleene arrived.

The doctor cut into the lung with his loafing knife to examine it. "Dr. Grady, he is showing clear signs of inhalation, so he was alive after the fire started. Let me check his stomach." He grabbed his scalpel and removed the stomach, holding both ends of it to not spill its contents. He turned back to his work station and dropped one end into a stainless-steel bowl that Greg strategically placed as soon as he heard the doctor say he wanted stomach contents. Sure, enough there was a strong smell of alcohol and a bunch of undissolved pills. "I think this is a murder-suicide, Dr. Grady," he remarked. "I will need the toxicology report, but I am certain with what's in his stomach is what more than likely killed him."

Just then the trooper burst through the door with his happy tropical accent. "Good morning, good morning, doctors. What do we have today? he said cheerfully while looking down at his camera to get it fired up. "I am pretty sure we have a murder- suicide from the house fire yesterday. You may want to call the fire investigators to see if it was an arson. Dr. Lowe's case over there has alcohol and pills in the stomach and signs of smoke inhalation, and my lady here has signs of strangulation and ligature marks."

"OK, let me get my photos really quick and then go make some phone calls." The trooper took his photos with Tracey's help while the doctor stood by and finally said to Tracey, "We will have to wait on her for a bit. I want to look at her x-rays again. We will need photos during the autopsy if we find anything. Trooper, can you have an investigator go to the house and see if they can find something that might have been used to strangle her. It looks like something between a shoe lace and an electrical cord. More than likely not going to be too far from where the body was found." "Will do, doc," the trooper replied cheerfully. "I am all set here. I will get on the phone now." He looked down at his display screen to double check his pictures as he exited the room. Tracey placed the woman's body back in its body bag and rolled her back into the cooler. There was no reason for Dr. Lowe to stop working on his case, so he finished his autopsy. Greg sewed him back up and reset the station for the next case and put that body away.

The next morning, Tracey and Greg were getting ready to go back out on the road and were doing the check on the truck and re-supplying it when Trooper Madeleene came walking by. "Anything on that case from yesterday, Arnie?" "As a matter of fact, yes. We checked with local police and they had been called to that house multiple times for domestic stuff and assaults, but the kicker is it was him calling on her. Apparently according to the local officer, she used to beat the crap out of him, if you can imagine that. The state fire marshal found traces of an accelerant in the kitchen and the remains of one of those fake fire logs in the kitchen, so he is calling it an arson fire. The final piece is the detective found a three-foot section of clothes line on the floor in the bedroom, which if I had to guess will match up perfectly with the ligature mark on her neck. So that is some good work you guys are doing. Congratulations!"

The story was likely that she went after him again, but this time he had had enough. They started an altercation that got the dogs upset, so one of them locked them in that room they were found in. They probably continued the fight, and he snapped and strangled her. Once he realized what he had done, he placed her in the bed and started feeling very remorseful then decided to end his life, too. It is too bad the dogs were caught in the middle of all of this, though.

WHAT'S THAT SMELL?

t was bright sunny day. Temps were going to be in the eighties, and Tracey and Greg were on the road again. They picked up their first two cases. Both were somewhat local hospitals, so they were back to the office and processing them by 9 a.m. Sharon came over to the processing area looking as casual and aloof as usual and calmly asked, "Hey, you guys want to go to a scene?" as she looked at the body they were processing.

"I am not sure what it is," she continued. "They called it in as body parts in a trash bag found about two miles in the woods. If it's still in the bag, don't open it until the doctor sees it, OK? They said it smells really bad, too - like nothing they have ever smelled before, so it has probably been out there a while." "Ohhh, sounds great," remarked Tracey. "I'll get the paperwork ready, and you guys can head out as soon as you are done here," Sharon said as she turned and slowly walked back toward the tech station.

They finished up processing the body and put it in the cooler and restocked the truck again just in case. The scene was southwest of Boston about an hour and a half drive again. Tracey texted away angrily on her phone. She had been telling Greg all morning about a fight she had been having with her husband over something stupid one of her teenagers had done and her husband's reaction to it the last two days. Greg always listened with a sympathetic ear, but he had his own problems at home these days. He was working sixty-plus hours a week, and on all three shifts, so his wife's big complaint was that all he talked about was the job and his coworkers. She had no interest in either and felt she was being left to deal with and raise their kids. On top of the personal matters, Greg had also been elected to act as the union rep for the techs when needed, so everybody, supervisors included, came to him with the job problems and possible union contract violations. The thing about the union, though, was it was almost nonexistent. The local union rep was almost impossible to reach. You would call and leave voicemail after voicemail, and you might get a call back by the end of the week. Not to mention she was personal friends with Dana Mahoney, the human resources manager at the office. Greg spent a lot of extra time in the office meeting with Dana to discuss issues and try to come up with solutions, but most of the time complaints went unanswered or not dealt with at all. The latest round of complaints was being filed by Nicky, Catrina, and a couple other people who Greg was sure were intimidated by the two of them to file complaints. Most of the complaints were aimed at proving Sharon and Ricardo incompetent as supervisors and that some of new techs who were hired were just not competent enough.

The conspiracy theory on this was that Nicky and Catrina thought that they should be day shift supervisors and deemed everybody else on the technical staff stupid. The theory was never proven, of course, but suspiciously Catrina was pregnant and was told by her doctor to see if they had any light duty work at the morgue, as lifting heavy bodies or dealing with stuff like Formalin chemicals could be dangerous. It was clearly stated in the union contract that there was no light duty and that if you could not perform the full duties required, you would need to take that time off until you could. As a supervisor, though, you could stay behind the desk and basically delegate everything and handle the phones and computer work, so basically light duty. Currently none of the supervisors except Sharon abided by this. Ricardo still did autopsies and went on the road if needed.

They were about halfway to the scene when Greg noticed that the gas gauge indicated the tank was just under half full. He had a thing about not letting it go below the halfway mark. Whoever had the truck last didn't fuel it up at the end of the shift like they were supposed to. Tracey was still angrily texting. With a loud grunt she threw the phone in her lap and then grabbed it and shoved it in her shirt pocket. "Ohhh, my God. That man is so damn stubborn sometimes. He drives me crazy."

"Trouble in paradise still?" Greg asked. "That man is impossible," she yelled back. Greg said, "Well, I am going to hit the next exit to get some gas. Maybe we will get lucky and they will have coffee, too." As luck would have it, there was a Dunkin' Donuts attached to the gas station. Greg pulled up to the pump, and Tracey hopped out looking at her phone again that had just vibrated in her shirt. She was smiling this time, though. Hubby must have said the right thing. "I am going to hit the ladies room. I will grab coffee on the way back out," she said. "Good plan." Greg smiled back at her. He hopped out and started to gas up the truck. About a minute into refueling his personal phone went off in his pocket. Tracey sent him a text - must have been from the ladies room. She had only just gotten out of the truck two minutes ago. She was just asking if he wanted a sandwich with his coffee. Greg responded with "sure." It took five minutes or so for the automatic stop to click on the pump handle. He replaced the cap and hung the pump back up just as his phone started to buzz again. He finished jotting down the numbers on his clipboard, logging that he filled the tank. He noticed no one had filled the tank for two days on this particular truck. He slid back into the driver's seat and looked at the text from Tracey. He assumed it was going to be they didn't have what he wanted or asking if he wanted anything else. But to his surprise, it was a full-on topless selfie. Greg never thought about doing anything with any other woman since he was married and was not really sure how to react to this. He sat there for a few seconds and put his phone back in his pocket to see what she was going to say about this. The plan in his head was to say he did not get another text from her if she brought it up.

Suddenly she burst out of the Dunkins carrying the tray of coffees and two small bags screaming at him. " Don't open that text! Don't open that text!" She ran toward the truck. "That was supposed to go to my husband! Don't open that!" Greg was thoroughly relieved. This was obviously not meant for him. He leaned over to open the passenger side door so she could get in with her hand full. Greg was smiling from ear to ear. He couldn't help it. This was too funny, but he managed a "What are you talking about?" Tracey now very red faced said, "Oh, my god. You saw it, didn't you?" Greg was still grinning. He could not hide it. "I don't know what you're talking about," he replied trying not to laugh. "Please delete it!" she pleaded with him. "That was supposed to go to Jim. He sent me a picture of him standing there with an erection saying "'someone is missing you' so I figured I would tease him a little with a shot from me. Please, please, please delete it," she begged. "Well, I don't know what you are talking about," repeated Greg. "Are you sure you didn't get that last text?" she questioned him again. "Last text I got was 'do I want a sandwich,'" smiled Greg. "Oh, thank God. How embarrassing that would have been," she said very relieved as she slumped back in her seat. Greg pulled his phone from his pocket. "Well, the last text I got was about a sandwich. The last picture I got, however - I may need if I ever need to file a harassment suit," he said now laughing out loud as he handed her his phone. "Ohhh my God!" she squealed grabbing at his phone. "Feel free to delete it," laughed Greg. "So, do you remember a while back when you asked me about things I have seen on this job that I won't forget? Well, this is going to be one of them." Greg was laughing out loud now.

They finally arrived in a very small rural town. The main street in the middle of town barely had a convenience store with a couple of gas pumps. Greg drove down the main drag at the posted speed limit of twenty-five miles per hour, trying to look at the GPS screen on the dashboard when an unmarked state police SUV came up on them, fast lights and siren blaring. He quickly went around Greg's truck. Greg barely had enough time to move over all the way. "He must have been doing sixty at least," remarked Tracey. "Look up over there, Tracey. There are two helicopters circling around." Tracey leaned forward to look up through the windshield. "One of them is just a news chopper, but the other one is a Blackhawk, I think, with a thermal camera mounted on it. This must be big."

They continued at the speed limit down Main Street and could see all the flashing lights down the road. They cruise past a few news crews alongside the road with reporters doing their live reports - more than likely interrupting people's daytime television shows to break the news that the medical examiner had arrived on scene. This always made Greg chuckle a little. The local news perpetuated the idea that the medical examiner went to scenes to investigate.

The only time Greg had seen an actual M.E. go to a scene was when one of the newer, younger doctors was hired. A woman named Catherine Carlyle. She came from the Midwest, and she was highly intelligent and already really good with the medical stuff. Shortly after she was hired, she happened to come down to the tech station when Greg was working the desk early on a Sunday morning, around 7 It was supposed to be Greg's day off. She told him she was not scheduled to work that day at all but wanted to see if she could go to a scene if one came in just to get a firsthand look. Greg had no problem with this at all. He thought it was a great idea. "At the moment there is nothing, but I will let you know as soon as something comes in." "That would be great," she said. "I will be upstairs in my office catching up on paperwork. Give me a shout if we get one, not that I am wanting anybody to die today, but I would like to see a scene in person."

Ricardo showed up right at 7:00. Greg filled him in on what happened on the overnight shift and that Dr. Carlyle was upstairs and wanted to go to a scene. He also had no problem with that and then threw in, "Hey, why don't you stay and help us out today, too. I am short a person." "I can stay for a little while. I can give you until noon." "Great," he said. "You and Carlyle can go to the first scene."

The woman on case intake was upstairs handling the phones so things stayed pretty quiet at the tech station. None of the scheduled doctors were ever in a hurry to show up on a Sunday, so they would probably not start any cases until ten or eleven. Greg made a coffee run for everybody who was there and came back to the tech station to catch up with Ricardo to see what the general atmosphere in the office was. No surprises that nothing much had changed - not even any new rumors circulating.

Finally, around 9:00, case intake was called downstairs. It was a small plane crash at a privately-owned airport about thirty minutes away. It looked like the pilot, the only occupant, had a mechanical issue on takeoff and nose-dived at high speed into the ground. He had been pronounced at the scene by local paramedics when they arrived. Greg used the overhead paging system to have Dr. Carlyle call the tech station, which she did. She sounded a little excited and said, "I will be right down."

Greg went outside to get the truck ready and make sure it was stocked. By the time he pulled it out of its parking space, the doctor and Ricardo were walking out the garage door. "I am going to go, too," smiled Ricardo. "I have not been out of the office for a while, and Nicky can watch the desk." The three of them piled into the truck. Dr. Carlyle, a petite woman, sat in the middle. "Are we using lights and siren?" she asked Ricardo. "No, not on this one, doctor, sorry," he said as he put the truck in drive and started to head out.

They arrived at the airport and pulled into the back gates. It was not a very big place, and they could already see where the fire engine was sitting with its lights flashing so they pulled up along-side of it. The pilot had already been removed from the cockpit and was lying in the grass behind the fire engine covered by a blanket. The three of them walked over and the doctor knelt down and looked under the blanket. "Oh, dear, he is pretty messed up," she remarked. "Can I go see the plane? Should I be taking some pictures?" she asked. Now no one knew exactly who she was asking. By all technical accounts she was the medical examiner, which for some reason made it her scene in everybody's mind. "You are the medical examiner. You can go sit in the cockpit if you want to," he said with a smile. She walked toward the plane. There was no fire and did not look like there was any threat of fire. She leaned over to look in the front side window of the plane wreckage then walked back over to the truck. "One of the seats was gone and the other one was all messed up. I think I will skip looking inside the plane."

Ricardo and Greg loaded the body for transport back to the office, and the three of them climbed back into the truck and started to head out. "That was so cool!" said Dr. Carlyle after they cleared the gate exiting the airport.

Back at the small rural town, they approached the parked local police car that was blocking a side street by parking right in the middle of the road and running crime scene tape to the corners off of either side of the cruiser. The cop hopped out of his cruiser and broke the tape so the truck could pass. Greg stopped right alongside him for his instructions. The cop told them to go down the street about a mile and they would see a trail head that was also taped off, and a cruiser was parked there. The trail saved about a mile walk into the woods to the bag. The Blackhawk buzzed the truck and flew by at a really low altitude, scanning the woods with its thermal camera.

They finally reached the trail head entrance where the cruiser was parked. There were two men in suits and one uniformed officer. Greg assumed the men in suits were detectives. All three men wore surgical masks. Greg and Tracey parked and approached the men. It was obvious right away why they were wearing the masks. The smell was horrendous. The older looking detective turned as they approached. "You guys might want to get some masks on yourselves. It gets a lot worse the closer you get to it. That bag is about a mile away, and you can smell it all the way down here."

"Are you sure it is a body or body parts?" Greg asked. " I have never smelled anything like that. It doesn't smell like a decomposing body." "We don't know what it is," said the detective. "No one wants to go near the thing, never mind open it. All we do know is that it is heavy and tied to a tree and stinks like hell. It feels like a torso with no limbs. We can't figure out why it would have been tied to a tree, though."

"Well, we have been instructed to not open it until we get back to the office and have a doctor open it. So, we are just going to bag it the way it is and take it back, but I am willing to bet this isn't a body." Greg told Tracey to get the sled out of the truck. The stretcher wouldn't roll very well on a dirt and rocky trail. They would have an easier time pulling the flat sled when it was loaded. "I think we might want to double bag this, too. The smell is awful." Tracey grabbed the sled and two body bags and started to drag it down the trail, following the younger detective. The older detective was correct. It seemed with each step the smell intensified. They were accurate in the judgement of distance. It seemed to be pretty close to a mile in and about one hundred yards off the side of the trail. The smell was really intense now. The detective said to Greg, "This is a close as I am getting. I can't take it." He handed Greg a folding lock blade knife. "Use this to cut the rope tying it to the tree."

"You ready for this?" Greg said to Tracey. "Ready as I am going to be. This is just gross." They approached the tree. Greg opened the knife to cut the rope. Tracey had the first bag spread out and un-zipped. "I am going to try and lift it straight up. When I do, slide the bag under it, and we will get it closed up as quick as we can." Greg stood on the other side of the tree, so when he had to bear hug this thing, he would have the tree between him and it. It only needed to come up an inch or two to get a body bag under it. The tree was only about four inches around, but it was enough of a buffer that he did not have to touch the bag with his chest. He didn't want to try and just lift it from the top of the garbage bag it was in. If that ripped it would be a disaster, and the way it smelled probably a haz-mat situation. Tracey was on her knees with the edge of the body bag in hand. Greg squatted down, reached around the tree, and stretched his arms out around the bag without touching it yet. "OK, ready on three, One.... Two... Three!" He closed his arms around the bag and managed to raise it just enough for Tracey to get enough of the bag under it. She rolled it in the bag and started to zipper it as fast as she could. "Ohhh, this is disgusting," she squealed. A uniformed officer from the local department had the second bag unzipped and ready to go. Greg and Tracey picked up the first bag, placed it inside the second bag, and zipped that one up too.

"I hate to say this, but it did kind of feel like a torso. It is at least as wide as me maybe a little wider, and I thought I felt ribs." Tracey and Greg picked up the bag and placed it on the sled, strapped it down, and started to drag it out. It felt unusually heavy for just a torso. "I don't think two bags are going to be enough," Tracy commented. They continued to drag it out on the sled until they got to the road side at the end of the trail. Tracey dropped the rope attached to the sled, pulled a stretcher out of the back of the truck, and collapsed it next to the sled. They slid it over and strapped it to the stretcher. Granted, the stretchers were not very wide, but this thing overhung it on both sides. They loaded the stretcher in the back and closed up the truck. "I think we are going to switch to another truck when we get back," Greg told Tracey. "I would have to agree with that," Tracey said.

They made a three-point turn on the side road and headed out the same way they came in. The Blackhawk was still making low altitude passes, but they could see the news copter much higher in the air seeming to follow them. "I am pretty certain we are the live shot on television right now," commented Greg. "Lucky us," said Tracey. They drove the speed limit down Main Street again, heading back to the highway. The news cameras on the side of the street were focusing the cameras on the truck to get the footage for the 6 o'clock news. All the main stations were there. "Hopefully we can shake this smell once we get on the highway," she said to Greg. Unfortunately, they were not able to shake the smell, but nobody tailgated them on the ride home.

The office cell phone started ringing. Tracey picked it up. "Hello? Tracey speaking." "Hi, this is Sharon. You guys on your way back yet?" "Yup, we should be there in about an hour, but we really need to come back with this before we go someplace else." OK, that's fine. I just needed to know when you guys were going to make it back. The chief wants to take a look at this right away. He thinks it might turn out to be a big deal media wise." "We would be happy to go lights and siren and break all the speed limits if you want, Sharon. This thing stinks!" "No, that's OK. An hour is fine." Sharon apparently didn't get the joke. "I'll see you when you get here. Thanks, and good bye." Sharon hung up the phone.

They arrived at the office and backed the truck in the courtyard. "I think we should suit up and put on some Tyvek," Greg says to Tracey. They both entered the garage and headed for the anteroom to suit up. As they walked by the tech desk, Sharon commented "Is that you guys that stink like that?"

The chief was already in the anteroom doing his paperwork getting ready to take a look at this case. Arnie and another trooper from the area where it was found were already standing by with cameras ready. "Is the body in the deco room?" he asked. "Not yet," responded Greg. We need to suit up before we handle it. We will get a quick body weight on it, and we will get it set up for you. We only need about five minutes." "Sounds good," said Dr. Cavanaugh

They both get fully suited up, pulled the stretcher out of the truck, and transferred it to a stainless-steel table and rolled it on to the scale. "Only sixty-five pounds. It felt much heavier when I lifted it," remarked Greg. "Can you tell the good doctor we are ready, and I will get this locked into the deco room." Greg locked the table in place and unzipped the first body bag. The bag apparently did something to hold back the odor because it just intensified ten-fold opening that outer bag. He hesitantly unzipped the second inner bag. It was like getting punched in the face by the stink.

The deco room door opened, and in walked the two troopers and Dr. Cavanaugh. Tracey popped her head in the room, already stripped of her Tyvek suit. "You don't need me for this, right? Thanks, Greg." She retreated from the room as quickly as she popped in.

The troopers both started snapping pictures of the dark green heavy-duty trash bag sitting on the table. "Not much to see so far," laughed Arnie in his perpetual happy mood. Greg handed Dr. Cavanaugh a scalpel that he'd just attached a blade to, and the doctor started to slice down the center of the bag very gingerly. "Well, look at that." Both troopers lifted their cameras to take a photo of whatever the doctor was about to expose. "It's another bag." Separating the inner bag from the outer bag with his fingers, he made a much faster cut down the middle and folded both halves to the side.

"Let's try bag number two," he said, once again making a slow gingerly cut down the center, cutting slowly but still opening the plastic bag with his other hand. A gray-colored fleshy skin started to appear as the bag was peeled away. It didn't take long to see they were scales. This was just some big unidentified giant fish head that someone tried to dispose of in the woods. The doctor now completely sliced open the rest of the bag and opened it up nice and wide for the troopers to photograph. "Arnie, I am going to need this fish identified by the end of the day so we can make the proper notifications," joked Cavanaugh. "Seriously, though, what kind of fish is this? I have never seen one this big or this stinky. I don't know how we are going to dispose of this. We can't just toss it in the dumpster. Look at the stink it has already caused on the news, pun intended. "Greg, just wrap this back up as best you can. I guess we are going to have to store it in the deco cooler for now until we can figure out how to get it to a landfill or something. I am at a complete loss. No wonder this person just tied it to a tree in the woods."

Arnie and his happy-go-lucky attitude smiled under his mask and said, "Well, I guess I have to go make some phone calls and let everybody know we don't have a serial killer on the loose." The other trooper chimed in, "yeah, I guess the locals down there might want to take a look in the bag next time before they call the news stations to get some attention."

Greg zipped it back up in its double body bag and placed it on a shelf in the deco cooler. This smell was not going to go away anytime soon. He stripped off his Tyvek and placed it in the trash and left the deco room. He headed over to the tech station. Sharon was still sitting behind the desk playing on her phone. Greg called Jay in building maintenance. "He is going to bring you down a pressure washer to clean out the back of that truck and then you can go to lunch if you want."

Unfortunately, this case was only going rank as number two on the smelliest of all-time list. Another case that had come in some time ago was a body that had been placed in a chest freezer and put inside a storage unit. The estimated amount of time until the body was found was five years or so. There weren't a lot of details on the case, but a man from across the country was charged with murder and finally confessed to the crime. He said he murdered the man in his state then dismembered him and placed the body parts in the chest freezer. He drove across the country and rented the storage unit in Massachusetts. The freezer was not plugged in but did have a fairly tight seal. The body was only discovered after a person reported a foul odor coming from a neighboring unit. Upon investigation of that unit the freezer was discovered. At that point it had dissolved into a slurry-type liquid with the bones inside. The freezer and its contents were giving off such an odor that the whole thing had to be done outside in the courtyard. About the only way to handle the case was to extract DNA for testing. There was nothing left to autopsy and really no way to determine cause of death.

STRIKE ONE

The office was still taking in more cases than it was releasing. There had been a new directive issued to the medical-legal staff, and cases that were being held up could now be released. There was a huge backlog of bodies in the facility with two or three to a shelf and some two on a table. It was finally decided to unload some of the unknowns and give them a state burial. The majority of these cases had been decomposed badly on their arrival to the office.

One day, Greg was working with Dr. John and had started his day at 6 a.m. and had done several cases. It was around 1 when he finally finished up with him and was going to go take his lunch break. As he was about to exit the building, he heard a page from Sharon, calling him back to the tech station. He had no idea why he was being paged. He approached Sharon at the desk, and she looked at him with a sad disappointed look on her face and asked, "Would you mind working with Dr. Carlyle until I can send someone in there to relieve you? Everyone else is at lunch or on the road already." Greg already knew that no one would be coming in and he would be stuck in the room until the end of his shift if not longer.

This seemed to have become a standard practice with the newer younger doctors. They would be assigned their cases at the morning meeting, which started at 9 a.m. But there were so many cases on the daily roster that the meeting would last a minimum of an hour. They would go back to their offices and research the case and get their paperwork together, taking them close to lunch time They would have their lunch and then come downstairs to start the cases. This was a fine practice for them and almost made sense that it would happen regularly. The problem with it was if the techs were not busy on cases, they were more often than not sent on the road to a scene or to grab hospital cases.

It was not uncommon for everybody to be out of the building. The techs who were supposed to be on autopsy for the day would time their break so they knew they would not be around when the doctors came down. The other main problem was day shift ended at 3 p.m., and second shift did not have extra people for autopsy. So that meant that cases that were not picked up during the day had to be contracted out to a livery service or would have to wait. Most of the time the doctors would be done by 5 p.m., but by the time the autopsy room was cleaned it was about 6:00 at night. So, second shift was now only able to grab two cases for the entire shift to bring them into the office.

James, the supervisor, was usually left on his own in the office when the other two techs went out on the road. So, most of the time, he was left to clean up the room to send the techs out an hour earlier. It still didn't matter. By the time they got back, they would all take their break and then there would not be any time left to go on removals. The late doctors were causing an avalanche of delays and problems for the technical staff.

Greg knew he really didn't have a choice, though, and had to go get suited up again and get Dr. Carlyle's cases ready. Maybe he would get lucky and someone would come in. She only had three cases. Two of them looked like they were going to be easy. One was a standard possible drug overdose found in a restroom of a local fast food place and the other a suicide by hanging at home with a note. The third case was going to be a little more involved. It was a middle-aged woman with no real medical history, other than being a little on the heavy side but not on any medications. The doctor was going to do that one last, so hopefully the first two would take him to the end of the shift, or someone would come in to send him out.

It was about 1:30 when the doctor finally came down. They did the externals and drew toxicology on all three cases. She did, however, want to autopsy all three. They started with the drug overdose. He was a sickly looking very skinny man in his late twenties maybe early thirties. It was easy to tell he had a tough life, but he did test positive for opiates. The situation where he was found and having a needle on him was making it pretty clear cut. The autopsy went quickly with no real surprises. It only took about forty-five minutes to complete. Greg just pulled him out and set the next case up before sewing up and cleaning him off.

The second case was not bad either, also an obvious hanging suicide with a note left near the body. The doctor did take a little extra time with the neck so that was about an hour. It gave Greg time to sew up the first body and get him cleaned up and re-bagged. She told Greg she was going to do paperwork on the first two cases and would be back in twenty minutes or so. That would put the time she was back right around 3 p.m.

As Greg had figured, no one was coming in to relieve him so he could go to lunch. At this point, he was just going to go home as soon as he could. He took off the dirty gloves and apron and went to the tech station to see Sharon and let her know that he was going to leave at three, so someone from second shift was going to have to come in to work with Dr. Carlyle. Not really to his surprise there were four techs hanging out in the back room. He was a little bit flustered and asked Sharon, "No one could have come in?" "They all just got back from lunch - no sense sending them in now. It's almost time to go home," was her response. Greg was a little pissed off and said, "Well fine, but I have to leave at three, so someone is going to have to come in."

He went back to the anteroom to get a fresh apron and gloves. The doctor was still sitting at one of the desks going through the folders and paperwork. Greg was obviously agitated, and she could tell. "Everything all right?" she asked. Greg filled her in on the situation, that he did not get lunch and started at 6:00 this morning with Dr. John. To make matters worse, everyone else got their break today, and when he went back to the tech desk to find a replacement, there were people sitting around just waiting until the end of the shift. In retrospect, he probably should not have vented to the doctor, but this seemed to be happening more and more often.

She tried to console him a little by telling him that the last case was going to be a little more involved, but if he could stay long enough to open the skull, she would handle the case by herself. It was better than having to stay until 5:00, so Greg was polite and said, "That's fine, doctor. That would be great'.

Right at 3:00, the doctor said she was ready. Greg was suited up and had already drawn the toxicology and blocked the body. As he stood by with his scalpel to start on the skull, the doctor told him he could start as soon as she had the chest cavity opened. Greg gave her the standard "that's fine, doctor" response and waited patiently.

The chest was finally opened. Greg figured, in his head anyway, that he could be done in a couple of minutes and get out of there. He made his cut from ear to ear and started to peel the skin back from the skull. He was only able to free up about an inch. This instantly became very frustrating. Every now and again skin was very difficult to peel back. Generally, on a normal case you just use your thumbs to separate the skin form the skull. This was going to be one of those cases where you need to delicately use the scalpel to slice whatever was holding the skin down. This added at least ten more minutes. The doctor was moving right along on her part. By that time Greg had only half the skin peeled back. He started to work at a much faster pace, trying to make small fast cuts to separate the skin. He started making progress, and another two inches peeled back. He stuck the scalpel back under the skin to work the next section. The skin was coming off so tight to the skull that the peeled-back skin slipped off his wet and slightly bloody glove right onto the tip of the scalpel blade causing what is known as a button hole. That was going to be an extra stitch or two now. Greg, very frustrated now, started to mumble under his breath about the situation. You have to be very careful when there is a button hole as you can now easily tear the skin and open the hole even wider or split the scalp altogether. The big problem was the skin was still very tight and not peeling from the skull like it should. This was turning into a disaster. He had no choice now but to drop the blade and start using just his thumbs. He continued to try and work the skin free. This had to be the worst case he'd ever done.

The doctor was just about ready to remove the brain. She stopped what she was doing and watched Greg for a few seconds. "Are you having a hard time?" she asked. "Yeah, I don't know what is going on with this. It won't peel back," he said while still trying to use his thumb and peel back with the other hand. "Just leave it," she said. "I will finish it." "Are you sure, doctor?" "Yeah, I know you are here later than you wanted to be. I will take care of it." Greg gave up on the skin and said, "Thanks, doctor. I really do have to go," and started to remove his protective clothing and exited the far side of the autopsy room to head right for the locker room to change.

A few days passed and Greg was called to Dana's office. Dr. Carlyle had filed a complaint against him for what she called "butchering the head" and walking out of the autopsy room before the case was finished. She also stated he was very angry that he had to work on the extra cases. Greg was flabbergasted by this, by the incident despite trying to defend himself. Even Dr. John came to his defense with his own report filed on how many cases he had done with Greg with no incidents. But that seemed to fall on deaf ears, and no real action was taken as far as discipline. Everything seemed to be proceeding as normal as it ever was in the office. Greg could not help but remember all the warnings he was given by Charlie and Dale about how quickly people in this place would turn on you to protect themselves.

STRIKE TWO

The office was in complete chaos. Bodies were being released in an attempt to get things under control in the coolers. Morale among technicians was extremely low. Some even refused to work with certain doctors or constantly took sick or personal days. Management seemed oblivious to all of it and just expected things to continue without any attempt to fix the situation.

Then the day came that caused drastic changes in everything in the morgue. It was another day of autopsies for Greg. He started with Dr. John, who was not even scheduled to autopsy that day. He still took cases every day, though, coming in at 6 a.m. and working until morning meeting. That day there were five cases off the first page, three views, and two autopsies.

The three views were all elderly people with medical histories who unfortunately passed away at home with no one around. One autopsy was a woman in her thirties who went into the hospital with complaints of a severe headache and ended up passing away in the hospital. That turned out to be some kind of brain hemorrhage. The other was a man in his fifties - a suspected suicide by an overdose. None of these cases would take long to complete.

After morning meeting, he was assigned to Dr. Grady for his cases. He had five that day, three autopsies, and two external views. Autopsies one and two were a motor vehicle accident - two young men in their early twenties. They were travelling at an excessive speed and lost control of the car and hit a large tree. The third was a woman in her forties - another suspected drug overdose. These cases were all too familiar. All in all, that was not as bad as it seemed. Greg would more than likely be out of the room by noontime.

Dr. Grady came down a little later than normal, so they got off to a late start. They managed to get through the cases and finish up around after noon time. Greg made quick work of cleaning up just a little past 12:30. This was going to be the first day in a few weeks that Greg actually got to take his lunch break. He finished cleaning up in the room just as two of the newer doctors were coming down to start their cases. Greg managed to slip past them through the door located on the far end of the room just in case, and he headed right for the locker room.

He took care of business, got himself cleaned up, and was going to head right for the front doors and avoid the tech station altogether. Just as he was exiting the locker room, the tone from the overhead paging system went off. It was Ricardo, who was running the desk that day, paging Greg to come to the tech station. "What the hell," he thought. "I am not taking on a third doctor today, not again." He wondered if it is was now too late to sneak out the front door and just say he didn't hear the page as he went to lunch. He figured it was worth the shot, so he headed for the front lobby taking the left from the locker room instead of the right. He opened the door in the hallway and headed in that direction. Janine the front desk receptionist was sitting at her desk and on the phone. Just as he was passing her, she waved her arm to flag Greg down. "He is right here, Ricardo. Hang on. I will put him on the phone." She handed the phone receiver to Greg. "Hey, buddy, could you come down to the tech station? I need you to do me a favor." "Can it wait until after I take lunch, Ricardo?" Greg asked hopefully. "No, I don't think it can. Can you just come see me? I will fill you in when you're down here. Thanks." The receiver clicked. "Goddamn it"! Greg mumbled almost to himself.

Greg headed back down the long hallway to the tech station. He almost had himself convinced that if he was going to be asked to take a third doctor, he would say no - he was going to lunch.

He hit the button to open the sliding glass door that separated the hallway from the tech desk. Before Ricardo could utter a word, Greg started speaking. "I am not going back in the room until after

I have lunch, Ricardo!" "Well, here is the thing, Greg. I have a scene in Cambridge. The only people I have to send are you and Nicky." Nicky won't go in the room either, and I can't get a livery service that is available, but she will go on the road with you. If you don't want to go on the road, then I have to pull someone else out of the room to go and you will probably have to work with both doctors or at least clean up after them when you come back from lunch."

Greg and Nicky got along just fine. They even joked around a little once in a while. If Nicky was harboring any hard feeling toward Greg, it was only because he didn't take her side or trash talk about the other technicians she didn't like. So, the lesser of two evils would be to go on the road. He knew Nicky would be more than willing to hit a drive through or at least get coffee.

"Fine," said Greg. "I will go to Cambridge with Nicky, but that's it. When I come back, I am going to lunch." "That's fine, buddy, thanks. I knew you would help me out. This shouldn't take too long anyway. They said they are ready for removal as soon as we can get there. Mapquest says it is only fifteen minutes away so you should be fine. You can be at the scene about 1:15, grab the body, and head back here by 2:00 or so." Greg looked at Ricardo. "Yeah whatever, Ricky. You know it never works out that way," he said in kind of a joking sarcastic way. "Nicky is already outside checking the truck. She is just waiting on you. The scene is not bad. There is a visiting nurse who came to see one of her patients, and it looks like a heart attack or some kind of cardiac event, no major thing."

Greg grabbed a body bag from the closet just in case Nicky hadn't and headed out back with the clipboard, office cell phone, and body bag tucked under his arm. Nicky had already pulled the truck out of its parking spot and was firmly planted in the driver's seat. Greg went around and jumped in the passenger side and hopped in the seat. "What's up, buttercup?" She smiled at him. "We haven't been on the road together for a while." Her seemingly happy attitude started to turn disgruntled and frustrated. "I was not going back in that room. I am sick of that shit, and no way was I going to a scene with one of those other idiots that work here.

They're all morons!" "Did you get lunch yet?" Greg asked trying to change the subject. " No, I did not get lunch yet again. My first stop is a drive through. I need the Micky D's fix, unless you have a problem with that, too," she said kind of jokingly. "Nope, no problem at all. I am starving." Greg smiled back at her.

They headed off for the scene taking the small detour for the drive through stop - not that big of a deal unless the scene called to see where they were at with the removal. They got food and ate as they worked their way across the city to Cambridge. Mapquest was accurate. It only took fifteen minutes even with the extra stop.

The house was huge, obviously a well-to-do family. It had a small front yard that was meticulously maintained as was the house. They rolled the stretcher with the clip board and body bag on top of it and carried it into the house. Arnie was already on scene looking down at his camera to look at the pictures he had taken. "Right this way, guys, toward the back of the house. This is an easy-peasey one. We just have to wait for the detective." "What detective?" demanded Nicky. " Ricardo said you were ready!"

"He just called. He will be here in a few minutes. He got tied up," said smiling Arnie. "No worries." They waited for another fifteen minutes, still no detective on scene or a phone call. Nicky's patience was now gone. "Can you call somebody, please?" she demanded of Arnie. "A little more patience, Nicky. He'll be here soon." " I am about to leave, and you will have to wait for another truck. I am not working late again today with no lunch!" She stormed off toward the front door. "I'll be waiting in the truck. If he is not here in the next fifteen minutes, I am out of here!" She did not slam the front door, but you could hear the truck door slam hard. "Oh man, she is perpetually in that time of month," laughed Arnie, with his smooth accent.

Whether he realized how lucky he was or not, the detective finally showed up right at the fifteen-more-minute deadline Nicky had set. He came into the home with Nicky following close behind him. He extended his hand for a handshake with Arnie. They exchanged pleasantries and the standard "have not seen you in a while" type conversation. Nicky's patience was paper thin. "Can you please go look at the body so we can go? You can have your reunion after," she said to the detective. He turned and looked at Nicky with a little surprise on his face. Greg was certain the detective was going to say something that would cause an incident. Nicky just did not care about what she said. He stared at her for a few seconds and must have used his detective powers to see that the look he was getting from her was not going to be worth the fight. He just gave her a smile and said, "Sure, where are we at Arnie?"

"No big thing here, Rich, nothing suspicious. You can go take a look if you want. I already took my pictures, and I will send you copies." "That would be great," the detective replied as he went into the back room to take a look. He was only in the room for a minute and came back out. "Yeah, it all looks OK. You guys can take the body."

The stretcher was already collapsed in the room outside the door where the body was. The bedroom it was in was small and had some medical equipment and machines in it as well as a wheelchair. There was no sense working in a room that crowded. They could just bag the body and carry it to this room to load it on the stretcher.

Greg grabbed the body bag and went into the room. There was a body in the bed under the blankets. The wheelchair was right against the bedside. Greg moved it out to the other room and started to unfold the body bag alongside the body in the bed. Just them Nicky came into the room. "What are you doing? Are you an idiot, too? The body is in the chair." Greg had not even noticed the body that was slumped over in the chair. It was the visiting nurse who had passed away. The person in the bed was the patient she was coming to see. Greg looked quickly at the face of the body in the bed. His eyes were wide open. He obviously couldn't move or speak. He must have been completely paralyzed and at this point probably terrified. Greg yanked the body bag off the bed and apologized profusely to the patient. He felt sick that this just happened. With all the Nicky attitude and the tension, it was causing, he never bothered to look around. He just wanted to do the removal and get out of there.

Nicky grabbed the bag off the floor and set it up at the feet of the body in the chair. They carefully slid the body down inside the bag in the proper position to zip it up and get out of there. Nicky had the zipper at the top and Greg the one at the bottom. They both zipped and ended up meeting in the middle of the bag. Nicky just looked at him and said, "I can't believe you. Let's get out of here." They picked up the body and took it in the next room to the waiting stretcher and got it strapped in and started to head for the door. Finally, they got in the truck and backed out of the driveway.

While all of this was going on, time had been slipping away. If they got back to the office now, they would probably get their lunch breaks in but would have to sit around or worse for the last thirty minutes of their shift. Just then the cell phone started ringing. Greg answered. It was Ricardo." Hey, how you guys doing? Are you almost back?" Greg spoke. "Hi, Ricardo. No, we are just leaving the scene now. They weren't ready. We had to wait for a detective to show up." "Oh, sorry," Ricardo said. "They told me it was ready, but, hey, since you guys are in Cambridge, medical-legal just dropped off a request for us to pick up some x-rays at Cambridge hospital. Mapquest says it's right down the street only about a mile and half away." "OK, what's the name and case number?" asked Greg. Ricardo gave him the information, and Greg wrote it down on a new case sheet from the clipboard.

Picking up x-rays, charts, or blood from a hospital was common for the technical staff. The problem was it could go one of two ways. They were either ready for items to be picked up and you could literally just run in and sign their forms and be off with what you needed. The second way was the person working the desk at the hospital was afraid of violating HIPAA laws and not willing to give out information. The general rule was the medical examiner could request whatever they want regarding a patient form a hospital, as it is now their case and the patient is deceased. Some hospital staff did not know this, so it usually involved making several phone calls and waiting for those in power to call back and approve the request. The second scenario could tie you up for an hour or more sometimes.

Nicky was not having any of this. She grabbed the phone from Greg and called the tech station directly. Poor Ricardo never knew what hit him and didn't get a word in edgewise before she hung up on him. As soon as he answered, "tech station," she let him have it, calling him as big an idiot as everyone else working there and saying they were idiots for making him a supervisor and putting him in charge. There is no way in hell she was going to pick up x-rays at this time of day when she had not had lunch and she was dropping this body off and going home. She hit the end call button and bounced the phone of the front seat of the truck. She dug in her pants pocket for her own personal phone and started dialing.

She direct dialed Deborah Wingate, the technical manager on her personal phone. Deborah answered. You could hear the muffled voice over the phone. "Hi, this is Deb." Nicky started right in. "Hi, it's me. What kind of idiot did you put behind that desk today? I have not had lunch and have been busting my ass all day and now he wants me to go to pick up x-rays at some hospital!" "You haven't had lunch today yet"? Deborah responded. "Where are you now?" "Just leaving a scene in Cambridge, and he wants us to go to the hospital and pick up x-rays for medical-legal clowns on a case that was done weeks ago." "OK, don't worry about it. Just come back and drop off the body and you can go home. It's late enough now as it is. Thanks, Nicky." She hung up the phone. "There, I took care of that!" Nicky put her phone back in her pocket.

Two or three minutes passed as they worked their way back to the office when the tech cell phone started ringing. Greg was afraid to answer it. If it was poor Ricardo with another scene, he probably would not live to see his next birthday." Greg answered, "Yes, Ricardo." "Hey, buddy, don't worry about those x-rays. Deborah says we will just send someone from second or third shift. When you guys get back, you can just drop the body off and take off if you want." "OK, Ricky, if you say so. We should be back in ten minutes or so. See you in a bit." "OK, buddy, see you in a bit." Greg hung up the phone. "I told you I took care of that," Nicky said smugly.

It took them about ten minutes from the call as predicted to get back to the office. Nicky grabbed the clipboard off the front seat and got out of the truck and stood out back while Greg removed the stretcher with the body. She walked in front of Greg as he pulled the stretcher. As they passed the tech station, she slammed the clipboard on the counter in front of Ricardo and then leaned forward on both of her hands right in his face. "I am leaving!" She stormed off down the hallway. Greg was a few steps behind her as this happened. He stopped to write the body into the logbook. As he was writing it in Ricardo said, "You can just leave her in the processing area. I'll take care of it." Greg finished entering the information in the book and in a mocking manner to Nicky slammed the book closed with the pen in it and took the same position on both of his hands to lean into Ricardo's face. "Because I am leaving, too!" They both got a laugh out of it. "This place is unbelievable sometimes." Ricardo continued to laugh as Greg walked down the hall to the locker room still laughing.

WHAT IS HAPPENING?

It was unusually slow all of a sudden. There were not a lot of cases coming in, and the daily roster was a reasonable level of a dozen to two dozen cases. Techs took advantage of this by using personal and vacation days to recharge their own batteries.

One night ended up being a single-coverage night by one of the newer techs. A young guy named Steve, just twenty-three years old, kind of on the stocky side and strong with a slightly annoying know-it-all personality. He worked as an EMT during the day and was in school to become a paramedic. With all of this going on as well as a longtime girlfriend and new baby, he was in a constant state of exhaustion. When he had coworkers on with him, he would go on the road and someone else would drive so he could sleep in the passenger's seat until he was needed.

Working the night shift could go either way. You could sit there staring at the wall for most of the night until the hospitals decide they needed to call their cases in, or you could get calls from scene after scene that needed immediate removals. If it was a lot of scenes nights, you had to process these cases in and handle the constantly ringing phone.

Steve was obviously lucky that night, and the phones must have stayed quiet. When Greg got to work about 5:30 in the morning to work with Dr. John at 6:00, Steve was nowhere to be found. Greg walked by the tech station, and it was abandoned. Steve could have been off doing any number of things. Maybe he needed a bathroom break and was in the locker room or headed upstairs to grab a cup of coffee. Greg headed to the locker room to get changed. Steve was not in there. He threw on a set of scrubs and figured he would just head upstairs to grab coffee and walk the long hall upstairs and take the back stairs to the tech desk. Maybe he would run into his ghost again. No such luck. No ghosts that morning. He grabbed his coffee from the kitchenette and headed down. Still no Steve at the tech desk. A little weird Greg had not run into him. With no Steve at the desk, Greg figured he would look at the calls from last night and the roster on the counter top to see what the day was going to be like. He took a seat behind the desk and started to look at the paperwork. Steve must be here. He took three calls, all declined cases from different hospitals, but the last one was taken at just after midnight. So, it had been dead silent for the last five hours. Just as Greg decided he was going to sit in the back room to not jinx the phones, as it was getting close to the time when hospitals called in their potential medical examiner cases, the phone rang. "Damn it," he thought to himself, "too late." The phone rang a second time. Greg reached to grab the cordless out of its charger. It was not there. The cradle was empty, but the phone was not ringing anymore either. "Steve was somewhere in the building with the cordless," Greg thought. He rolled the chair back to its spot under the countertop where Steve was supposed to be sitting. Greg was going to head into the back room and pretend he didn't know anything. Just as he was about to back away from the counter to head for the back room, one of the doors on the closet that the new body bags were stored clicked and slowly started to open. The doors did not have doorknobs. They had handle-type hardware. Greg stood there staring at the door still slowly opening with the handle pulled all the way down to open the door. He didn't know if he should be scared of what was happening or not. He could hear Steve's very sleepy voice. "Medical examiner's office, do you have a case to report?" The door was fully open, the other still closed so Greg could only see half of Steve as he rolled himself out of the closet. Steve finally spotted Greg smiling and thinking this was pretty funny. Steve had piled the body bags into a make-shift bed inside the closet and apparently had been sleeping in there most of the night. He finally spotted Greg standing behind the techs counter. He gave him a little smile and a wave hello sign with his free hand, acting like "nothing to see here, just go about your day." He took his spot behind the desk and started entering the case information on the computer. Greg stood in the doorway leading to the back room holding his coffee listening to Steve take the case information to see what was being called in. Steve finished taking the patient's demographics and paused while listening to the voice on the other end describe the details. "OK," Steve said finally, "and her doctor will sign the death certificate. OK then the medical examiner will decline jurisdiction. Thank you," He hung up the phone.

It was required that hospitals call in cases that passed away within twenty-four hours of being admitted. This case happened to be an eighty-five-year-old man with significant cardiac history who came in with chest pains about twelve hours earlier. He was in the cardiac intensive care unit, but they were unable to keep him alive and he coded several times since admission.

"What a great night," Steve said loudly as he stretched his arms out way over his head. "I didn't have to accept any cases all night. We have three that are ready to come in, but I got a memo saying to not use livery services to save money because it has been slow his week."

The slow down on taking cases had helped to clear out some of the bodies that had been overloaded in the cooler, not quite enough but there were a few free tables and some gurneys only had one body on them now. The shelves were still overloaded. Sadly, everyone knew this slower pace would only lead to a surge eventually. Maybe the grim reaper was on vacation and his replacement wasn't as efficient.

REALITY CHECK

A s predicted, it didn't take much longer for the cases come in at full force again. The office had decided that they needed a new protocol for releasing the unclaimed or badly de-composed bodies that had been sitting in the coolers - some for months, even a few that were there for a year or more.

Generally, they would not release a body until a positive identi-fication had been made. This meant some cases like the unknown fisherman who was found floating in the ocean would not be re-leased for cremation or burial for more than a year. He had been found floating in the ocean by another fishing boat and was already badly decomposed and had been getting picked apart by sea life. The problem with identifying him was no one from any of the fish-ing ports had been reported missing. No family or anybody, for that matter, had reported that someone didn't make it back from a fish-ing trip. There was no way of telling where he came from or how he ended up in the ocean or even if he was a fisherman.

While he was there, though, he was used as a training tool for new state police cadets who had to observe an autopsy. The unknown fisherman and a couple of other select cases in various states of decomposition were pulled out to be used as a teaching tool on what the new troopers should look for and to give them some exposure to what they could possibly have to deal with.

It was always amusing to watch when a soon-to-be-graduating class of troopers came in. They would line the back of the autopsy room usually two dozen, sometimes more of some pretty tough-looking men and woman. Dr. Lowe took particular interest in being the doctor to show the bodies to the cadets and explain things. The techs and doctors in the building were pretty used to this sort of thing and these cases, so other than the foul odor, it was an easy day. It was not uncommon for a trooper or two to have to leave the room or faint right on the spot when the bodies were presented.

Now, however, the unknown and a bunch of other were set to be released and given a proper burial in a state cemetery. The problem was that a lot of bodies going out and a lot of bodies coming in usually backed up the processing area when both were happening at the same time.

Greg had just finished up for the day in the autopsy room. It was another day of working with three doctors and not getting a lunch break or any break to speak of. He was frustrated and just wanted to get out of there. The shift had ended, and second shift had already started by the time he got his station in the room cleaned up. There was absolute chaos in the processing area when he finally got to leave the room.

James was behind the desk by himself. His two techs had already left to go to a scene for a removal. The truck that had been sent out on first shift had just returned with two cases of their own, and they were processing them in. There was also a livery service that had transported two cases in and three livery services there to pick up their own cases.

It was not an easy task to release some of these older cases. They were usually two or three deep on a shelf somewhere in the cooler, which meant you needed to find two empty gurneys - one to place the front two bodies on and one to place the body being releases on. James had his hands full with the constantly ringing phone and several funeral directors waiting impatiently. The first-shift technicians had bailed out already like rats on a sinking ship. Morale was still very low, and day shift was getting hit just as bad as any other shift, sometimes worse with administration micromanaging and autopsies going on all day.

The processing area and the hallway were jammed with bodies on tables, gurneys, and stretchers. The funeral homes that were there to pick up these older bodies also had their own stretchers with a cremation box on them. The cremation box was literally a rectangular box made out of plywood, used to put the decomposing bodies in They had a wooden lid to seal the body in to keep the smell down and went right into the oven for cremation.

Greg tried to walk past all of this to get out for the day, but James was pleading for some help to clear some of these people out. He stopped Greg and begged him to pull a couple of bodies for him before he left. Greg reluctantly said OK, and James handed him a Post-it notes with two case numbers on it. Both bodies were on the same shelf in the deco cooler. Of course, they were in the back of the cooler, which was much smaller than the main cooler, and Dr. Cavanaugh was autopsying a decomposed body in that room with a new tech who was willing to stay late to finish that case.

Greg double checked the bodies' location on the database system. James had given him the right information, so he had to go find an empty table or gurney to pull the front body off. Fortunately, these were two of the cases they used for the cadet training. They were on a lower shelf, and he didn't need to get the lift in the cooler. He grabbed one of the now-empty stretchers for the truck that was sitting in the hallway and rolled that into the deco room to use for the front body. The deco cooler was at capacity. All the shelves were full, and four tables took up all of the floor space. This was not going to be easy, especially with the doctor in the deco room working on a case.

He pulled the tables with bodies on them that he didn't need and placed them around the deco room, trying not to take up more space than he needed and giving the doctor and his tech the room they needed to finish their autopsy. There was not much room left, just a skinny pathway to the cooler door. He rolled the stretcher in and loaded the front body on it and rolled it back out. There was no room left inside the deco room, so he had to take it out into the hallway.

There were still at least three funeral homes and livery services waiting. Someone may have just come in, but it was so chaotic and crowded it was hard to tell. There was also a livery service dropping off two more bodies. This was becoming a nightmare. Greg placed the body he'd just removed from the cooler in front of the sliding glass door leading to the garage as there was no more room in the hallway or processing area. He bobbed and weaved his way through all the people and their empty stretchers to find another empty to pull his two cases. If he had to move bodies around to try and free up a table, he would have to go into the database and change all the locations of the cases he moved. One terminal was being used by the two techs processing their cases in, and James was on the other trying to find locations of the other cases going on. It was taking him a while because the damn phone would not stop ringing.

Just as Greg was about to pass the processing area, the two techs processing had moved their second body off of their second stretcher that was supposed to go back in the truck. Greg grabbed it, saying, "Sorry, guys. James will have to replace this for you." He rolled it back through the obstacle course to get to the deco cooler and loaded the first body on the note James had given him. By the time he had taken that one out into the hallway, James had managed to get rid of one of the funeral homes and his two bodies, so that freed up a little room. Greg pulled his case and parked it up against the wall. "Is that one of the ones I asked you to pull, Greg?" James asked. "Yes, this is one of them. The other one is on the same shelf. I just need to find another stretcher to put him on." "That's good enough if you want to take off. I just need to be able to get access to it, and I will probably need that stretcher to put him on anyway," said James. "Are you sure?" I had to pull everything out of the cooler. You will have to put them all back?" Greg questioned back. "Yeah, go ahead. You can take off." Greg headed right for the back door, happy to be out of there.

A few weeks had passed, and as Greg showed up for work one morning, he noticed the local news truck on the street in front of the office. A female reporter stood on front of the section of wall that had the medical examiner's lettering on it. Must have been a big scene last night or someone famous, he thought to himself.

He headed into the building to see if he could find out what was happening.

Steve was sitting behind the desk; the other two techs were in the back room. They must have already come back from any overnight removals. "What's going on? Something big happen last night?" Greg asked. "You haven't seen the news?" Steve asked back with a little surprise. "No, I haven't heard anything. What happened?" Greg said. "Someone released the wrong body. We seem to have one missing. Some family filed a lawsuit saying we gave them the wrong body," replied Steve. "Really, do they know who did it or when this happened?" Greg was already thinking of the day a few weeks ago as he was trying to leave. "Well, the shit is about to hit the fan," said Steve. "They are bringing in some investigators from the state to try and figure it out." "Yeah, they told us to not even go on the road last night," chimed in Phil standing in the doorway leading to the back room.

"It all came to light yesterday afternoon and made the 6 o'clock news. They had James going through the logbook all night looking. I guess they are going to check the video from the hallway cameras today to see if they can figure out when it happened and who released it. So, for now, the directive is everything that gets released has to be signed off by three people minimum. Someone is in a lot of trouble, though, if they get it figured out."

As foretold by Steve, sure enough five big wigs from the state showed up from various agencies, including the state police and county sheriff's department, and even a man on the State's Board of Funeral Directors to investigate and check the video. James was already back in the office at 9 a.m. Somehow he had been recruited to participate in the investigation. At this point all they know was a funeral home came in to pick up a body that could not be found in the coolers. According to the logbook, it was not signed out and should still be in the building.

James' first task was going to be to make a list of everybody who was here and find out which one was signed out that should not have been and which one was not here that was signed out.

With the state of decomposition, the body had already been buried at this point. There was no way it was going to be viewed by family or an open casket. This meant it would probably have to be exhumed and then reburied.

The office was on lockdown for the next few days. No one was allowed to go out to lunch. Staff had to stay in the building. They couldn't even go out back to smoke. News cameras were set up on the parking garage that overlooked the courtyard. If staff were caught talking to the press, they would be immediately terminated from the office.

After three days, they started calling different technicians upstairs to give statements. They must have narrowed things down to a time on when it happened. A few day shift techs were called up first. The only information that they could pass along was that investigators had them sit and explain what was happening on the video they were watching. It was not long before Greg was called upstairs, but he kind of new this was coming. He still suspected it had to be that day, but he knew he pulled the right body.

He knocked on the office door that the investigators were in and was told to come in and take a seat. Sure enough, they had the video on the screen cued up to the point where Greg was at the computer terminal double checking the locations James had given him. "Can you just tell us what you are doing as we play the video?" the woman sitting across the table asked. "I will do my best," replied Greg.

He explained everything that he saw on the video and what he was doing from looking up the locations in the cooler to trying to find an open stretcher and pulling all the other bodies out of the cooler. Then he saw exactly what they saw on the video: the first body that Greg had placed in the hallway and pushed up against the wall while he went to get a second stretcher and rolled that into the cooler. When Greg was in the cooler to get the first body that James put on the sticky note, James and the funeral director with one of the cremation boxes on it just pushed his stretcher up against the stretcher that Greg had pulled out first and had nowhere else to put it other than in front of the sliding glass door. They both grabbed an end of the body bag and slid it into the wooden box and sealed the cremation box with the wooden lid. Neither of them checked the case number or toe tag. James had just assumed that was his first case.

Greg did not want to rat anybody out, but this clearly was not his fault. He never told James or the director which case that was, and they clearly did not even look at the case number or the toe tag. They just dragged it over and closed the lid, and off the funeral director went. They asked Greg a few different ways if he had ever indicated that was the case James had asked for and why he just seemingly left after pulling the first case if he was asked to pull two. All Greg could do was give his version of what happened, which was he never told James which case that was , and he never pulled the second body out of the cooler, James told him he could leave.

They then questioned him on leaving all of the cases he pulled from the cooler and didn't put back and why he used the stretchers that were supposed to be in the truck for removals. He gave them all the explanations they needed. All three of them stood up and extended their hands for a handshake and thanked him for coming upstairs to review the video. They said he was all set. Greg did not have a very good feeling about any of this, but he didn't want to take the fall for a wrong body being released.

Over the course of the next week, there was a lot of news coverage of the incident. The body had to be exhumed and moved to its proper burial spot so the family could bury their actual relative in the family's plot. Greg and James' involvement was officially labeled a miscommunication between staff. This didn't sit very well with Greg though.

DRASTIC CHANGES

This incident caused a huge outcry for sweeping changes in the medical examiner's office going all the way up to the governor's office. The press was relentless in trying to pursue a story and going after anyone who would talk to them associated with the office. Cavanaugh was put on administrative leave while they continued to investigate every policy and procedure in the office.

Three of the people who were brought in for the investigation now had a permanent office in the building to help oversee the changes that were going to be ordered after the investigation filed its report. The office was already at the bottom of the rankings for the nationwide standards for a medical examiner's office, largely due to lack of funding, proper equipment, and staffing. The staff that was there from administrators, doctors, techs, and clerical staff were all good people and good at what they did, but the office had much bigger problems that good people alone were not going to fix.

A private consulting firm was hired to observe and give recommendations on how to right the sinking ship. It took them a few months to come out with their full report. It contained comments like "The office needs a complete overhaul, no written procedures for transporting bodies, jeopardizing the health and safety of its staff as four recently tested positive for inactive tuberculosis." It also detailed weak, inept leadership and mismanagement that was leading the office onto the verge of a complete collapse.

After the report was filed, the state fired the chief and his right-hand man, Richard. A lot more money was added to the budget.

There was a large remodeling project for the upstairs offices with new office furniture. The techs still got the hand-me-downs for chairs. Three brand new ambulance-style trucks for removals were added, and new protocols for storing stock jars and evidence were introduced. The biggest addition was a new cooler for bodies that was built outside in the courtyard that took up about one third of the entire area. There was even talk of opening a couple of satellite offices to ease the workload in the one building. A few more new technicians, a few doctors, a Safety officer and building maintenance guy were also added. They happened to be brothers with a very prominent last name. To try and help with the growing backlog of cases, doctors were now allowed to do only three cases per day, but there would be more doctors scheduled to autopsy on a daily basis. With all the new hires more supervisor positions would open soon.

The building was fixed and patched where needed pretty quickly, and the new safety guy made sure all the techs knew the proper lifting techniques and even gave out back belts. He went on removals randomly to make sure everything was being done properly. Of course, certain techs didn't like that very much as it interfered with coffee and lunch stops.

One removal that he went on was with Greg and Dale. He happened to still be in the building around 9 p.m. when a local scene was called in. He wanted to work all three shifts to try and identify problems specific to each shift. This didn't happen often but every once in a while.

This scene was about twenty minutes from the office in one of the Boston suburbs. It should have been a fairly quick removal. It was a college student who was found hanging in his bedroom closet, an apparent suicide after some difficulties getting through school and meeting his parents' expectations, according to the note found.

The local police were on scene, and Trooper Madeleene was on his way, so all three men hopped in a truck and started to head over. They got the truck ready and left the courtyard and were about to pull out to the main road when Vinney, the new safety officer, suggested stopping at the local Dunkins to grab a coffee for the road. Well, that was a surprise.

They arrived at the scene. It was in an apartment building complex with three multi-story buildings shaped like a "U" with a large courtyard in the middle. They pulled the truck up behind the local cruiser with flashing lights and could see other officers standing in front of the building at the farthest end from where they were parked. This is as close as they could get. Greg grabbed the stretcher from the back of the truck, a body bag, and a backboard, while Dale carried the clipboard. There were about eight steps to the front door, so they collapsed the stretcher right at the bottom at Vinney's suggestion, so they did not have to carry the extra weight. The back board was also Vinney's suggestion.

The local cop was standing at the top of the stairs holding the glass door open and said, "You guys might want to hurry and get him out before people start coming outside." this kind of fell on deaf ears as they were not really dilly dallying. They headed up the stairs with the backboard and body bag. "Is the trooper here yet?" asked Dale. "No, but should be here anytime now," was the response. They continued down the long hallway, following the officer to the apartment door but could not help but notice that almost every door on the way down was open with someone standing in it.

"We can't take the body until the trooper gets here and says it's OK," Dale said to the officer. "Then you are going to have trouble getting out of here. All three buildings are the same race and religion. It is part of their custom to want to touch the body as it is being carried away. You probably have only about ten minutes before you have a crowd of about a thousand people out there that are going to want to touch the stretcher on its way by."

"Well, I am sorry to say we have to wait for the trooper to take his pictures," responded Dale. " Let me go check out front and see what is happening in the courtyard. If there is a crowd, I will see if I can get some backup here."

It took Arnie another fifteen minutes to get to the scene. He walked into the room camera at the ready and in his perpetual good mood, "Man, what a crowd out there," he said with his big smile. "The uniformed officer says he some backup coming, but we will have to make the run across the courtyard quickly." Dale informed him

Arnie snapped his pictures and took a quick look at the note. "OK, guys, I am all set. You can take him." Dale lifted the legs off the floor while Greg slid the body bag up the length of the body all the way up to the bar in the closet the rope was tied to. Dale zipped the bag all the way to where the rope entered the bag and pulled out his pocketknife. "Ready," he said looking at Greg. Greg bear hugged the body bag to keep it from falling when the rope was cut. It worked like a charm. He easily was able to lay the body down on the waiting backboard on the floor so they could strap him down. He tucked the remaining rope in and zipped it up the rest of the way.

The uniformed cop was now joined by two others. The plan was to carry the body down the hall as quickly as they could. The three cops would try and keep people inside their apartments as they passed, and Arnie could lead the way out. It turned out the hallway was quite a gauntlet. As soon as the police passed by the doors, people would pop out and try to touch the body by coming up behind, all while chanting and wailing prayers as they followed the body as closely as they could.

"This is going to be the real test," said the local cop, as they approached the front glass doors. This was no joke. There were about a thousand people in the courtyard, maybe more wailing and chanting, waiting for the body to come out. They were literally crowded so close to the stretcher that you could not put the body on it if you wanted to.

"I have a few more uniforms outside. They will push the crowd back from the stretcher. We will do our best to keep the front stairs clear. I would suggest you just get him on the stretcher, but don't waste time trying to strap him down you won't have time. Once you have the stretcher up and rolling, we will form a wedge through the crowd to your truck and hopefully we can get there without any incidents, said the local cop. "Just keep up with me, guys. I got you. I won't leave without you," said the still-cheerful Arnie.

Vinney now suggested getting the stretcher lifted and ready to roll right up against the steps, which actually makes sense, but he was very nervous about this. Dale stepped outside. The level of noise from the wailing and chanting went up about twenty decibels when he opened the glass door. As the police outside formed the blockade enough for Dale to lift both ends of the stretcher and place it in position, he ran back up the steps into the lobby with the rest. Vinney spoke. "You guys get ready to lift. I will count to three and open the front door, and we will make a run for it." The outside uniforms were doing a good job keeping the crowd back from the stairs, but they would easily lose control when the crowd pushed forward.

Dale and Greg both squatted at opposite ends of the backboard ready to lift on three. Arnie and the three cops and Vinney were ready to move out. Vinney started counting. "one...two...three," He popped open the door as wide as he could. Greg and Dale lifted and started on their way out. The three uniformed cops who were inside joined the four outside. They made enough room to get the backboard on top of the stretcher and started to roll forward. The crowd was deafening with the chanting and wailing and pushing forward, moving the uniforms all the way back to just about hitting the stretcher themselves. Arnie was about five yards ahead of everybody in the crowd. He yelled back, "I will get the doors on the back of the truck open." The stretcher was having great difficulty moving forward. Hands were reaching in from every direction. People even grabbed at the wheels all the way down on the ground, grabbing at Greg and Arnie as they passed, pushing and pulling in different directions. They finally make it to the back of the truck. The local cops did a great job at holding the majority back to at least keep the stretcher moving toward the truck. Greg was pretty sure that everybody in the crowd in some form or other did manage to touch the stretcher or the people walking by. He looked around for Arnie. What happened to Arnie? Did he get trampled? He made the final swing on his end of the stretcher to line it up to slide in the truck. The crowd was still trying to advance, and the police were still struggling to hold them back. Then he saw Arnie's taillights about fifty yards away just about to pull out of the parking lot. Hands still reaching in from everywhere, Greg managed to slide the stretcher in and close the back doors. The crowd almost instantly started to retreat back from the truck. The chanting and wailing were still going on, but at least they were not trying to grab the body anymore. The crowd pulled back away from the truck. The cops could now breath again. One of them said, "Wow, that was something." "Yeah, it was. Let's get out of here," said a shaken Vinney.

They transported the body back to the morgue, and within thirty minutes or so there were about two hundred people in the courtyard. No more trucks were going to be able to leave for the rest of the night.

TROUBLED TIMES STILL

Catrina had her baby, and had taken her maternity leave only to come back and hear another young female tech named Kim was pregnant. Kim was not in Catrina's clique and avoided her altogether. When Kim was training, Catrina was confined to autopsy, and assigned to work with her until she was fully trained. Kim quickly picked up on the autopsy procedures and which doctors she wanted to work with. For some reason, Catrina, as she did with most of the new people, had deemed her an idiot. The obvious reason was Kim did not allow herself to be pulled into the drama and cliques among the techs. She tried to stay neutral and friendly with everyone. Unfortunately, with Catrina if you were not with her, you were against her. Even though Kim tried to be extra helpful and do most of the heavy lifting for Catrina while she was pregnant and she was being trained, Catrina still considered her to be against her and made numerous complaints about Kim to Deborah the tech manager. This caused several performance reviews and warnings. After the third warning, Kim requested someone else continued with her training and she was moved to Greg.

Greg had no problems with her work or ability to learn new things. Catrina was good at autopsies, and Kim was able to copy her style very well, so autopsies were not a problem. She was not trained on removals though since Catrina was office bound during the pregnancy. When Greg was asked to give a review of Kim's work on autopsies by Deborah, Greg had no problem letting her know she could start training on removals. Kim was so happy with finally being allowed to go on the road that she sent an email to all the management and Greg thanking him for saving her from Catrina's wrath.

One of her first days on the road with Greg was early October. With Halloween fast approaching, decorations were all over the place. Some neighborhoods went all out - others were just OK. One neighborhood went so all out. You would think there was a zombie apocalypse with mannequins and stuffed creatures all over the place. Some were so life like that one home at the end of a cul-de-sac went unnoticed for several days until a strong odor was noticed by neighbors. The police were called to do a well-being check on the home and found that the wife had murdered her husband inside the home by stabbing him several times and then hung herself from a tree in the yard. With the neighborhood being all decked out and looking realistic to begin with, no one seemed to notice the real body hanging from the tree in the side yard. The woman was there for at least five days before being noticed. As Greg had figured, Kim handled it all just fine - no problems with the state of the bodies or the strength needed to do the removal.

Although Kim was pregnant, she did not have the same issues as Catrina. Her doctor did not feel she would need to be on light duty for quite some time. When Catrina found out she was pregnant, she wanted light duty right away to run the desk and give out the orders for the day. Kim had no interest in that. She wanted to perform her day-to-day tech duties until it was not allowed by her doctor. Catrina felt this made her look very bad in people's eyes, and it was rumored that she was making statement like she hoped Kim miscarried or lost the baby. Once word started to spread about these statements, she was finally called into to answer these complaints.

She pulled Greg aside one day as he was the union rep for the techs. She asked what she needed to do to defend herself from these charges. She knew their severity as she could barely keep herself from crying as she spoke. A lot of people were happy that she was finally being put in check for once. But as usual, there was not much more than a slap on the wrist.

The autopsies that were done on the man and woman were pretty standard except for a white powdery substance found in both of their lungs. It was not identifiable by eye. Samples were taken from both bodies. Two vials went to the lab, and two vials were placed in the storage area of the cooler for analysis. The autopsies were done by Dr. Lowe, and he remarked in all his years that he had never seen anything like it. He was not sure if it was something they inhaled or some form of bacterial infection, but he was sure the lab would figure it out. The new safety officer insisted that they get sealed before storage and not handled without the special hazmat suits with respirators. Of course, it was too late now for Dr. Lowe and Tracy who had worked on the case.

There were a couple of young guys hired as well. Both of them were students in some of the same classes as Katelyn Fletcher, the director of operations. She was given the job but did not quite have the degree she needed to qualify, so she was at least working on it.

Both men could have been GQ models, both early twenties and in good shape. Gary the lighter haired one was in school to learn forensics. He had a great sense of humor and was always joking. He seemed to get along with almost everybody. He was smart and didn't stay at the morgue very long. As soon as his school was done, he found a good job in another state as a crime scene investigator.

The darker haired one named Brad was going to be a pre-med student as soon as the core classes were done. He finished his regular school and had been applying to medical schools waiting to be accepted so he was around a little longer. He was also a very likeable guy and good to work with.

Greg had taken Brad on the road when he was being trained, and they had been dispatched to a scene on the south coast of the state to a fishing port town. Some fishermen had a night in town drinking after being at sea for a few weeks. It was 2:30 in the morning. This was one of the times that everything was captured on video cameras set up for security purposes on the dock, so the whole incident was able to be seen and went something like this.

The boats on the pier were lined up along the dock. Their ship was the farthest out, so they had to walk the length of the pier past the other three boats to get to theirs. All three were very drunk and the walk back to their boat from the end of the pier was about forty yards or so. They were staggering and bumping into each other as they made their way down the dock. After a few more steps of bumping into each other, it quickly turned into roughhousing and pushing. One man bumped into another man, knocking him to the ground close to the edge, nearly knocking him into the water. The man standing extended his hand and leaned over to try and help the other man he'd just knocked down back to his feet. The man on the ground reached up and grabbed his wrist and pulled hard trying to pull him over as well. He did not realize his own strength when he did this because it pulled him right over the edge and into the ocean between two of the parked boats. The third man staggered his way over as best he could to look over the edge to try and find him and help him out. But in his inebriated state, almost as soon as he leaned forward over the edge he fell in as well.

The man still on the ground now rolled over on his stomach and was hanging his head and arms over the edge trying to reach them for at least a minute. Then he rolled himself toward the middle at a safe distance from the edge and got up and started to walk very fast almost at a jogging pace away from the dock. It is not really clear if the men were at the surface or had gone under at this point.

According to the time stamp on the video, it took him nearly thirty minutes to call 911 to report two men in the water who had not come out or even surfaced at this point. The local police, fire, and ambulance responded to the scene. The fire department had a dive team that quickly suited up and went into the water to try and find the men. After several attempts on their own, the state police dive team was called in as well as some other mutual aid. By 5 a.m., the parking lot of the marina was packed with local and state police and fire apparatus, which brought out all the news truck with the cherry picker booms to get the best overhead camera shot. There was even a state police chopper and news helicopter buzzing overhead. All the boats were towed out away from the pier to make the search easier. The incident commander from the state police was now running the scene. He had the big state police Command center RV brought in to run things from, but there was barely enough room to park it on the scene. They had to shuffle a lot of vehicles around to fit it in. One of the first things he did was call the case into the medical examiner's office reporting two bodies that would need to be removed. Greg and Brad were the first out road team, so they got the truck ready and headed to the marina.

When they arrived, there were no parking spots in the lot. Greg went into the command RV to let them know they were there, and they informed him that they had found one body. He did not want the media seeing the body being removed, so the commander had people once again shuffling vehicles around to get the medical examiner's truck as close to the dock as possible. After fifteen minutes of vehicles being pulled on and off the lot like a wooden slide puzzle, they managed to get them to the very end of the pier waiting for the bodies to be brought up.

They backed down the narrow path made by all the exiting equipment and could see the booms of the cherry pickers on the news vans all jockeying for position as high up as they could go as they backed up. The parking area filled back in quicker than it was cleared out, like water filling in empty space.

The first body was finally removed from the water, and they managed to load him in the back of the truck. The dive teams were having a very hard time with the search. The water was dark and murky with very low visibility, and there were remnants of old pier posts, moorings, and trash on the ocean floor where they needed to search.

One of the state police asked Greg if they minded waiting around until they found the second body. Obviously, the answer had to be yes. Greg figured he better call the office to let them know they would be tied up for an unknown amount of time. He called the tech station, and Sharon answered the phone. Greg filled her in on what was going on, but she did not want to make the final call. She transferred the call to Deborah, the tech manager.

Greg explained the situation as best he could to Deborah, but he got the feeling she was not listening to a word he said. Sometimes you can just tell when someone is not listening, and he was probably right. She said they could not afford to have a truck tied up there, and other removals needed to be done. Extra doctors were cutting today, and people had called in sick etcetera, etcetera. Greg tried to plead his case again, really trying to emphasize how difficult it would be to have all these vehicles moved again so they could leave with just one body. The other body, for all he knew, could be found in a matter of a few minutes. Of course, there was the possibility it could take a few more hours. Not to mention the embarrassment of having to go back into the command unit and tell them they had to leave and needed all those trucks moved again.

Greg tried to get Brad to talk to the commander. He just sat there with a grin on his face refusing saying, "It's all you, good luck." Well there were no two ways about it. Greg had to go see the man in charge and let him know they had to go. He got out of the truck and started to head toward the command center thinking of how he could possibly approach this. Just as he was about to step on the first step of the RV, the commander came out. "What's up?" he asked Greg. Greg still did not know what he was going to say so he started with, "Ummm, you are not going to like this, but I was just told we have to leave." "What do you mean leave?" he said looking very confused. Greg continued. "I was just told by my office we need to take the first guy back, and we will send a service for the second one when you find it." The commander still looking befuddled said, "You are kidding me, right? I don't have the time to have guys moving trucks around again on top of they are going to find the body sooner than later. When will you have a removal service here? We can't wait around all day for one."

Greg tried to explain to him that his boss insisted they leave the scene now and go do other removals. The commander was very frustrated now. "This is unbelievable. What is your manager's name? Have her call me." He handed Greg a card with his contact information and walked away as several other first responders came up to him with questions.

Greg, now embarrassed with butterflies in his stomach, already knew how his next phone call to Deborah was going to go. He walked back to the truck slowly and slid back in the driver's seat. "Well how did that go?" asked Brad. "As expected," said a dejected Greg. "So, what are you going to do now?" Greg filled Brad in on the commander's request to have Deborah call him. Brad laughed. "You know if you told me this office was run like this and this happened, I would probably not have believed you, but here I am seeing it live."

Greg sat in the driver's seat for a minute or two thinking about how to revisit this issue with Deborah. "No chance you are going to make this call for me, is there, Brad?" Brad responded, "You have a better chance of hitting the lottery and being able to quit and walk off now before I would make this call." He laughed. "Good luck but make the call in the truck. I want to hear it."

Greg made the call to Deborah and told her what the scene commander said, emphasizing that they are going to find the body sooner than later. Despite the pleas to save more embarrassment and how much effort would be needed to move all the vehicles out of the way, she didn't care. She had made her decision and that was that. She had no intention of calling the scene to speak with anyone.

Once again Greg had to go find the commander and let him know Deborah refused to call and wanted the truck released from the scene immediately. Greg completely mortified walked around the scene looking for the man in charge to explain to him one more time he needed to go. Needless to say, when he found the commander, he was obviously angry and didn't have time to deal with this nonsense. Greg told him Deborah was not calling and not letting up. The truck had to be on its way back now.

The commander made several threats to make calls of his own when this was over. He wanted names of people he could call to make sure this didn't happen again. Greg told him who was responsible for making the call to have the truck leave and gave the director of operations' name and headed back to the truck.

He got back in the driver's seat again as a uniformed trooper came over to ask if they actually had to go. He was as confused as the commander. Greg told him it was true the office did not want the truck sitting there waiting. "Wow, that's unreal," the trooper said. "OK, hang on let me see if I can get some people to move things around again." Brad slumped down in his seat jokingly trying to hide his face. "This is unreal," he said.

One by one, vehicles started to move, starting at the back end by the news crews. This sent cameras and reporters into a tizzy assuming something was happening. All cameras were now focused on the newest activity. After a fifteen-minute wait, they were finally able to start moving forward to exit. Trucks filled back in the empty gaps left by the ME truck's departure. They were driving out slowly, and as they passed local firefighter, he asked," They found the other guy?" "Not yet," replied Greg. "Then why are you guys leaving?" he asked. Greg came to a stop and told him his office wanted the truck for other removals. " This how you guys always do it?" he asked even more puzzled. "Not usually," Greg responded as he started to drive forward again.

They finally approached the end of the lot toward the gate, and all the cameras were now focused on the truck. Greg had to drive through very slowly. The reporters and cameramen didn't care about stepping or being right in front of the truck as it tried to leave. He heard one reporter announce on camera that they must have found the second man because the medical examiner was leaving the scene. Brad was still slouched way down in his seat on the passenger side.

They made the drive back to the office, discussing the embarrassment this was and would cause to the office. It took them a little more than an hour to get back. Ricardo was now running the desk as they pulled the first and only body they had by the desk. "Wow, you guys made really good time," he commented as they stopped to sign the body in the log. "What are you talking about, Ricardo? We were there for a few hours waiting?" "Yeah, but they just called about thirty minutes ago to say they found the second body. You do have both of them, right?"

Apparently, no one had told Ricardo that they were leaving the scene with only one body, and he just assumed that since the truck was on scene that they had both. He had not even started to try to find a removal service for the second. Greg and Brad went to process the first guy in while Ricardo tried to find a livery service that was close to the scene. He wasn't having much luck. They were either too busy already or didn't have the staff to handle it.

Greg and Brad finished processing the fisherman in and were about to load the stretcher back in the truck when Ricardo told them, "I don't know how to tell you guys this, but you have to go back and get the second one. I can't find any one available to get him. It's been an hour since they called it in, and it's an hour drive so use lights and siren to try and cut some time down."

They made the drive all the way back down, siren screaming all the way, which didn't do much more than give both guys a headache. They only managed to cut fifteen minutes of the normal travel time. Fortunately, when they arrived, the scene had cleared of all the dive teams and command units. Just one local fire department rescue truck was down by the end of the pier where they had been parked. They had loaded the body inside it to keep it out of the sun and public view. They made the transfer to their truck with the help of the two paramedics. One of them commented that there must have been something else big going on to pull the truck from the scene when they did. Brad just smiled at him and said, "Nope, just bad management." Both paramedics chuckled a little, probably thinking he was joking. Once again, the incident just seemed to disappear and was not brought up again. There was, however, a policy change that all removals had to be handled within one hour. Of course, there was no way to enforce this as trucks could be anywhere in the state and livery services were not paid well enough to go out of their way to help the agency.

SATELLITES

The consulting firm's report made some good changes in the office prompting the hiring of more people at a better pay rate. It soon came to light that the new people were coming in at a level-two technician rate. The office felt it would attract better quality people, but it turned out that it was so the people hiring could bring in who they wanted. This immediately caused resentment among the level-one techs who had been there for a while. This is when it came to light that Brad and Gary were classmates of Katelyn.

One of the major changes in how things were to operate was the report's recommendation to open a couple of satellite offices in the state to alleviate the workload in Boston. They'd already had an office in the western part of the state for several years, but it only covered a limited section of the state dealing with only the western portion. Boston was responsible for about three-quarters of the state, making removals difficult if they were in central areas. The first satellite office would be in one of the largest hospitals in the central part of the state to handle all of the cases in those counties. It would be staffed by one tech, one doctor, and one administrator. They decided to set up the first office in the hospital's morgue and share the cooler for the bodies. It was practically ideal. The hospital already had an autopsy room and cooler. Greg's commute would be about the same time and distance but with much less traffic. The hours of the satellite were much better too and would be a Monday through Friday job. This made Catrina even more angry as it would really be a long delay to get the office in the southern part of the state she wanted to go to.

As soon as the job was posted, Greg submitted his resume and cover letter expressing his interest in the position. Unfortunately for him, Bill and Adam both lived closer to the new office and had seniority over him . Adam, the most senior technician, was initially given the job.

Adam had the office running smoothly with no problems for about three months, but he was in the reserves as a medic and was to be deployed for a year in the Middle East. Once again, when the job was posted Bill and Greg both applied, and once again Greg did not have the seniority over Bill. So, Bill got to take over the office. Things didn't run quite as smooth though as they did with Adam.

The hospital management called and complained about where Bill was parking the truck and the cleanliness of the autopsy and morgue areas. Dr. Grady, had gone to a part-time position to take the job there as it was closer to his home and he was starting to think about his retirement. He also started to have a few complaints about Bill being late or sloppy with his work.

Deborah, the tech manager, had spoken to him several times already about the standards not being met. After the last complaint by the hospital, she decided to go out there and see exactly what was happening. She did not want to deal with another news story about the medical examiner's office. This would be her first visit to the new office since it had opened.

One of the main complaints by the hospital was where the truck was being parked. The hospital had very limited parking for employees, never mind what they considered an outside contractor. The three who worked for the medical examiner had to park their cars up the street at a local funeral home that offered some spots for free to the medical examiner staff. It was about a half mile away from the hospital, but it beat giving up half your paycheck to park in the parking garage, unless it was in the middle of a rain or snow storm, of course.

The hospital had an underground garage where contractors, vendors, and supplies came in. It was completely isolated from view to the general public and had a long ramp that funeral homes and livery services had to back up when they needed to retrieve or bring a body into the morgue. The ramp was about two hundred feet long, between two cinderblock walls, with only a matter of about two feet on either side of the truck if you managed to back up straight enough. There was a flat spot on the top of the ramp, not quite big enough for the full-length pick-up truck. Bill had taken to routinely backing the medical examiner's truck all the way up to the top of the ramp.

One of the more frequent complainers of this practice was an organization that sold animals to the hospital for experimenting and testing. They would deliver live swine to the hospital on occasion, and the pigs had to be delivered up that ramp into the facility. Due to health codes, they could not go through the regular shipping and receiving dock. Bill parking the truck there made it very difficult for the animals to move through. Certain funeral homes had also filed complaints as they would have to park on the steep angle to pick up or deliver a body, and it was much more difficult to load and unload when the back of the vehicle was at an angle.

Deborah arrived unannounced, and Bill had no idea she was coming. She decided to check the ramp to see what the complaint was and sure enough saw the truck parked at the top of the ramp as well as a minivan from a funeral home that was there to pick up a body. She walked up the ramp and was looking over the situation when she noticed a bag on the floor of the truck. She walked around the truck to the passenger side and opened the door to check out the bag and found a six pack of beer inside with one missing.

Bill's job was now in great jeopardy. He was given the option to go to rehab with counseling and be transferred back to Boston or be terminated. Or he could just resign his position. He chose to resign immediately and went on to other things.

Once again, the position in the central Massachusetts office was open. Greg jumped on it for the third time and was finally getting away from all the drama at the main office. He was immediately sent to take over. It was liberating. He no longer had to deal with bad morale, infighting, or cliques. It was a Monday through

Friday position, so his weekends were now free. He liked working with Dr. Grady. Cases were done fast, and there were no unnecessary autopsies.

He didn't really know Brenda, the woman who handled the administration tasks and acted as Dr. Grady's assistant, but they seem to hit it off pretty well and got along fine. There was a lot of banter between them in a matter of days. She was about his age and had a sharp wit. She didn't put up with the doctors' or anybody else's antics. She was a long-time employee with the state and looking forward to her retirement eventually. She had built up a lot of sick, personal, and vacation time and knew how to use it. One of Greg's favorite things to bust her chops about was to ask if work was interfering with her social life.

This was turning out to be a dream job. All three got along great. They had a daily routine. Greg was the first one to arrive in the morning and would get things set up for the doctor to come in, usually around ten or so. Brenda got in at 8:30 and handled any phone messages and let Greg know which cases were getting picked up for release to the funeral homes. Dr. Grady usually called around 9:00 to see what came in, and Brenda would give him the run down and instructions on what he wanted Greg to do and who to set up for autopsy. It got to a point where it was running so smoothly that the bodies in the cooler were sorted out by medical examiner case to be done, ready for release, and hospital cases.

There were no homicides or decomposed bodies that had to be dealt with in this building. All of those were still sent to Boston. There were very limited cases that came through that were considered high profile or even news worthy. The hospital staff that used the same areas as the medical examiner's office were all friendly and helpful when they were needed. Greg even got to participate in an x-ray class taught in the hospital and was asked to demonstrate to students how an autopsy was performed.

Most days Greg had everything ready to go when the doctor arrived, including drawing and labeling all the toxicology and photos. The cases were done by noon time. This had become such a no-stress environment for all three that they often went to lunch together and even had a 3 o'clock ice cream break in the hospital cafeteria in the summer. Greg really enjoyed working in this office. It was so stress free he was even able to quit smoking.

SMOOTH SAILING TO STORMY SEAS

After a few months of smooth sailing, Greg started to get calls from Deborah wanting to know what was going on. As the office representative for the union, Greg was inundated with phone calls with people wanting to file complaints. The morale in Boston had gotten much worse with no one there to act as a buffer between Catrina and most of the new techs. He found himself having almost daily phone calls with Dana in human resources and constantly trying to get the regional union rep to rectify the situation. The majority of the complaints were against Catrina, including that she created a hostile work environment and even bullied.

Catrina even called Greg to try and get some union representation and wanted to lodge complaints against other techs. Somehow she managed to get Sharon demoted from supervisor down to a level-two technician. Her plan backfired, though, when the office decided that with the new satellite office they no longer needed or could afford two day-shift supervisors. So, Catrina decided to launch an assault on the central Mass. location to try and prove it was not needed but the southern Mass. office should be opened.

It was not hard to understand her prejudice against the central Mass. office for Greg. He now had what he considered a great job with low stress, and she was going to be stuck in what she called her own personal hell for quite some time more. He was not worried about her ranting to management with her opinions on whether the new office was needed though. After all, they were doing just as many cases with three people as the western Mass. office was doing with three doctors, three techs, and two administrators, right?

It didn't take her long though to put a bug in Deborah's ear about the workings of the office, though. Deborah made another unannounced visit to the office to try and "catch" people in the act, but it just so happened on that day it had been busy with six cases on the roster and three autopsies. For two of the cases the local police wanted to have a detective present. The state police also wanted to attend, so the considerably smaller autopsy room was looking crowded and busy. Had she read her email that Greg had sent earlier that morning when he arrived and sent his report, she would have known that. Deborah only stayed about five minutes and when she found out Greg was going to be too busy for quite some time to be able to talk with her, she decided it would be best if she left. She told Greg that she would like a phone call when he had things wrapped up. Greg assured her he would call when he had time to talk.

He called her later that afternoon. She stated her concern was that the office was not pulling its weight to take the pressure of Boston. She was requesting that central cases be postponed. He should come to Boston in the morning to cover staff shortages and help with autopsies when needed. And then return to the central office to handle the case load there. This was one of the most absurd things Greg had ever been asked to do by management. Although things were well under control in his office, there were still a lot of extra duties that needed to be handled after autopsies. He was responsible for arranging removals, delivering toxicology to the lab, and processing incoming and releasing cases. When Brenda took a day off, he was expected to handle the phones all day and deal with Dr. Grady. None of this was a problem as long as he was left alone by Boston interference.

The next morning when Greg came in to get set up for the day, he noticed one of the cases on the roster was an off-duty state trooper who had died in an automobile accident overnight, as well as four others for the day. Three had already been brought in overnight by funeral homes or livery services, and they all needed to be processed and logged in. The trooper's body was still at a local hospital but was ready to be picked up. There was already a voice-mail on his phone from a state police lieutenant, asking to be notified of when the body was going to be transported to the medical examiner's office so he could have the proper police escort to the morgue.

Greg figured he could get Dr. Grady all set up. That would give him about two hours before he came in, which should give Greg plenty of time. He called the lieutenant back and made the arrangements. He was fine with having the proper escort at the hospital at 8:45 in the morning. That would give Greg about fifteen minutes to pick up the body and plenty of time to get back to the office for the anticipated 10 a.m. anticipated arrival of Dr. Grady.

Just then his phone rang. According to the caller id it was the Boston office. Greg answered the phone. It was Deborah. There was no hello or good morning. She started right in with, "I thought I told you to report to the Boston office in the mornings?" Greg really was not in the mood for a confrontation with her this morning, but figured he was now on the defensive, so he responded. "Well, I am sure you saw the case roster this morning. I have to pick up this trooper first thing this morning, and they want to give him the police escort to the office." An angry Deborah snapped back, "I don't care if they want an escort to the office. That case should be coming here anyway. The chief sent me an email and wants three stock jars from your office brought to Boston, and they need to be here before he arrives. You need to grab those jars and start heading to Boston immediately."

Greg was now frustrated and angry. This was all part of Catrina's ranting to Deborah about the office not being busy enough. "I already made arrangements with the lieutenant for the escort. I can grab the stock jars and pick up the body and be there by 10:00, 10:30. Of course, I have to tell him that the body is going to Boston. I am pretty sure he assumes it is being done here." An angrier Deborah responded, " I told you those jars need to be here by 9 a.m., and you should have been here at 7:00 for your shift to start. The state police escort is not our problem. Tell the lieutenant that we will have to make other arrangements to pick up the body when we can transport him to Boston. You need to have those jars in this office by morning meeting and then work with a doctor to clear some cases."

Greg was truly flustered. He was not going to go against the state police again like at the fisherman's removal. He decided he would deal with the consequences and keep to his original plan, but he did have to call the lieutenant back and inform him the escort was now going to be to Boston, and he needed to make it a little earlier if he could. The lieutenant was as confused as Greg as to why the body was going to Boston and informed him he would get the escort there as early as he could, but there was not much he could do about it.

Greg processed the bodies in as quickly as he could, which would make his arrival to the hospital around 8:15. Hopefully the lieutenant would have his escorts there. This would only fifteen minutes or so earlier than originally planned, but it would help. The hospital was not far away. Usually the trip took fifteen minutes. He hopped in the truck and started to head over. About halfway there, he realized he never grabbed the three stock jars. He had to turn around and go back to the office. Now he still wouldn't make it there until the original time. He hightailed it back to the office, drove right in to the underground shipping receiving area, and drove the truck straight up the ramp. This didn't really save much time because now he had to back all the way down instead of up. He ran through the hallways inside the hospital and took the stairs down the two flights instead of waiting on the slowest elevator in history. Bursting into the morgue, he ran right to his desk to grab the case numbers for the jars, grabbed a box to put the jars in, and started to run back out. The elevator doors had just started to close as he exited, so he stuck his arm in and the doors slowly retracted. Greg jumped in and started repeatedly hitting the "close door" button. Damn this thing was slow.

Finally, at the ground floor he was in a full stride heading for the exterior door to the truck and backed all the way down the ramp in record time, just as a tractor trailer started to pull in the only door for incoming and outgoing traffic. He had to sit and wait, tapping his fingers on the steering wheel while the obviously new driver tried to figure out where he was going and how to negotiate the area with a fifty-foot trailer. Greg saw his opening to get out and took it driving much faster in the garage than he should, have but at least he was out and had the jars. He still didn't care about the consequences of being late to Boston. He just hoped the escorts were ready and waiting at the hospital.

Arriving at the hospital having lost an additional fifteen minutes due to forgetting the jars the first time, he grabbed his clipboard and ran into the hospital to grab the copy of the medical chart from admissions and sign the body out. Greg ran back to his truck to drive around to the back side of the hospital. Coming around the final corner he could see the dumpsters at the far end of the building. The morgue entrance at hospitals was almost always near the dumpsters. He could see a marked state police cruiser, an unmarked SUV, and one motorcycle. He backed his truck up to the door, hopped out, and briefly gave his condolences to the troopers and told them he would be back in a few minutes and they could get on the road. The motorcycle cop told Greg, "Take your time. We are waiting on one more bike cop. I just got off the phone with him. He will be here in about another twenty minutes."

"Damn," thought Greg. He was really screwed now. He wouldn't get to Boston until at least 11:00 with traffic and an escorted speed limit ride all the way to Boston. Well, it was too late now. He went into the door heading toward the morgue to pick up his case and load it into the truck. After he had him loaded and secured, the trooper in the unmarked SUV filled Greg in on what he already knew. The marked cruiser would take the lead, the two bikes would ride along the sides of the truck, and the unmarked would be behind all of them. All the lights would be flashing but would be a speed limit ride and to just follow the bikes' lead if they needed to change lanes or something.

The second motorcycle finally arrived about thirty minutes later instead of twenty. He shut down his bike and exchanged small talk with the other troopers for another ten minutes before it was decided it was time to start moving out. Greg fell into place behind the cruiser. The two bikes stayed behind him until they were on the highway. When they finally got on the highway, Greg couldn't help but think this was going to be the slowest ride to the city ever. He was going to be in a lot of trouble if the chief was waiting on those jars.

They finally arrived at the Boston office. Someone had called ahead because there was a line of state and local police lining the roadway to the office and courtyard area to pay their respects as the body passed by in the truck.

Greg backed in the courtyard to the garage door and opened the back doors to remove the body when two uniformed troopers grabbed a door to hold them open as he pulled the stretcher out and gave him a walking escort into the building. Greg pulled the stretcher all the way down to the processing area, hoping the cops would move away before he transferred him to a table for processing. He put the stretcher on the scale and told the cops he needed to sign the body in as he started to walk back to the tech station desk.

Ricardo was running the desk, and as Greg was signing in the body, he told him, "Deborah said she would like to see you when you get here. I will have someone else process the trooper for you." "OK, Ricky. I have to get the stock jars out of the truck first." Greg walked back outside and grabbed the box from the floor of the truck and brought it back in. As he was walking by, he told Ricardo the box was for the chief, and he would leave it on the table by the processing area.

Greg went down to Deborah's office. She was on the phone and motioned for him to sit down. He sat there kind of nervous. She was noticeably pissed off. She hung up her phone and asked Greg, "Did you bring the jars?" "Yes, I did. They're in a box on the processing table," he answered. Without acknowledging his response, she picked up her phone again and dialed an extension and waited to leave a message that the jars were here and hung up her phone again.

"You realize you are going to be written up for this?" she said looking at him coldly. "I did what I thought was the right thing to do. The arrangements were made to transport the body with an escort. It's called a professional courtesy," replied Greg. Even more angry, she snapped back, "You disobeyed a direct order from the chief and from me! I told you I needed you here in Boston at 7 a.m. to assist with services here!" Greg, very frustrated and not really caring anymore, responded back in his own frustrated tone. "There are eight Boston techs on today. With four doctors cutting, that leaves plenty of people for autopsy and removals. If handled correctly, everyone would get lunch and all the cases would be done. The Boston doctors don't start doing autopsies until nearly noon if not later most days. I have to handle everything that comes into my office on a daily basis. No one has ever offered to send me help no matter how many cases there are. I won't be able to do any of the cases on my roster today. Dr. Grady will be long gone before I get back. That means I will have double the work load tomorrow, which is not going to make anyone happy, right down to the funeral homes that want to pick up their clients. It would have made a lot more sense to have a Boston tech drive to Worcester and pick up the jars than for me to waste four hours of my shift driving back and forth. If you check the numbers, I am doing by myself just as many cases as western Mass. does with three technicians, on top of releases and intakes. Not to mention removals, evidence collection, toxicology, and dealing with the phones when I need to. It does not make any sense to start my day in Boston and them drive to Worcester every day. We have a good system, and we work well together. Not getting there until noon time every day will not get the cases done." Greg got a little carried away with his tone. After all, she was still his boss, but this was ridiculous in his mind.

"Well, you will do what you are told to do by management whether you think it makes sense or not. And on top of disobeying a direct order, I am going to add insubordination for your general attitude. This could mean that you are going to be removed from central Mass. and transferred back to Boston permanently." "I will bring in my union rep to fight any and all charges if I need to," Greg responded. "You do that, and we will see how much union protection you think you have. Now make sure Ricardo is all set with his staff and if you need to stay here and help. If he doesn't need you, then go back to Worcester, but report here in the morning." A still very angry Greg said, "I still have four cases from today plus whatever comes in tonight. If I come here in the morning, then I will need help in my office tomorrow." "You know what, fine," she snarled back. "Go directly to the central office tomorrow. I will come up with a solution on how to handle your workload out there. You have had it too easy for too long at this point."

Greg left her office and walked quickly down the long hallway. Two of the newer technicians who Greg did not even know were processing the trooper. He breezed right by them without saying anything. As he was about to pass Ricardo at the desk, Ricardo asked, "Everything OK, buddy?" Without missing a step as he said as he passed, "Yup, just fine. I have to head back to Worcester. See ya later." There were still several uniformed officers milling around in the courtyard. A few came to Greg to thank him for the escort with a handshake and a few kind words. Greg did not show any of the anger or attitude he was feeling and hopped back in his truck to head to the office. He took his time driving back, thinking of the interaction he'd just had with his boss, but he really didn't care he knew he was right. Of course, now she was going to make his life miserable with the micro-managing.

STRIKE THREE

It took about a month, but as predicted, Deborah was micro-managing everything that Greg did. One of the major changes she made was he now had to come to Boston every morning to check on the status of things. If things looked OK in Boston, he could hop in the medical examiner's truck and head to Worcester. This was another one of the most ridiculous things he would have to do in his life. Drive from home to Boston and then Boston to Worcester, work on his cases, drive back to Boston, and then drive home.

It was an attempt to break his will was all he could think of. When Brenda took a day off or a vacation, he could go directly to the central office to handle the phones in her absence. One day when Brenda was out, Greg spent the entire day at the office when a funeral home called to give the information needed to pick up a body, and they wanted it that afternoon. This was not a problem. He didn't have to go to Boston, so he could wait. Dr. Grady had left for the day a few hours ago, so he had time to try and catch up on all the things he had not been able to do.

Shortly before the funeral home was due to come in for their client, the phone rang. It was a family member of one of the medical examiner's cases. They were looking for information on the case and how they needed to proceed. Greg didn't mind giving them the information they needed, but these calls usually took a bit of time with a lot of questions and then trying to explain the answers until they had a good grasp of how things would and needed to happen.

As he was on the phone, the funeral home arrived for their case. The funeral director poked his head in the office door and saw that

Greg was on the phone. He made a gesture with his hands looking like he was writing on a piece of paper, indicating that he was looking for the death certificate and paperwork for his case. Greg still on the phone handed him the folder with everything he needed, and he ducked back out of the office.

The cooler was being shared by the hospital, so they had several cases of their own in there. It was common practice for funeral directors and livery services to enter and exit the cooler with their bodies. Greg could hear the funeral director banging around in the cooler, as he went in to get the body on his own as if it was a hospital case. By the time Greg had finished up the phone call, the director was standing at the log book signing out the body he had already loaded and strapped to his stretcher and covered with the velvet cloth bag. He finished signing him out in the log, and Greg double checked it and added his signature where he was supposed to. The funeral director said, "Thanks, I am in kind of a hurry. I have an appointment with the family in a little bit." Greg joked, "You sure you have the right body?" He knew he should have insisted on seeing the toe tag, but he wanted to go home, and the director said he was in a hurry. He figured the man was a professional. He signed out the right body and had the correct paperwork, so it should all be good.

The next morning Brenda called Greg on his personal cell phone. "You need to get here like right now. We have a problem." "What's the matter?" asked Greg. "The crematory just called. They have the wrong body. You need to get here and check the cooler. I am not going in there." "Damn it! I knew I should have double checked that toe tag," said a panicked Greg. "I will be there as soon as I can. I have already left Boston."

He arrived at the office and went to see Brenda, "does anybody know this is going on?" Greg asked. "Not yet, but I have to let Boston know in case the crematory says something," she replied. "OK, who is the crematory supposed to have? I will take him over there and bring the other one back." Sure enough, it was the body that went out late yesterday while Greg was on the phone. This was going to be a huge deal. Deborah and Catrina had won. He was sure he was getting fired. He loaded the correct body and headed over to the crematory, which was all the way across town and swapped the bodies out.

The woman who worked at the crematory was pleasant enough about it. She even commented it was a good thing they caught it and thank God for all the double checks they perform. She added, "You would be surprised at how many times this happens, but no worries. It's all good now."

Greg asked tentatively, "So do you have to report this to some-one?" "No, no harm, no foul. It's best people don't know when this happens," she answered. "Thank you, that's great," said Greg. He loaded the body in the truck and grabbed his phone to call Brenda to let her know he had made the switch and that no one was filing any reports. "Oh," she said solemnly. "I just got off the phone with Boston. I'm sorry, but I had to let them know just in case." Greg now had a huge knot in his stomach. He was as good as fired now.

It was less than an hour before he got the phone call he was expecting from Deborah. Greg tried to make a joke in his own head. This was the first time she had responded to anything in a timely manner. Deborah spoke with almost no emotion in her voice and just told him to report to Boston immediately. Any cases out there that day would have to wait. She ended the call.

He drove to Boston and headed straight to her office. She was sitting there with Katelyn, who spoke first. "We are going to need you to write up a statement on how the wrong body was released and then you are suspended pending our investigation." Katelyn stood up and walked out of the office to head back upstairs. Deborah now chimed in. "Well, what happened?" she asked with a bit of attitude. Greg explained the situation, with the phone call and the director loading the body by himself. But the funeral home did have the right paperwork for the case they were pick-ing up. The director grabbed the wrong body. Unfortunately for him she was correct about the fact that Greg did not unstrap and open the bag to check the toe tag before the case left. "Go write up your report and then you can go home. Your suspension starts immediately."

It took three days for them to call Greg in for a hearing. It was scheduled for right after the daily morning meeting in the conference room. It was a full house. The hearing included Greg and his regional union rep. Greg thought to someone must have a direct line that he didn't to get the union that quickly. Representing the office was Deborah, Katlyn, Dana from human resources, Chief Cavanaugh ,and the office lawyer, Catherine Brady. He was seriously outnumbered here.

They asked for his explanation again for to get everyone up to speed while they all looked at copies of his written statement from the other day. Katlyn said, "They had the funeral director write up a statement, and it pretty much told the same story, He added that he thought his body was in the front of the cooler since Greg knew he was coming in. He knew he was picking up an elderly man and that is who was in front."

There was no more questioning from anyone. After an awkward silence while they looked over the funeral director's statement, Katlyn spoke. "Your suspension is extended for the rest of the week, and Monday you will report to Boston to work first shift here, someone else will take over the central Mass. office." Then almost simultaneously they all stood up to leave. Greg was the only one who didn't. He must have missed the rehearsal. As they all exited, the union rep stood with Greg, and the only thing, she said to him was, "I knew there was not much to worry about. OK, I have to run." Greg thought to himself, "You have nothing to worry about because you did not just lose a week's pay." He was also wondering why his rep did not attempt to reach him. He had left two messages for her that she never returned. There was no prep or discussion of what could or was going to happen.

BACK TO BOSTON

Greg reluctantly headed to Boston the next Monday morning. This was embarrassing, and he had no idea how anybody was going to react to it. His fears were soon put to rest, though, after people started coming in. Most were happy to have him back in the main office and were quite welcoming. Even Dr. Lowe made a point of poking his head in the tech station's back room to tell Greg, "Welcome back, and today's news is tomorrow's fish wrap so not to worry about it." Deborah had nothing to say, and Catrina's welcome back speech was "This is what happens when you try to defend all these idiots."

It didn't take long for Greg to be back in the full swing of being the office union rep and to the almost daily meeting with Dana. He had spent a lot of time in Dana's office. She seemed genuinely aware of the problems and even sympathetic and was always encouraging Greg to get people to put things in writing so changes could be made. The sad part was people did put things in writing and filed complaints with the office and the union, but nothing ever changed. It just seemed to poke the hornet's nest, so no one did that much anymore unless it was major. About the only attempt to make all the this go away was to require all the technicians go through a workplace sensitivity and workplace violence class.

One of the subjects discussed with Dana and on occasion with the union rep was getting the techs a pay increase and a better title. It was almost contract negotiation time, and the current pay rate was an important to the techs and to be able to have some kind of advancement if they stayed long enough.

After several weeks, Greg finally managed to convince the union rep to try and negotiate an increase for most of the level-one techs and create a new supervisor position. Cindy, the union rep, was able to get a provision added for negotiations. The office seemed to agree the techs deserved more money, according to Dana, and they were all for it.

The catch with the supervisory position was it would have to be on third shift as day shift had one. Sharon was demoted but still was seen a supervisor, and second shift only needed one. To top it off, third shift would also lose one technician, so removals at night would become a problem until they hired or created a third-shift job to take cases over the phone. The shift would run with two people taking cases and doing some mundane cleaning tasks.

There were also rumors that the new budget would include money to open the other new satellite office to lighten the load on the Boston office, which still covered a large portion of the state. If Greg could grab the tech-three spot it would be a nice pay increase.

Catrina was infuriated by this development; she felt the next supervisor spot should be hers. The new satellite office was close to where she lived, and she wanted nothing more than to be out of the main office and away from everybody she deemed stupid. Catrina had spent the last few years trying to discredit the current supervisors and attempting to manipulate management to get her way. Several people told Greg that she was telling anyone who would listen that she could take that tech-three spot away from anybody if she wanted it. The problem was she could not work third shift and could not manipulate the union contract. Catrina also made statements that she would ruin anybody who took that spot, thinking if it was left open, they would open the satellite office and make that person the tech three.

The job position was finally posted for the third-shift supervisor as well as a third-shift case taker. Whether people were actually intimidated by Catrina or they really didn't want to work third shift was unclear. Greg had a clear shot at getting the position anyway. He had seniority over just about everyone except Freddy and Mary, but with their track record, they would be destined to stay as tech twos for the remainder of their careers. Greg knew that Catrina had some influence over the tech manager, but as far as he knew, she did not have any influence on her or Katelyn. It would be a good move for him to take the job.

He submitted his resume as required and waited for the panel interview. This seemed kind of silly to him as he has worked there for a few years, but that was part of the requirements. He was concerned about the suspension and the couple of write ups against him, but maybe they would see it really wasn't his fault. He did have seniority. A couple of other people also submitted resumes for the position, but no one he had to worry about. His time served worked in his favor. It took them about a month to make it official, but he got the promotion to supervisor.

Greg started the third shift as a supervisor after they made it official. They still had not put someone on as a case taker upstairs for third shift. It was going to be Greg as the supervisor, Phil who had been working third shift all along, and another new hire named Steve. Phil was great to work with. He knew his job and was willing to do whatever needed to be done without much complaining He even went out to handle a removal by himself on a homicide case that was called in in the pouring rain as no removal services were available and it was very local. The agency would have looked really bad if they could not handle a removal only a few blocks away in a timely manner. Steve, on the other hand, was a bit more challenging. He was a touch on the lazy side and would not willingly do anything extra. He took the job thinking he could sit at his desk and watch DVDs all night and answer a few random phone calls when Greg was already tied up on the phone.

Greg had a lot of other responsibilities now after the missing body. There had to be an inventory of everybody in all three coolers every night, physically checking each toe tag and matching it with what the computer system said was there. In addition, he made sure the floors were done and the autopsy room was spotless and stocked up for the day-shift activities. Some nights the phones would be non-stop, and other nights you would only handle a few calls. But Greg managed to handle the inventory, reports, and other tasks assigned no matter what kind of night it was.

The third shift was for the most part uneventful. There were no autopsies performed at night. After the reports and inventories were done, it was handling some on the mundane mindless cleaning chores, stocking up the autopsy and anteroom. Removals were on an as- needed basis unless it was a scene, so on a quiet night there were no road trips. The office had instituted a new policy that hospital cases had to be put on hold until the organ bank people released them to the medical examiner. The common trend with this policy was the organ bank only had to call and say they are reaching out to family in the morning, so most hospital cases would sit overnight.

There was one special project that was an ongoing nightmare, though it would have to be done in small doses. They decided that stock jars, with pieces of organs and brain in them, no longer had to be saved if they were older than five years, unless they were a homicide case.

The plan was to reuse the jars for new cases to save some of the budget. So, the agency purchased and had installed two commercial-grade dishwashers. The jars that could be dumped were printed out in a report by Deborah, and she would give it to the tech station on a nightly basis.

The process was slow and had to be done by an open garage door as the fumes from the formalin were pungent if not toxic unless you were wearing a mask. Then the jars had to be soaked in a hot soapy sink to remove all traces of evidence tape and labels. This was very time consuming. Then the jars were run through the dishwashers to be reused. The whole process was disgusting. No one wanted to do it, but it had to be done. It didn't take long for Deborah to start dropping the ball and not print the report for the jars to be dumped and with no new jars being ordered, supplies soon started to dwindle. She was seemingly working later and later. It was not uncommon for Greg to see her in her office sometimes as late as midnight. It was a weird dynamic with her these days.

After a month or two of being back in Boston, she seemed more friendly and was even asking Greg's opinions on things. It was quite a development.

On one occasion when Greg came in for his shift, he saw a stack of papers on the tech station desk. She had printed a report so jars could be done that night. The autopsy room was just about out of them again. He went to the locker room to change and noticed Deborah sitting in her office typing away on her computer. She called him into her office. They had a friendly conversation about things and then some work-related talk about needing some jars done for tomorrow. She mentioned the report she had already delivered to the second shift. The second-shift people did not do any jars though.

Greg put on a pair of scrubs and started scraping labels and evidence tape glue off the jars that had been soaking. Deborah was leaving for the night. She walked by and stopped to watch Greg struggle with a razor blade, scraping at the label remnants stuck to the jar. "You know what? You don't have to do any jars tonight. I am trying to find some kind of acetone or glue remover to make this easier," she told Greg.

Phil could not help overhearing the conversation, and as Deborah walked out the garage he started to laugh. "Something funny, Phil?" Greg asked smiling "She is so clueless about every-thing around here," said a still-laughing Phil. "There are only twelve jars left in the autopsy room so not enough for tomorrow already. The report she printed out is about one hundred pages of the same case numbers. The only reason she is looking for an acetone is Catrina was going to do jars today because we are out, and she didn't want to go on the road with anyone. When she started do-ing the jars and realized this sucks, she went to Deborah's office to complain and told her she will not do anymore until the glue can be removed without all the scraping.

Greg looked at the report she had printed out. Sure enough, it was one hundred copies of the top page. This meant he could only do about two cases worth of jars. It would be enough to get through tomorrow, but that would be about the end.

He did what he could and started the dishwasher, and then went to do his inventory report. Phil could handle the phones. The calls were kind of sparse, and it was after the shift change at the hospitals so it should stay quiet unless there was a scene. They did what they could for the rest of night. Greg could not help but notice the box of jars he brought from Worcester a few months ago were still untouched in the box in the processing area. He even opened the box to see if the evidence tape had been broken, but nope still intact.

RUMORS

R umors started to spread that the office was not getting the budget for the second satellite office, which did not sit well with Catrina. She was gunning to terminate anybody to free up money. It was happening slowly, but people were removed for no apparent reasons. Freddy and Mary, both long-term state employees, just vanished and if anybody knew what happened to them, no one was talking. The rumors were that they were forced to retire. No one believed either would have retired willingly. James was fired for supposedly making a racial slur. The rumor about him was that he was going to expose his relationship with Francine, jeopardizing her marriage to the state politician. Steve supposedly had some sort of argument with Dana and stormed off and quit. Karen had also finally had enough and sought other employment.

The really strange thing was Greg, the office union rep, was not informed of anyone filing complaints, and no one came to him for advice or to contact the main union rep. People were just there one day and gone the next. There were no jobs being posted for re-placements either, so something was definitely happening behind the scenes.

It didn't take long for Greg to be questioned on things. There were complaints filed that the autopsy room was not being cleaned and stocked at night., in addition to not doing or arranging remov-als at night intentionally to avoid processing, causing backups on day shift.

Greg was called upstairs to the conference room for his an-nual review. Once again, it was with the panel of Deborah, Dana, and Katelyn. He was questioned on his role as a supervisor and for allowing people to slack off at night, not performing the required duties and such. He defended himself as best he could but was really caught off guard. The annual review process was usually just the employee and Deborah, and the evaluation was checked off as "meets expectations," and that was it for the year. No one ever received a higher or lower mark on the review. It was just a standard practice.

This time it was apparent that there were no friendly faces on the other side of the table. Deborah was going to have him stay late after working nights to perform autopsies to keep his skills sharp. This was absurd all around. If Dr. John was not cutting, he would be there until afternoon. No other supervisor had ever done autopsies on any shift. She also wanted him to make himself available for removals on both first and second shift by coming in early or staying late.

Katlyn questioned him about why he never put himself on call for removals on his off hours. He gave her the practical reason that he lived an hour away. The office wanted cases picked up within the hour of the call. That would be impossible.

Dana questioned him about not able to control the technicians he supervised and having them perform tasks and allowing people like Catrina to yell back and say "no" to things she was asked to do. Greg was not sure if he should throw Deborah under the bus on this one or not, but Deborah herself insisted on an answer. So, he gave the perfect example of the time they were asked to pick up x-rays at a hospital after a removal that was right down the street. Katelyn questioned Deborah on this, and she denied it all. Greg left the room with his head spinning. He had no idea what had just happened. For some reason, he felt his head was back on the chopping block.

As the weeks went by, Greg decided to be a good boy and stay late in the mornings to work with Dr. John when he came in for 6 a.m. At least two days a week, he would work the last four hours of second shift to do removals.

One Tuesday when Greg came in for his shift, one of the second-shift technicians told him he needed to take a personal day on Friday. He asked Greg if he could cover the hours for him. Greg said sure as long as Deborah was OK with it. The technician told Greg, "Deborah told me no one can take a personal day anymore unless they find their own replacement, but that seems to only apply to me right now." Greg said it was fine. He would take the whole shift for him.

Greg worked his next two days without any trouble. Things seemed calm for the moment. His regular Thursday day off was fast approaching, and he was looking forward to it. He had been working a ton of hours for several weeks. Thursday would be a good rest day, as he was working the double shift on Friday.

Thursday morning, he was finishing up his nightly report and getting the day's roster and case folders organized when Catrina came behind the desk and grabbed the daily roster, quite rudely out of his hands, to see what was going on that day. She immediately flew into a rage after looking at the roster and demanded to know why the four cases at hospitals had not been brought in on the overnight shift.

Greg, trying to stay calm, explained the newer organ bank policy and that they placed the cases on hold. Catrina didn't care. She was livid. She was scheduled to go on the road, and one of the few people she actually liked was not coming in. She would have to go on the road with someone else. She stormed down the hallway toward the locker room yelling all the way. "I am so sick of this shit; things are going to change around here! I am tired of third shift just sitting on their asses all night and sleeping!"

Ricardo, who was standing nearby waiting for Greg to give him the nightly briefing, smiled and said, "Maybe we will get lucky and she is quitting." "I wouldn't count on it, Ricky. She pretty much runs the place at this point." "Ain't that the truth," Ricardo laughed.

Greg filled Ricardo in on the night, which was unusually quiet. They had only taken two calls early in the shift and both were declines. The organ bank had called at 6:45 and released the hospital cases, so those were now ready to be brought in. So really not a good day for Catrina to go ranting to Deborah about the shift not doing anything.

THE END OF AN ERA

Greg's day off came and went. He didn't get much rest, but at least he didn't see any dead people. It was going to be a long night in the morgue, though. The one day off in the middle of the week messed up his sleep schedule, so he was up a little too early. He had to go work a double shift on a Friday night. This could really go either way as far as workload. He jumped in his car and headed for Boston. Nearly halfway there, his cell phone rang. He glanced down at the caller i.d. It was the medical examiner's office, so he answered.

"Hi, Greg. This is Dana. Are you supposed to be working today?" "Yes, I am. I am on my way in now. I am working a double." "Ummm OK. I was told to give you a call and tell you to not bother coming in until you are called. I don't really know what is going on yet, but apparently they are investigating something about you and Phil on the overnight shift." "You have got to be kidding me, Dana. You have no idea? Is there a body missing again?" " I'm sorry, Greg. I really don't know. Katlyn just called me and told me to call you and give you that message." "Is this another suspension?" Greg asked. "I really don't know what they are doing, Greg, but as far as I know, this is a paid leave pending the investigation." "Well, I guess there is nothing I can do except turn around and go home. Can you please call me and let me know what this is about when you find out?" "I will. I promise. Just sit tight until you hear from me or the office. Again, I am sorry for this call. I have to go. Good luck, and I will let you know as soon as I do." She hung up.

Greg truly had nothing else to do but turn around and go home. He tried calling a couple of people he was friendly with at the morgue, but they didn't know anything and seemed just as surprised. His phone rang again, and it was Phil. He'd just gotten the same call from Dana as Greg, and she didn't tell Phil any more than she told Greg. This was not looking good. Neither man could figure out what the problem could possibly be. Everything they did was by the book, no matter how often Deborah changed the policies.

So, on a late Friday afternoon they were apparently under some kind of internal investigation. Even the human resources manager didn't know what was going on. There wouldn't be any answers until at least Monday. "Would calling Deborah be out of line?" Greg wondered.. "What the hell do I have to lose." He found her name in his phone contacts and called. The phone didn't ring - just went straight to voicemail. He ended the call. It was useless to leave a message.

Monday rolled around finally. Greg had not heard from anyone all weekend. He waited until 2 p.m. and called Dana office's direct line. There was no answer, so he left a voicemail asking if she has found out anything yet. He made a few other phone calls. All he got to do was leave voicemails. He waited on pins and needles for some kind of answers. his phone rang. It was Phil again. They talked for a few minutes. Phil was hitting the same roadblocks as Greg. No one was answering their phones.

"Well, at least it's a paid leave for now. I suppose that's something," Greg said." "I think I am getting a lawyer," Phil replied. "Well, let me know what he says. I might need to get one too," Greg responded.

The entire week went by with no phone calls returned, no union reps calling, and no one working at the morgue taking Greg's calls. He received a certified letter in the mail Friday afternoon from the office. The letter notified Greg he had been suspended with pay for an indefinite time period pending an investigation of sleeping at his post, failing to perform duties as assigned, and failure to supervise. He would be notified by certified letter of the hearing date. "What the hell," he said to himself. This had to be Catrina's doing.

Part of him was actually a little relieved. He had never slept on the job and followed every instruction given to him by management. As far as he knew, there were no issues with his work. The days crept by at a snail's pace, waiting for some kind of response from the office. Finally, the following Friday Greg received another certified letter informing him his disciplinary hearing was going to be the following Wednesday at two p.m. He called Phil to see if he got his letter. Phil said he'd just gotten it, and his hearing was Thursday. "I guess they don't want us to be there at the same time," he remarked. Greg checked his bank account. His full paycheck had been electronically deposited, so that was good.

THE HEARING

Greg was driving into Boston for the hearing, still wondering what they could possibly have to prove their charges against him. His union rep had finally called him that morning and told him how the hearing should go and not to say anything even if they asked questions, not even a yes or no answer.

Again, it was Greg and his rep against Deborah, Katelyn, Dana, and Catherine. This was a very official proceeding, and it was being recorded. It started with a formal reading of the charges against Greg. Katelyn posed the question, "Have you or anyone you know fallen asleep while you were on duty?" Greg sat silently with his hands in his lap and glanced at his union rep, who just gave a slight headshake indicating to stay quiet. Katelyn asked again, "Have you ever disregarded instructions or requests by your manager to perform certain tasks?" Once again Greg sat silent. Deborah now said, "Have you allowed your subordinates to sleep or not perform duties while on your shift?" Greg still sat silent and motionless. He glanced at his rep and got a nod of approval.

Catherine said, "Well, obviously we are not going to get any answers here today. I would suggest we move on with the process to terminate employment." The union rep now asks, "The union has submitted a request in writing to see the supposed surveillance video showing this employee sleeping, and we have not received any tapes or evidence you are claiming to have." Catherine responded, "We will present all of our evidence at the termination hearing." For now, the employee will remain on paid leave until a determination is made. I suggest we wrap this up for today. The termination hearing will be on Friday at 10 a.m."

The four managers all stood up and started to exit the conference room. As Katelyn walked past, she said to the union rep, "You can use the conference room for fifteen minutes to speak with your client." The union rep waited until they exited the room and closed the door. "So, as I expected, they do not have any video or proof you blew off work duties." "I did not sleep at my post or not perform any tasks. The only thing that comes to mind is the stock jars, but Deborah told me not to bother until she got some acetone, and I still did enough of them to get through the next day," Greg told his rep.

"This is going to turn out fine," he said. "They don't have anything, or they would have brought it up today. When was your last review?" he asked. "Just a few weeks ago. I still have my copy. Everything is checked off as meets expectations," Greg told him. "Excellent," he said. "They can't rate you as above expectations or they would have to give you a raise or below expectations, they would have to bring you in for hearings. So, it sounds like everything was fine." "Honestly, I did not think I had an issue with anyone or anything here," remarked Greg. "Do you have any emails or written instructions from Deborah?" "No, they blocked me from my email account the first day of the suspension," said Greg

TERMINATION HEARING

The day of the final hearing was here. Greg arrived early to meet his union rep to go over anything he needed to know. The union guy was in full-blown lawyer mode, briefcase and all. "OK, I have everything I need in here - your employee reviews and a copy of your work file," the rep said. "Can they use the other suspensions and write ups against me?" asked Greg. "Anything they use has to be less than a year old, and I don't think they have anything this time either."

It was time for the hearing. All involved sat around the conference table. It was as official as the discipline hearing had been and started the same way with reading the charges against Greg. "Sleeping at his post, not performing required tasks, and allowing his subordinates to sleep at their post and failure to supervise."

They had a video screen set up, hooked to a laptop after the complaint was read Katelyn said, "Let's start with the video." She made a few clicks with her mouse, and the video surveillance of the tech station popped up on the monitor. It showed Greg behind the tech station doing something on the computer, but the screen was not visible. "Can you tell us what you are doing here?" Katelyn asked. "I am checking my email for any instructions or directives for the night from Deborah," Greg said calmly. The video showed Greg walk over to the stack of papers and shuffle through the stack that Deborah had printed out. "Now I am looking at the report that Deborah had printed out of stock jars that could be dumped," Greg continued. "Why are you shuffling through them? Are you looking for something in particular?" Katelyn asked. "No, actually. Phil had just informed me that the stack of papers was useless. It was just the top page copied about one hundred times with all the same case numbers." "Did you report that to anyone?" she asked. " I sent Deborah an email later that night about it, yes," replied Greg. "Did you receive an email that morning from Greg, Ms. Wingate?" Deborah adjusted herself in her seat. "I don't recall, Ms. Fletcher. I would have to look," was her response. Greg immediately jumped in "I am sure you will find it in my sent folder. I currently do not have access to my email account."

"OK, let's move on," continued Katelyn. "You are now seen leaving the tech station. Where are you going?" " I am either going to do some of the stock jars that second shift left soaking all night or going to do my cooler inventory. I am not sure which," Greg said. "I thought you could not do any jars that night because of the report?" "There was already a sink full of jars soaking, I do not know who dumped them, but the autopsy room needed jars for the next morning, Even though Ms. Wingate previously told me to not bother to do jars until she was able to find an acetone, I still needed to have some jars for the autopsy room." Greg still remained calm and started to realize they really didn't have anything.

"And where is your co-worker while you are doing all of this?" asked Katelyn. "He is in the back room handling calls," was Greg's response. "You did not take more than two calls all night though, correct?" she says. "That is correct. It was an unusually quiet night," Greg said. "You are gone for quite some time from the video doing the jars and inventory," she continued. "Sometimes it takes longer than others to finish," was Greg's response. "I may have gone to the men's room at some point as well. I do not recall. "Well, you do not reappear on camera for at least an hour, maybe a little longer. When you do finally come back, you go into the back room and not at the tech desk. Why is that?" "I had finished whatever I was doing and went to check with Phil on how the phones had been," Greg responded. "And how were the phones?" Katelyn asked. " Phil had only taken two calls while I was gone, and they were both declined." She continued with, "Why does Phil work in the back room?" "The chair is more comfortable back there, and I am usually at the front desk"

"Could it be that he likes the back room because the security camera has a box placed in front of it on a top shelf so the room cannot be observed?" she asked. Katelyn clicked her mouse a couple of times, and the image on the monitor switched to show the back side of a large box of Tyvek suits. "I did not realize the camera was blocked. I never thought about the cameras in the back room, but if it is blocked by a box on a shelf then the camera should be relocated, I would think," Greg said smugly. "Well, you do realize that camera is supposed to be monitoring the evidence located at the back of that room, don't you?" she said. Greg responded, "A person would be seen entering the back room from the front cameras, and the door has a card access lock so you would know who entered if something went missing."

Katelyn asked, "After you finished whatever it was you were doing and went into the back room that cannot be observed. Phil can be seen on the front desk camera going upstairs for a few minutes and then coming down with two containers of presumably food, is that correct?" "Yes, that is correct. Phil brought lunch in for both of us and heated it in the microwave upstairs. Since it was quiet, we figured we would both have lunch at the same time," Greg answered. "Do you usually take lunch at the same time? What if a call comes in?" asked Katelyn. "Then one of us would stop eating and answer the phone. It happens quite often," Greg said with a bit of a surprised tone at the question.

"So exactly what did you do the rest of the night?" "At this point, there was not much left to do. My reports were done, the autopsy room was all set, and I was told by Deborah to not bother with jars that night. I am sure you have seen on the video that I ran the floor machine up and down the hallway for about an hour to clean the floors. Usually in the early-morning hours, we start getting calls in from hospitals before they change shifts so after the floors, I was at my desk waiting for calls. Phil was at his desk waiting for calls as well." Greg did not like admitting that there was some sitting around, but sometimes it happens.

"Were there any cases that needed to be brought in? I have the roster from that night, and it appears there were four hospital cases that needed transport to the office?" Katelyn questioned. Greg adjusted himself in his seat a little because he knew what Deborah's response was about to be to his answer, but he answered it anyway. "Deborah had instructed the technicians that the organ bank could place a hold on cases pending talking to family. The second-shift supervisor had told me in his end-of-shift briefing that the organ bank had placed an overnight hold on those cases, so, no, they could not have come in overnight," Greg said while glancing over at Deborah who was now adjusting herself in her chair.

Katelyn with full confidence said, "I have no further questions." Catherine, the lawyer, spoke. "Does the union have any defense?" The union rep passed out copies of Greg's most recent performance review done by Deborah. "As you can see from his review, everything is checked off as meets expectations, which means there are no work ethic or related problems. If you read Greg's personnel file, I am sure you will notice he has been promoted twice in the last three years from a level-one technician to a level-three technician supervisor. I would say that is a good indication that he is an excellent employee and has posed very few problems. There is nothing you presented here that would indicate any of these accusations or charges are true. His employee record speaks for itself."

"Thank you," Catherine said. "This hearing is adjourned." Everybody stood up and left the conference room. Greg followed his union rep who headed right for the stairwell leading to the front lobby as the management team headed back to their offices. He stopped in the front lobby. "I don't think you have anything to worry about. They have no proof on anything. It is all speculation. It should take them about a week to make a decision, and then I will be in touch." He gave Greg a firm handshake and headed for the door out to the street.

Greg figured he would walk down through the morgue area to the tech station to see if he could talk to anybody, but his i.d. badge had been deactivated. He no longer had access. He went out the front door and walked around the building. He got to the parking area and started to head for his car. No one was out back smoking. It was pointless to try and see anybody, so he decided to head home. Maybe he could get someone on the phone later. About halfway home, he called Phil to fill him in on the proceedings.

Phil informed Greg that he had spoken to someone in the office. He would not reveal their identity and was told that anyone caught talking to either Greg or himself would be facing disciplinary action. Phil was also very confident that this whole thing was a farce and that they had nothing and could prove nothing.

THE OUTCOME

The days passed slowly. The whole thing caused a lot of tension at home and was now starting to cause problems with Greg's marriage. His wife was not very supportive and even seemed to be siding with the office on the charges, which was pretty tough for him to figure out. He had a few local friends he could talk to, but it probably didn't come off than much more than everyone complains about their job. If people only knew what really happened in that place.

The day finally came when he received his certified letter, just less than a full week since the hearing. Greg could not ever remember a time when he was this nervous about anything. He opened the envelope slowly and carefully. There was a cover letter explaining that the outcome of the hearing was enclosed, listing the charges and who attended the hearing, so no news there. He separated the two pages and folded the top third of the letter down to start exposing the actual results letter of the hearing. There it was the first thing on the letter and no way of avoiding seeing it first. In bold letters, the letter said he was **"terminated effective the date of the hearing last week."** Now he had lost this week's pay, which quite frankly he was counting on to pay bills. He had no idea what to do now. His wife was going to be pissed and anything but sympathetic or supporting.

Phil called shortly after Greg opened his letter to bitch and express his disbelief in this as well. He vowed to hire his own lawyer and sue the state. Greg spent fifteen minutes on the phone with him but really had his own problems to deal with right now. He called the union rep's office and left a voicemail. He wondered if that call would ever be returned. After all he was no longer in the union with no job at the morgue.

He sat at home waiting for his wife to come home from her job, dreading how that conversation was going to go. His phone rang. It was Tracey. "Oh, my God," she said. "I just heard they actually fired you over this and Phil, too. I am so sorry. What are you going to do?" "I have no idea right now, Tracey," Greg said solemnly. "I am sure you will find something soon," she said trying to be consoling. " Oh, and I just found out from Dr. John, the lab could not identify that powdery stuff we found in that couples' lungs a while ago. They think it is some kind of spore or bacteria, but they have not seen it before. Dr. John thinks we should both get some testing done."

"Oh, that's terrible, Tracey. I hope that works out OK." Greg really was not concerned about that at this point. He cut the call short and told her he needed to try and figure out what to do but thanked her for calling. A few other people from the morgue called to extend their sympathies that afternoon. One or two even called the following week, but that was about it. For Greg, it was the end of Life at the Morgue.

CPSIA information can be obtained
at www.ICGtesting.com
Printed in the USA
LVHW091943050520
653768LV00004B/22